P9-EAJ-680

Elsewhere

IN THE LAND OF

Parrots

ALSO BY JIM PAUL

Medieval in L.A.

Catapult: Harry and I Build a Siege Weapon

What's Called Love: A Real Romance

The Rune Poem

JIM PAUL

Elsewhere IN THE LAND OF Parrots

HARCOURT, INC.
Orlando Austin New York San Diego Toronto London

www.HarcourtBooks.com

This is a work of fiction. Names, characters, and incidents are either products of the author's imagination or are used fictitiously for verisimilitude.

Library of Congress Cataloging-in-Publication Data
Paul, Jim, 1950–
Elsewhere in the land of parrots/Jim Paul.
p. cm.
ISBN 0-15-100495-1
1. Poets—Fiction. 2. Parrots—Fiction. 3. Recluses—Fiction.
4. Exotic bird owners—Fiction. 5. Telegraph Hill (San Francisco, Calif.)—Fiction. 6. Americans—South America—Fiction.
7. South America—Fiction. I. Title.
PS3566.A82624E47 2003
813'.54—dc21 2003007918

Text set in Meridien
Designed by Linda Lockowitz

Printed in the United States of America

First edition
A C E G I K J H F D B

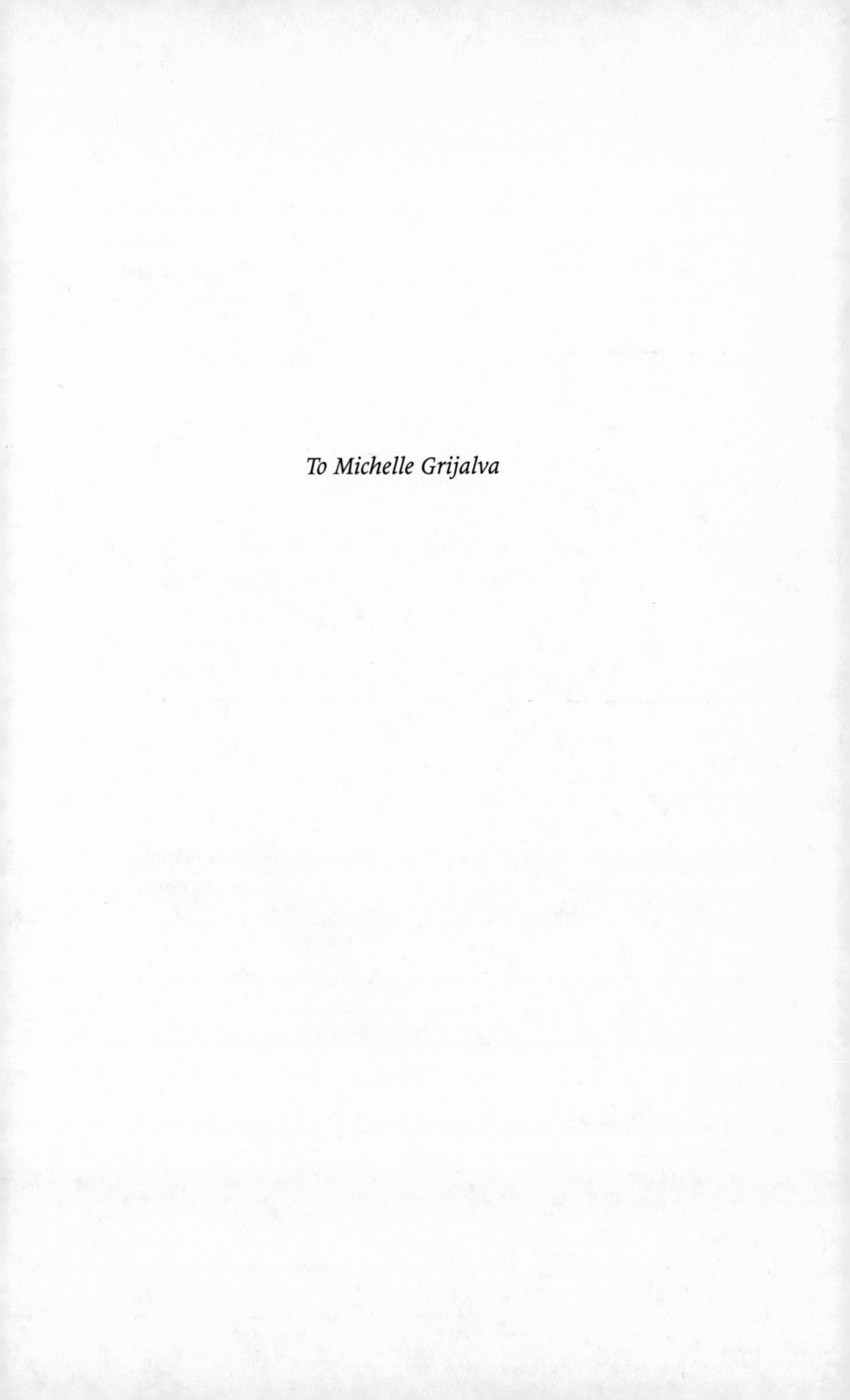

To Michelle Grijalva

How do you know
but every bird
that cuts the airy way
is an immense world
of delight, closed
by your senses five?

—William Blake

The World is All
that is the Case.

—Ludwig Wittgenstein

Elsewhere
IN THE LAND OF
Parrots

1

David didn't go out much. Hadn't for years. Even though he lived in a beautiful city, San Francisco, and had lived there since his birth, the outside world had not really existed for him. His bookcase blocked the window in the bedroom of the third-floor apartment where he lived. Out there, out in the larger world, was trouble, difficulty at best and bad trouble at worst. People were a problem, but it wasn't just people. The elements of nature were to be avoided. The earth itself bore explosive forces that might shatter whole apartment buildings. The sea was frigid and murderous. Animals had teeth and were not to be trusted. The seemingly innocent sky harbored huge destructive forces, or at least rain, a watery nuisance.

As a child, without ever mentioning it to anyone, David had begun fearing the world. If anyone had asked him just where this fear had begun, he might have said, facetiously, that as a child he had been bitten by a swan. This was true. In the park at the Palace of Fine Arts, he'd run toward the beautiful creature, his arms out, his four-year-old self ecstatic, and the big bird had let him have it, biting him on the hands and face and sending him screaming to his mother. It was more likely, though, he had derived his sense that the world was not safe from his father, who was himself not safe, subject to deep moodiness and sudden swings of temper.

But probably David would not have been able to completely justify his fearfulness, to himself or anyone else. Though he had heard of terrible things, nothing very awful had, in fact, ever happened to him. Occasionally the elements got in his way, a big storm soaked him on the street or an earthquake shut off his lights for a time. But that was all. So his fear had mellowed into what appeared to be a simple lack of interest. Mostly he managed to live inside, both inside his apartment and inside himself, writing his poetry. This was his main interest and his chosen work. David was a poet.

All his life he'd been a voracious reader—devouring a book or two a week. He had immense powers of recollection, practically memorizing all that he read. David could write before he went to school and had always written things down, making up little stories and poems, which, if they were very good, were posted by his mother on the back of the front door of the house. He'd grown up in the Sunset District, a protosuburb west of downtown. When he got out of high school, David stayed in San Francisco, going to State. He would have preferred to remain at home while at college, but his father, wanting to get him out of the house, rented him one of the apartments he owned in the Haight.

His father did not give him a break on the rent, however, and he was forced to take roommates. He chose two as mild and bookish as himself, boys who looked to him as the head of the household. This admiration, combined with the natural nonchalance of the eighteen-year-old and the peace of a house without his father in it, had brought David into the most outgoing time of his life. He liked the neighborhood. That it was not the wild Haight of the '60s, but the Haight of the '80s, a rather staid and funky place, suited him. David was staid and funky in his dress—usually a plain brown shirt and black pants hung on his tall and angular frame—and he wore his dark curly hair long in the style of the old neighborhood. He ventured out. The streets and restaurants of the Haight, the park, movies at the Old Vic, these became his haunts. The place grew tolerable, even comfortable to him after he'd lived there awhile.

At the height of this brief extraversion—because of it, actually—he met and married a young woman named Rosalind. Married life allowed him to return to the more inward existence he always preferred. He moved with his new bride to the Mission District, to the apartment where he still lived, though by himself at this point.

He never took up the Mission as he had the Haight. The Mission felt altogether more urban to him, and it brought his old fears back. When he went out, he moved in the circumspect way that he thought big cities required. He developed his mental corridors through the urban core, his ways and means. To go downtown or to the East Bay, he rode BART, San Francisco's squarish and limited subway, which he knew so intimately that the train had come to seem merely a mental conveyance, bringing the public library to him, rather than vice versa. He spent as little time on surface streets as he could. Up there he watched his back far more than he had to. He ducked into doorways a lot.

He did not travel far. Once friends from college had convinced him to go with them to Mexico, down to the Yucatán. The plane ride itself disturbed him. It wasn't just that the huge heavy mechanism did not belong off the ground. What bothered him most was the violent change of place it effected. The jet switched everything, one setting gone and the other there, like a conjuring act. This disorienting and instantaneous change of scene made places seem like channels on TV. Unsettled by the swift substitution of Mexico for his hometown, David had fallen ill a day after their arrival and had spent the week in a darkened motel room, miserably throwing up, while his friends ran around outside, happily throwing a Frisbee across the white sand.

He stayed home after that. And he did all right. Though his childish fear at times took possession of him, in general, David was not paralyzed. He had his defenses, and they worked. He didn't sleep well, but he got his rest. At night, he put on a blindfold to block out the light, that coppery glow that surrounds big cities. To ward off the traffic noise and the sound of the elevator, the shaft of which ran just past his bedroom wall, he wore earplugs.

Near his bed was his desk, at which he wrote in the mornings. On some morning in the now-distant past, he had simply left the earplugs in, and now this was his habit. So as David typed all morning—he wrote his poems with a computer—he heard only the wind of his own breath in the passages of his head.

His rejection of the larger world had its complement in his embrace of the inner one. He was a stubborn man, deeply attached to his attachments, and he had managed to turn poetry into a profession. He made a small living at it—at teaching it, anyway—and his work was known, as such things are, by a few people beyond his immediate friends. That is to say, he was a successful poet.

Could such an internal man write poems? True, certain kinds of poetry had eluded David, kinds that might have taken him out of doors. He was not a poet of sublime scapes, depicting lakes and meadows, still less a poet of outward wit and social chatter, a nabob of the salon. As he conceived of it now, David was a very late poet, writing when neither sublimity, nor wit, nor even simple description was possible. The poets of the past had used all that up.

As a poet, David felt that he lived at the end of history. Actually he took some pride in it. It was a special fate, to live at the end. But it limited things. By the time he had come along, he could find only a little rind left at the bottom of the big barrel of literary possibilities, this to scrape up and publish as he might. Hence David had become a deconstructionist, a practitioner of an art form that he and a few others called X poetry.

State was a hotbed of X poetry. David had met his compatriots there; others he knew through the obscure journals in which they published. Among these few, X poetry had arisen in the most painstaking manner possible, in conclaves where innocent-sounding terms were assigned the most arcane meanings, and with nobody in the larger world the wiser. A "book" was not a book, a "word" was not a word, a "letter" was not a letter. As an X poet, David wrote verse that avoided any conventional narrative or even conventional sentences, all of that rational structure deeply suspect to practitioners of his ilk. The result was as opaque as mud, and that was the way X poets liked it: a mire of words, available to any and to no interpretation. And at this David had become expert, had labored these long years. He had a dozen books to his credit, none of them with three words in a row that made any "sense." This is what he did all morning, his ears stuffed with plugs.

He'd been dedicated to this pursuit for fifteen years. In

the thirteenth year, his wife, Rosalind, a sensible and patient woman who had loyally and strenuously attempted to comprehend what he was doing, finally gave up and left him. As a sophomore living in the Haight, he had wooed Rosalind with the most romantic verses possible. But by the time he had graduated college, the poetry had changed, and after that so had he. He found that opacity had its personal as well as its aesthetic virtues, as a kind of stuffing, and by the time he was thirty he was fully insulated by it. He had X-poeted himself.

Rosalind had thrown up her hands at last, having followed her husband into this rarefied existence and having eventually decided she didn't really like it. His already internal existence become more and more so, to the point that he rarely went outside unless coerced. She had proclaimed him at last "impossible," a term that might have been applied to his work. For her part Rosalind had exited the marriage after igniting an affair at the software company where she worked, a romance with her cubicle mate, a man called Mango. Mango liked the club life; he had a tag for a name.

David remained on regular speaking terms with his ex-wife. He was solid, even stolid, in his connections. He did not have that many, and he made few new ones. But after the divorce, he drew his life even more closely about him. He lived alone in his apartment on Guerrero Street, a literate fortification. He threw very little away, and the place was more and more jammed with his books and papers. Papers and texts covered his bed, and occasionally when he was very tired, he simply cleared a small space among this litter, where he lay and slept.

Of course David was still required to go outside. For a long time, he had worked in a copy shop, where he had risen to manager, his chief qualification being that he did not despise the job. He deemed it a proper occupation for an X poet, the reproduction of text as text. But then he attracted academic attention by managing to publish his poems. His literary career had been an odyssey, a wending from tiny press to tinier press, often just before they'd gone out of business. David's work had ushered more than one small publishing enterprise out of the world. Still, it was notice of a sort. His X poet colleagues who had been employed by colleges recommended him, and David found work teaching.

So by the time of this story, David taught a class here and a class there in the Bay Area. He commuted by bus and subway to San Francisco State and to Mills College, where he wrought great muddy depths of ennui upon hapless undergraduates. And really, that might have been that, for David. Whole lives are spent on less, after all. And David himself would not have said he was unhappy. He might have confessed, had he known you very well, that he wanted a female companion. Badly, profoundly, wanted one. Still, he would never have told you that his life was small, interior, utterly consumed, every day, with thoughts and things not a soul in the world but David cared about. If he yearned for more, for a life in the larger world—he did, and who wouldn't have?—you would never have heard this from him.

Then, in the middle of a spell of that splendid weather, clear skies and bright air, that sometimes occurs in San Francisco in February—weather unnoticed by David himself, of course—things changed. A letter arrived in the mail from the Wadsworth Foundation. The procedures of the Wadsworth Foundation were secret; they took no applications and gave away big monetary awards to artists and writers. And they were giving him one of these big prizes—a thousand dollars times his age, which added up to $37,000, granted each year for five years, in recognition of his work and of his genius. "I am honored and delighted to inform you . . . ," the letter began.

David read on, entranced, just then not hearing the parrot for the first time in a couple of weeks. His father had given him the parrot, and it had been noisy from the start. The bird said nothing in English and made just one main noise, a call, a loud two-part trumpeting that sounded like the bark of a long-frozen hinge. In spite of its sameness, the call seemed to vary in import and to be oddly, even unsettlingly, appropriate to whatever situation David found himself in.

David savored the letter. Though this reward had arrived while he was still relatively young, David himself felt that the prize had been a long time in coming. He was, in spite of his inwardness, an ambitious man as regards his work, all of which now seemed justified. The years at minimum wage seemed justified. Even his divorce—the biggest sacrifice to his work, he felt—enhanced the glory of the day. Somewhere a committee of scholars had decided that David Huntington should receive this honor. God knew how it had happened. But everything was changed by it. He'd have money. He'd get offers at the best schools. He'd be famous. He would *be* X poetry.

But he still had an immediate problem: whom to tell? Overjoyed, he had to tell someone. So he told the parrot.

"I got it!" he shouted at the bird, who just then was perching on the refrigerator. The bird squawked back. "The Wadsworth!" said David. *Squawk.* "I'm a genius!" *Squawk.*

Even for David, this dialogue was less than satisfactory. So he thought of calling a woman he was seeing. Actually "seeing" would be putting too fine a point on it. He'd been out with her twice, once on a date arranged by his friend Lyle, and once after that, when she'd told him that she needed to take some time out. David called Caroline anyway, not that it mattered much, as he got her answering machine, so he had to leave a message at the beep. With the parrot still screeching in the background, he had let himself go and had shouted into the machine, "I'm a Wadsworth. I'm a genius. It's happened." Then he stopped, not knowing what else to say, hearing the wheels grinding away in the tape machine, and just hung up without saying good-bye or even identifying himself.

This, too, was quite unsatisfactory. Even if he had reached her, she would not have been able to rejoice properly at his news. Caroline was a writer herself, with some jealousy and no patience for good news about other writers, especially David. David knew he wouldn't have wanted to hear this news from another writer, either. That was why he hadn't immediately called any of the writers he knew—Marilyn the chair at Mills, Renny the curator, or Lyle his fellow X poet. He felt that they would take the news badly.

Then he called his friend Peter, whom he'd known since college and who worked with the Longshoremen's Union on the docks. But he got no answer, not even an answering machine, as Peter didn't believe in them. David held on to the receiver, letting it ring. The trill on the line alternated with the parrot squawk, and was similarly unfulfilling.

So he called Rosalind, his ex-wife, but got only her boyfriend, Mango. Mango answered the phone saying "Yah mon," like a Rastafarian. The guy had long orange hair, which had probably given rise to his nickname. He was a talented bass player, Rosalind had claimed, and was only biding his time at the software company until he got his recording deal. David took a deep breath and tried to explain the Wadsworth to Mango. It was a fellowship, an honor for his work, his poetry. It was money, said David, finally. How much? Mango asked. A thousand dollars times his age for five years, said David. How much is that? said Mango, who was twenty-six. A lot, said David.

Mango said he'd tell Roz, a name David had never called Rosalind, and David got off the phone, feeling that this effort to celebrate his good news with anyone had been fruitless and sensing the painful irony that, having labored so long to not be understood, he would not be able to make people understand at this point. So in a sort of despair, he returned to the squawk of the parrot, who *had* been answering him the whole time, as if it had been the bird instead of these distant electronic significations of human beings to whom David had been speaking.

The bird was making its same noise—that rasping, two-toned call, its raucous iamb. Over the past two weeks the sound had sometimes seemed to be a cry for help, sometimes a scream of rage, sometimes a simple emotionless bleat like a homing beacon. But this time, there could be no mistaking it. As David had been speaking into the dumb electronic webwork of the phone system, as he had tried to relay his news, the bird had been calling back in mocking mimicry. The bird was squawking; David was squawking. There wasn't much difference.

Then a real mistake: David called his father, a childish, demanding man, whom his mother had long ago divorced. His mother had moved to San Diego and remarried, but his father lived on in the old house on Taraval, forever restless and disgruntled and resenting. When David was in third grade,

Ben had changed the family name from Hirsch to Huntington. David remembered the difficulty at school, the questions the other kids asked about his new name. Maybe this was where the X poetry business had begun, in some defensive obfuscation about the essential names for things.

Ben was in real estate. He held properties, mostly light industrial lots south of Market, and sold them when the selling was good. Lately he had moved into converting and selling live/work studios for artists. Doing so he had taken up Bohemian airs. He wore a black racing cap on his bald pate, drove his black Porsche Carrera, took lunch at Postrio. Ben was rich, though he gave no money to anyone, including his son.

"Dad," said David, "I won the Wadsworth."

"You won the what?" said Ben.

"The Wadsworth, a fellowship, a big award for my writing."

"Does it come with money?" asked his father.

"Yeah, good money," said David, "Fifty thousand a year for five years." He was exaggerating slightly.

"Fifty thousand a year?" said Ben. "A good plumber makes more than that." Talking to his father was worse than talking to a machine, and just as predictable. The bird squawked again, mocking him for even trying.

"Is that my bird?" asked Ben. "How's he doing?"

"He screams," said David.

"Yeah, I hear him," said Ben. "He does that a lot. But you can keep the cover on. That shuts him up." David had already discovered this, but he hadn't the heart to keep the bird in the dark all the time. In truth, David hadn't even liked keeping the bird in the cage.

"Where'd you get this bird, anyway?" said David. He had

already begun to suspect that his father's gift was not the big-hearted gesture he might have imagined.

"Bought him in Serramonte, at the mall," said Ben. "So cute I couldn't resist him." David doubted this. His father could resist anything.

The bird had come out of the blue. Ben had stopped by with it, without calling first. He'd buzzed and told David to come down, as he didn't want to park. "I have something for you," he said. Outside, Ben stood by his double-parked Porsche. A large domed object sat in the passenger seat.

"It's a parrot," Ben had said. "I brought you a parrot. You always wanted a parrot when you were a kid. It's a present."

What it was, was the larger world, coming into David's life through a minuscule crack, an odd circumstance. But David did not see it coming. He wanted to believe that his father had brought him a present. That maybe his dad was finally feeling fatherly, was relenting a little in his selfishness.

"Gee, thanks, Dad," was all David had said, as Ben had put the big covered cage in David's arms. He was glad to do it, Ben said.

Ben got back inside the low vehicle. "Enjoy," he called out. "His name's Pepito." He pulled his cap down on his head and gunned it, blasting down Guerrero Street. He left David struggling with the cage and the door to the apartment building.

David had taken the cage back upstairs, placed it on a stool in the corner of his kitchen, and pulled the cover off. There on the swinging perch, looking back at him with piercing dark eyes, was a small green parrot. His parrot, David thought. It had a splatter of red feathers across its forehead and a crook at the point of its beak, from biting down too hard on something. The bird's eyes were especially expressive. The parrot could dilate its black pupils at will. A white wrinkled membrane framed and emphasized them. The bird gazed at David for about three seconds, focusing and refocusing its eyes, and then let out its cry, which made David jump. It was a louder sound than you'd think could come from a smallish bird. And it was the first of thousands, tens of thousands, of such squawks.

2

Fern was as far from home as she had ever been and getting farther every minute. She was in Ecuador, riding a bus from Cuenca down to Guayaquil. Her trip had begun in the early morning, high in the Andes, and would end after dark, at sea level. For Fern everything was new. Every tree against the sky on the ridgetop, every rock by the road. She had not been out of the United States before and had never traveled on her own. Proud of having come this far, she had, in truth, little idea of the magnitude of what she had taken on. She was not yet thirty and still naïve in an American way. Her confidence, however untried, had protected her, so far.

She had a plan. Every day was planned. On the bus from Cuenca to Guayaquil, she planned to read a book, a text about adaptive radiation. It was a difficult book, about animals, which were her main interest, but about them indirectly, as occasional illustrations of a theory in evolution. And out the window of the bus, Ecuador was intervening. Since she had been a girl, Fern had wanted to see Ecuador. In Ecuador you could see the whole world. It had more geographical range in less space than any other place on the planet. Within two hundred miles of where she sat were snowy mountains, some of the most extraordinary on earth, dry upland forests called *cerrado,* equatorial rain forests, and tropical beaches. The land leaped down from glaciers to lagoons.

When you went up in Ecuador, it was like flying far north, whizzing up to Banff, and if you went down, you went all the way down, to zero degrees, to the equator. Elevation could mimic latitude, so tiny Ecuador could encompass landscapes that would otherwise be thousands of miles apart. When Fern had first heard this in high school, she'd known she would see Ecuador someday, and here she was. She'd had to find a site for her field study, and Ecuador had come up, specifically the coastal region. But the idea of the country's geographic range had never left her, so she'd chosen to go first to the highlands, to start with the ice-capped volcanoes around Quito and then to climb down. She'd see everything.

Just then, she was not even watching the earth's range roll by out the bus window. With that song on, she could not *not* listen, and she gave up trying, putting down her book. The bus had a speaker system, and the driver played music. *The* music, you might say, as you heard the same music everywhere in Ecuador, in the streets and the plazas, in the restaurants and the clubs, sung by young and old alike. Everybody knew the words. The particular song capturing Fern was one she'd heard just the night before. She and her classmates had danced to it, in a disco in Cuenca, which was a university town in the mountains.

For the past three months, Fern had been studying Spanish in Cuenca. At the insistence of the others, Fern had gone to the disco—called Piccadilly, oddly enough—to celebrate the conclusion of their term. She did not usually dance and hadn't planned to. She had an early morning the next day.

She'd planned just to sit at a table, sipping *canelazo,* a sweet rum concoction she'd learned to like. But this particular song had everybody dancing, and the others had refused her refusal, actually pulling her to her feet.

So she had joined them, jumping around, which was what she thought to do when she danced, until she and everyone else were sweaty and singing along with the refrain of the tune. On the bus, Fern sang the refrain again—*Son Latinos*—under her breath, as the song reached its final choruses, then she tried to go back to her chapter on the continual and gradual mechanisms of evolutionary change. "Slight genetic differences can suggest chronological relationships between different species that have diverged over wide geographical areas."

She made a note in the margin, in her serious way. "Parrots?" By which she meant to remind herself that somewhere, sometime—when this year of field study was done, maybe, and she got back to Tucson and the library—she would check the literature on genetic research into parrots to see if any interesting DNA work had been done on them.

But then the music began again—another song she knew from her trip—and that was the last serious thought she could manage for a time. She looked out the window at the steep, thickly forested Andean countryside and hummed along.

Fern Melartin was an exotic, there in Ecuador. She had been born in Saint Paul, Minnesota, of Finnish pioneer stock. She was lanky and fair-haired and blue-eyed. Men and sometimes women found her attractive. She had learned how to tell when this was happening. There would be an overeager quality to the gaze or the words, a quality she had not understood for the longest time. Fern herself thought she looked odd and apelike. When she looked in the mirror, it was all she could do not to jut out her lower jaw and make those in-out ape noises. Part of this arose from her studies. She was a primate, after all, she'd reasoned. But, in truth, she was a beautiful young woman, and she did not much look apelike, at least not more than any other human being.

Fern's parents had named their daughter Fern and their son Forrest. They'd been librarians and amateur naturalists, people who lived for the outdoors. Every vacation and many weekends they'd camped out together, often paddling across the lakes of Minnesota in two canoes. So, as a little girl, Fern had come to love staying for days in some remote place, where ducks and geese moved among the cattails and at night no lights shone across the broad black surface of the water.

She'd come to South America to undertake the fieldwork for her dissertation in the Guayas River Estuary—Fern was studying for her Ph.D. at Sonora State University. She was writing about a species of small green parrot called, in Latin, *Aratinga erythrogenys.* To find and observe this aratinga was her quest in Ecuador. These birds were important indicators of the state of the earth. Once they had flown over the coasts in noisy flocks of tens of thousands. But now the human population had made changes in the birds' habitat, cutting down the upland forests, where researchers had observed them in the '50s and '60s. Those forests were 90 percent gone now.

Fern had read that the aratinga also bred in mangrove swamps, and she hoped to confirm this report. The mangroves posed their own difficulties. They were steamy, tangled, muddy, full of bugs and snakes, and accessible only by boat.

Still, Fern was determined to find this bird there. She felt that the success of her dissertation would depend upon it.

This was her goal then. Fern had always had goals. She had goals that extended for years into the future. She would find the aratinga, write her dissertation, get it published, get a great university position, get married, and have babies, two of them. She planned to do all these things by the time she was thirty-five, some five years in the future. And nobody who knew Fern would have doubted that she would accomplish them.

But unforeseen events had slowed her down. She'd had some trouble getting a fellowship in her third year in grad school. She had attached herself to the wrong professor—someone who had not been tenured—and at this point she had to work to pay for school. Still, she had kept on course. She'd gotten engaged in the previous year. And she liked working in the tree nursery. Though the extra job had cost her two years, she hadn't had to take out any student loans, and she had financed this year in South America by herself.

And now she was on her way. Fern's father had been proud of her for going, though he had not said so around her mother, who was terrified by the prospect of her daughter so far away and on her own. During Fern's last phone call to Saint Paul, her mother tearfully had made her promise that she would not do anything dangerous in Ecuador and that she would not go anywhere alone. But *dangerous* and *alone* seemed to be relative terms to Fern. This bus trip, for instance, was not dangerous and she was among others, if not with them. Her mother, she knew, would not buy this. For her own part, Fern had not let herself feel fear about her trip. She had her plans and her plans included going to

Ecuador. Only the night before she'd left Tucson had the whole enterprise finally made her afraid.

Fern's fiancé, Geoffrey, had tried to scare her into not going. During her last week at home he'd brought her magazine articles, one after the next, meant to convince her of the dangers of such travel: one on intestinal parasites, one on kidnapping, one on a woman in Peru imprisoned for years on dubious charges, even one on a bank failure. Geoffrey was doing his masters in Business Administration at another university in Tucson; for him bank failure was no small threat. What if you can't make withdrawals from your accounts? he had argued. Do you think they have the FDIC down there?

By her last day in the States, all of it had worn her down. The two of them had gone to dinner. Geoffrey had been angry because, in preparing for her trip, she'd cut off her hair, which had been down to her shoulders and now was at most an inch long all over. Then he had spent the whole evening trying to dissuade her from going at all. He'd reimburse her for the ticket, he'd said. But she hadn't given in and had gotten angry with him in turn when he had refused to stop. He just didn't understand, she'd said, and she'd slept that last night on her own side of the bed, lying on her stomach with her arms folded under her, her face away from him. They had not made love. Actually she had only pretended to sleep. She'd lain there all night scaring herself over and over again with horrible scenarios of what would certainly happen to her in Ecuador.

Still, she had left him behind, had left her town, Tucson, and her country. She'd gotten into a taxi as Geoffrey had turned away from the window of their apartment. She'd flown to Miami, then had made a connection to Quito, arriving late at night in cold high mountain air and staying at a hotel near the airport, where she had called Geoffrey and tried to make up with him. That night, so far away, she felt closer to him than ever. She loved Geoffrey. He had his stubborn ways, his narrow ways, but he loved her, too, and she still wanted to marry him. This would be the last time she'd feel so strongly about him.

The next day she explored Quito, a beautiful city so high in the air—at 10,000 feet—that she felt dizzy as she walked the avenues and markets. Even that first day, she'd felt safe there, safer than in Tucson. A few men had made comments to her, but she had learned to say *"No me moleste"* and to keep walking, and it had worked, every time. The taxi drivers and the people in the markets went out of their way to help her, and everything was interesting: the scattered pale houses on the steep hills, the blackened cathedral, the narrow stone streets, and especially the people themselves—all kinds of Ecuadorians in business suits and in ancient dark clothing—everyone outside, jamming the sidewalks, inhabiting a city in a way she'd never known before.

Things were connected here, was how she described it to herself. There wasn't the sense that you got in the United States of separation, rich from poor, old from young, natural from urban, old from new. For the past three months, she'd been able to look anywhere and see evidence of this. Looking out the window of the bus, she saw, on a bench by the road, miles from anything, in the middle of the jungle and the mountains, two girls, in old-fashioned skirts and new Mickey Mouse T-shirts and strange round hats, talking happily.

Still, she hadn't really been tested. People had taken care of her in Ecuador. In Quito the school's van had picked her up and driven her the several hours across the Andean ridges to Cuenca, where she'd lived in the town's old quarter for three months with her "Ecuadorian family," which was the way the school described her hosts, in their home, a hacienda with a thick carved front door on the street and tall cool corridors inside and a central garden with a fountain. The family had quickly become familiar to Fern. She'd eaten her meals, played cards, even gone to Mass with them, though she hadn't been to church in years and had been raised as a Lutheran. They had a daughter just two years younger than she was, a young woman called Monica.

When she hadn't been with the family, she'd been with her schoolmates. School went on all day. In school, they were supposed to speak only in Spanish, and the staff did everything they could to keep them in classes all the time. They took language classes in the villa overlooking the river, and on many evenings met for cooking class or ceramics class or dancing class. Fern had had to carry on in Spanish for months, and though occasionally it seemed easy and natural, for the most part she had to think in English and laboriously translate her thought into Spanish words. A teacher had told her that this would eventually give way to simply thinking in Spanish, but that hadn't happened yet.

The whole family had gone down to the bus station to see her off, Monica and her fiancé Paulo and her sister Maria Augusta, who at eleven was the youngest in the family, and even the Doña, Monica's mother. Fern and Monica had cried and hugged at their parting. So only at that moment on the bus had Fern been alone, forced to test her sense of connection and to confront her solitude and her distance from home.

The mountain road was not in good shape. Its pavement had been washed away in places, and the bus had to roll ahead over rough gravel. Even so, the driver raced along, passing on blind curves with a long honk on his horn. Beyond the road, the land was steep, nearly vertical, and dense and green with *la selva*—the jungle. Above the bus, the peaks were so high she couldn't see the tops. They just went up and up, green as park grass.

Some areas of the mountainsides had been cleared, plowed, and planted, but it still looked wild. Here in the mountains, the old earth might still prevail, if only through the potency of its slope and elevation. The people of the old earth persisted here, too: On the steepest slopes and on top of the ridges she could spot the occasional lone silhouetted figure, ghostly in long dark clothes, striding along. To the west, beyond the shoulder of the road, lay a broad white plain that was actually the tops of clouds. Far below was Guayaquil, and beyond the city, the Pacific Ocean. If the bus went off the road, they would fall for miles. Maybe never hit bottom.

But that did not happen. The bus traveled safely and steadily down for hours, switching back and forth on the narrow road, submerging into the clouds and coming out under them. Then, abruptly, the land went flat, and they proceeded across a plain, almost entirely planted, the fields bordered by a ruffle of low banana trees under a gray sky. Spats of rain struck the window now and again. It was still the rainy season here, and it seemed to be another country from the high mountain town where she'd been that morning.

As the land had opened up, she looked for birds and saw lots of them in the sky—herons, raptors, turkey vultures. Highways select for carrion birds, she thought idly. She watched for birds with the quick regular wingbeats of parrots, but saw none. This had been parrot habitat once, though now the big trees they needed for their nests were rare. Only a few tall native trees stood above the hedgerows on the wild margins of the fields. She'd seen no parrots in Ecuador yet. The closest she'd come had been hearing their squawks behind wooden doors off the narrow streets in Cuenca.

The bus came into the town of La Troncal, which was just a collection of concrete buildings lining the road. The buildings were white with Latin touches of bright colors, splattered with painted political ads, new and old. The dirt side streets stopped abruptly at fields cultivated with sugarcane and banana. Big parked trucks had DOLE printed on their sides. At the main bus stop, boys came aboard selling apples from Chile, melons, *pollo,* and drinks, and a woman got on carrying a cage with a parrot in it.

This felt fateful to Fern, and she decided to get a look at the bird. So she changed her seat to sit next to the woman and with only a little hesitation tried to start a conversation in Spanish.

"¿Tienes un loro?" said Fern, and the woman answered back, glad to introduce her bird. This was Mija, she said. Mija could count in English and when it was cold, Mija said, *"Hace frío."* Fern recognized Mija as a blue-headed parrot, though this one's head and flight feathers looked purple. Fern said, *"Mucho gusto,"* both to the bird and its owner, and then, at least for the moment, couldn't formulate any more Spanish. Some field biologist she was, she thought, interviewing a bird on a bus. So for a while she just sat there, looking at the parrot and the landscape, and thinking about Geoffrey.

Couldn't she do her fieldwork in Arizona? he'd asked for the hundredth time. There were no parrots left in Arizona, she'd answered. Then he'd wanted to get married before she left, though in the end she had wrung from him the concession that this year apart would be a good test for their relationship. In Cuenca, she had written him excited letters almost every day, trying to relate everything to him. And she talked to him on the phone once a week, as they'd planned, shouting, "I miss you!" over the international static, in the booth at the EMETEL, the phone office off the town square.

Her seatmate had gone to sleep, though the parrot, Mija, continued to observe Fern. Outside, things got more urban as they approached the sprawling mass of Guayaquil. The air was smoky. Many of the buildings had sprays of reinforcing bars sprouting from the rooftop pillars, as if they might yet proceed upward someday.

Geoffrey was terrible with letters. She had gotten only two from him, both of them sounding telegraphic. On the phone, he told her about his family—his father was the CEO of a local company, his mother a real estate agent—and talked also about his classes and his friends, how they had gone to the basketball game or gotten drunk at the Lonely Bear. The day before, when she'd made her last call to him from Cuenca, he'd been surprised to hear that she was heading down to Guayaquil.

"Already?" he said, not intending anything bad by it. But it made her feel disconnected from him. The months she'd spent in Cuenca felt like such a long time to her. And she didn't know when she'd be able to call him again. Remembering this, she took out her notebook and pen and began a letter—"Dear Sweetie, I met a parrot named Mija on the bus. A blue head from the Amazon." She looked at the bird closely as she described it for Geoffrey—"It has a red beak and the undersides of its tail feathers are red, too." Then she looked at what she'd written and it seemed idiotic, as if addressed to a child.

She held her pen out next to the cage, and the bird deftly pulled the cap off the end with its prehensile claw. It bit down on the plastic once and then dropped it. Fern had a flush of feeling actually *there,* on the bus in the presence of this bird. It was a feeling she'd been experiencing regularly since she'd come to Ecuador. She'd be looking at something and suddenly feel herself looking at it as if she and it and everything around her had been cast into real flesh, real earth, real stone. It made her feel as if her life back home had been a movie or something, a bodiless stream of images.

After a while the country grew marshy, and they reached a bridge over the Guayas, a wide stream flowing southward into the estuary where she would spend the next few months. The traffic thickened as they approached the city, and the bus moved slowly across the span. Her seatmate woke up with a start and said, *"Dios mío."*

The woman spoke partially in English and introduced herself as Dicna. She had acquired her bird seventeen years before on a trip to the Amazon. "Seventeen years old!" said Dicna to the bird. And to Fern, with dark zest, "She will be alive *cuando esté muerta."* Hearing this, Fern had a pang of sympathy for this woman on the bus. Would she end up like her, alone, if not with a beloved bird then with her beloved bird studies?

This was too much, and so she settled on a finite anxiety, something raised by what Dicna had said. Why hadn't she chosen the Amazon for her fieldwork? It was going to be a lot harder to find her aratinga in the swamps. So she spoke to herself seriously. She'd studied mangrove ecology. She'd be able to get a sense of the whole ecosystem more quickly there. Plus, fewer biologists had written about it. Wasn't that what she was, a biologist?

Beyond the blurred bridge railing, the river was broad and brown and at its far edge a low green fringe rose, where the mangroves began. They were both calming and forbidding, promising and threatening. Fern felt a ripple of fear at what she had undertaken, as well as a pulse of excitement. In her businesslike way, she tried to dismiss all that feeling and simply concentrate on the process. She had gotten all the way to South America and had come within sight of her goal. She knew about mangroves. She knew about this aratinga. Still, the fear and the thrill lingered until the bus cleared the bridge, and her view of the river and its far bank disappeared.

3

The parrot was a pain, noisy and unfriendly, and yet David liked him. It was good to have another living thing around during the day, when the building was vacant, the other residents attending to their jobs. Many of them were in software and often worked nights as well. But now the bird was there, calling attention to itself. It woke and slept, sometimes lying flat on its back with its birdy feet up.

The bird was mean, but the bird was real, and David found he didn't mind living with it. He even found himself grateful for its presence, as if he had wanted to pay attention to something outside himself for a long time. Now he had to. In fact, if David was going to be brought out of his long self-confinement, it would have to be by something like this parrot, something loud, for one thing. Even his earplugs didn't keep out the parrot's cries. They pierced his wadding.

He didn't like the name the parrot had come with, Pepito. It was a dumb name. Pepito was the name of a parrot on a cereal box and this was no cereal box bird, nobody's pet. If this parrot had indeed come from a pet shop in a mall, then he was a bad product, a failed consumer item. That was okay with David. Better a failed consumer item, he felt, than a successful one. David decided to call the bird Little Wittgenstein. It was the bird's blank, deep, universally signifying and ever-present cry that suggested the name. Wittgenstein, the philosopher–patron saint of the X poets, had argued that language had no absolute meaning.

It did not matter what the bird was called. He responded to nothing and to everything, and shed his human names like a boulder shedding the tide. David might have called him Moby-Dick, for all the good it did. Pepito, Little Wittgenstein, or whatever, he stared, screamed, spread his feathers, ate and drank and shat his pale guano, and was utterly indomitable, a bird unto himself.

And a bird out of his cage. On the third day he had the parrot, David decided to let him loose in the apartment. David's hatred for the cage, a tall, hooped, bustly item that took up a lot of the kitchen, won out over his fear of the bird itself. Besides its ungainliness, the cage reminded David of his father. For this reason David assumed that Little Wittgenstein hated the cage, too.

Actually the parrot liked the cage. It took a week of coaxing and leaving the cage door open to get him to emerge, first to perch atop the cage and then to leave it. David transferred the standing perch to the top of the refrigerator and found an old wooden ruler, which he extended to the parrot. After biting the ruler once, the parrot obligingly stepped aboard and was transferred to the perch. David stuffed the big cage into the hall closet, and Little Wittgenstein was unhoused, at least in the apartment.

So the bird was free, and David's own feeling of captivity, derived from seeing the bird in the cage, was relieved. But there was a price for this, David found. The bird was even harder to ignore. At first he could only fly off his perch, not up to it, and he did so to walk into David's bedroom at dawn to deliver his singular message. Within a week, he could flutter around and flap himself up to high vantage points as well. From these he looked down, magisterial and popeyed, only thin air between his sharp beak and David's flesh.

The Wadsworth Prize unsettled David, too. For a long time his friends had encouraged him to get out more, and now he was getting invitations. Not that he accepted any. Parties were dreadful to David. But the world was beckoning, and there was one reason David considered taking up its offer. He still needed to find a woman.

His friend Peter, the only one to whom David confided about women, had told him that if he were serious about finding a girlfriend, he'd have to go out. He would not find one here, Peter had said on one of his regular visits to David's apartment. David trusted Peter's judgment. Peter wasn't a writer, for one thing. He was a social worker and a trade unionist, a throwback, David thought sometimes, but a sincere guy. Peter wore a red star on his Levi's jacket and drove an ancient Volkswagen Beetle. On his visit, Peter looked at Little Wittgenstein with a cool eye and said nothing.

David decided he might take Peter's advice and begin going out for coffee in the morning. This was a luxurious period in San Francisco and the whole city was taking its coffee in expensive cafés. Why not me, too? asked David. It would give him a reason to get up and shower, for one thing, now that he had no job.

By then it was late spring, and he had finished teaching. At the end of the spring term, he'd always had to make strenuous arrangements to secure a class or two in the fall. At State, he'd have to go see Maxine, the chair, and endure her serious doubts, then agree to teach whatever, and even then to wait nervously until August when the classes came through or not.

But this time, he'd simply walked out, making no arrangements to return in the fall. And lo, Maxine had called *him*, to make sure he was coming back. He had answered with what he'd always wished he could have answered, that no, he would stay home and write in the fall. Maxine said she couldn't guarantee that she could get him back into the rotation, but David said that was all right.

He'd gotten lots of calls, finally. Caroline had called and rather dutifully congratulated him. She'd said, "That's great," and, "That's just great," and to get off the line, "Well, that's just great." Rosalind had called. Even a broker called him, a specialist in internet IPOs who was sure he'd want to invest. He didn't want to do that. But he did want to launch himself into his life as an independent writer, a free-and-clear individual who could, if he felt like it, go out to a café in the morning.

So David went out. He walked up to Noe Valley, that tony neighborhood of shops and pretty row houses, and on the first morning he did so, good things happened, as if he were being given a sign. First, when he stopped at an automatic teller machine on the way, he found that his new money had arrived. It hadn't come as a check, but as a wire transfer, like an intravenous pump from the reservoir of really big dollars. He'd been trying to take twenty out of eighty dollars and now he had dozens of thousands, the figures echoing his age in a fateful way. So he pushed the button for a hundred instead. Out they came, five new twenties. And then at the café, a new place called Savor, he met a woman. Or more or less met a woman. She'd been ahead of him in the line and when they'd been given their coffee, he had found the nerve to ask her where he could find the sugar, and she had pointed at the counter.

He thought about the encounter all day and began to rehearse for the next morning. And then the next day—he'd never have done this if not for the Wadsworth—after having to wait half an hour as if examining the racks of mugs and fancy grinders until she miraculously appeared, he nearly choked, but finally did ask if he might join her at her table and she'd said sure. Her name was Gail. His was Dave, he said.

She'd never met a real poet before, she said, when David told her—gently, not using the term *X poetry*—what he did. She didn't seem put off, and David was encouraged. Still, there was a difficulty. Finishing her *latte*, Gail had given him her phone number, telling him at the same time that he probably shouldn't call her at home, as Brian, evidently the man she lived with, wouldn't like it. They weren't "on good terms," she had added, by way of explanation.

For a couple of weeks, David's scalp sizzled with caffeine. He'd never drunk so much coffee, especially not the hair-raisingly strong coffee people in San Francisco were drinking then. But he hadn't gotten any further with Gail. She'd asked to hear some of his poetry and had listened to it, pie-eyed over the café table, but David hadn't been able to work up the nerve to ask her out, and she was no closer to breaking up with Brian than she had been before. She did tell him, however, that Brian was boring. She'd said this a couple of times, actually, and each time it had given David a little hope. "That's great," he said.

At home, man and bird coexisted uneasily. One morning, feeling brave, David extended a finger toward the bird, as the parrot sat on his perch atop the refrigerator. David had it in mind that he might eventually be able to touch or pet Little Wittgenstein, and he put forth the digit generously enough, reaching up in the gesture of Adam extending a finger to God. Not leaving the perch, the bird struck like a snake, gripping the meaty tip of David's index finger and not letting go. David gave a sharp, wordless shout, very loud, right into the parrot's goofy red face, and still the bird held on, until David pulled back his finger with force, not caring if he pitched the parrot across the kitchen, which he didn't. In fact, the parrot recovered nicely, seeming quite pleased with himself.

Still, David persisted, thinking of the swan at the Palace of Fine Arts and not wishing to sustain an aversion to his new roommate. The next morning he cut up some fruit, put it in a small dish, and gently edged the dish onto the top of fridge, keeping his distance. The parrot contemplated the offering for a second, then hopped down to eat. This method of feeding became the established pattern.

Having been bitten by the bird didn't make David less interested in it. Indeed, the creature took on a certain fascination as a result. David watched him trimming off bits of apple with his beak or working on cleaning his green wing feathers, occasionally spreading his wings broadly and showing the pale orange undersides. This Little Wittgenstein was the Other, David conceived—the Feathered Other. It was a concept he liked, an invocation of that which was inviolable, that which did not deign to conform to human expectation.

At that time, earplugs still in his ears, under a muffled barrage of parrot squawks, David was concerned with creating his magnum opus, the would-be fruit of this fellowship. It was to be a great nonnarrative epic, a volume of otherness, pages of X poetry, none of it deigning to conform to human expectation. It would thwart a reader for hundreds of pages.

Thwarting was the delight, the true art of the X poet. Of course X poets were perverse, withholding types. But beyond that, they weren't simply denying, they were deconstructing. And to hear them talk, this was no minor deconstruction job. Theirs was the final massive demolition of everything that had happened in the West since the Middle Ages, a pulling down brick by brick of the whole edifice of the Enlightenment and its diminishingly empirical aftermath.

David, in his heart, wasn't so grandiose about it. He'd simply learned early on in his career—such as it was—that clarity got you only so far. At first, he'd simply reached for ambiguity, for a teasing doubleness. And the more he obfuscated, the better he did. The new book was his dimmest yet. He was out to stymie the mental expectations of some ideal and inhumanly patient reader, perhaps even this lovely Gail from the café, who might admire the persistence of a poet who worked so hard not to be understood. David could almost see the book, finished and published, a big, deliciously difficult volume.

Still, the actual writing wasn't going well. It was a strenuous effort, he'd found, to make no sense. It required all his wiliness. A truly grand stymieing was a huge job. Sometimes he felt as if the work were not so much undoing the rational habits that the culture was founded on as reversing the evolution of the mind itself. The mind, having groped its way out of the swamp of nonsense—for its survival, mind you—was not about to stop meaning now. Often a whole page of seemingly random language could be unified by a single unwitting word, turned into a scene, something as coherent as moonlight on a riverbank. He had to guard against this.

It was a problem, too, to have been awarded a prize to write this way. The prize had removed the restrictions on his proceeding into this thicket of X poetry. It had helped to have restrictions—having to teach freshmen to diagram sentences, for instance—so that his work might react against them. The kind of writing he did was best done peripherally. Going straight at it was tough. So the spring went on, without his having to do anything for money, and he was having trouble. The work kept coming out logical and lyrical.

Even random selection didn't seem to help. Without thinking, he took an alphabetical list of dictionary entries with special usage notes—"principal, principle, prophecy, prophesy, prove, quash, raise, rational, rationale, ravage, ravish, raze"—and found that it was practically a sonnet. Or, taken verbatim from another list, one of irregular verbs—"go went gone/grave graved graven/grind ground ground"—worse. It reminded him of Gray's *Elegy.* None of it was acceptable, but he kept it all, thinking he might snip it into nonsense later. He wrote a lot, having nothing else to do, and the paper stacked up in the corner of his bedroom that was his study. Watching the parrot was more interesting.

Meanwhile, there was David's life in a higher financial sphere. He still shopped for food, of course. His habit had been to shop as quickly and as cheaply as possible, and to see no one if he could. From his apartment he'd walk downhill into the Mission and buy in bulk from a market on Capp Street. He got stacks of corn tortillas, which he saved in the freezer for months, also canned beans, big bags of rice, cheap beer. These had been his staples.

But in his new life, David felt called by the specialty shops up the hill. Almost without noticing it, he was buying clothes in Noe Valley and dressing like the others in the café called Savor, in soft leather and lovely plaids and really nice jeans. The clerks called him Dave. He walked amid shoppers who pushed strollers and sucked fruit smoothies through straws, and he bought reggiano and pâté in the cheese store, and shiitake mushrooms and arugula and Niman Schell steaks and wonderful Braeburn apples and other proper-nouned items in the little groceries, even beluga caviar and the finest tiniest-bubbliest Italian water.

And then the furniture stores began appealing to him, and one morning in a kind of terrified trance, thinking of Gail, he spent $3,000 on a sofa, a beauteous huge pale velvet item, and then put out another grand on chairs and a pair of black-lacquered bedside tables with drawers in them. For years his stuff had lain happily in piles on the floor by the bed, but no more. Then he found the Persian carpet store. All these items he had delivered to his apartment, and the deliverymen stuffed them in there with everything else. Having new things did not mean David would throw anything away.

The deliverymen enraged the parrot. He screamed and flew at their heads. He had claimed the apartment as his own domain. The parrot didn't like visitors in general. When David's friend Lyle stopped by, the parrot attacked him. Lyle wasn't good with animals. He was a fussy, funny man with a shock of silver bangs that was his trademark. He and David and Peter had become friends in college, back when Lyle's personality had appeared merely immature and he was therefore still likable.

On the evening of the attack, Lyle had come over to have a few beers, to celebrate David's fellowship, he'd said without enthusiasm. But Little Wittgenstein did not stop screaming, and finally Lyle, maybe a bit drunk by then, screamed back at the parrot, who then came down off the fridge like a harpy and flapped in Lyle's face. Lyle gasped and ran out of the room, hiding in the bathroom until David assured him that he had shut Little Wittgenstein in the bedroom. Lyle emerged, but could not relax much after that, and soon left.

Lyle had reported back to the others—in the bar called Babar, downhill in the Mission, where even David joined the coterie once in a while—that David's existence was weirder than shit. Lyle, who had been consumed with envy when David won the Wadsworth and grief-stricken that this honor had somehow slipped past *him,* took some comfort in giving this report to the others. David and his new furniture and his mountain of paper and his crazy, vicious parrot. It was just imploding, said Lyle, it was all just imploding. "It can't last," he told them. "No one can keep living like that. Something will give."

The next time Lyle came over, he was taking no chances. It was a pale, damp afternoon, and Lyle arrived in the company of their mutual friend Peter.

"Put that bird in its cage," said Lyle, "or we aren't coming up."

"I won't," said David. "And you'll come up anyway." David gave them a long buzz. Once inside David's apartment, Lyle wouldn't go into the kitchen, where the parrot was. The three of them talked in the living room, David on his big new couch, Peter springy in a cantilevered chair, and Lyle nervous in the shallow bunker of the old sofa.

Lyle talked a lot, anyway. He liked to talk—in blurts without verbs—about poets he hated. "Wendy Patkin," he was saying this time. "Those goddamned horses. Steeds, they might as well be. Steeds in subordinate clauses."

From the kitchen came a chirrup and a flutter of wings, and then around the corner flew the green avenger, having heard his enemy. He landed on top of a bookshelf and chewed maniacally at something deep in his feathers. Lyle looked ready to flee.

"Can he be elsewhere?" asked Lyle. "Can you put him somewhere?"

"He goes where he goes," said David.

The bird squawked at them, as if he knew he was being discussed.

"Does he mean anything by that?" said Peter.

"What do you mean *mean*?" said Lyle. "He does that constantly."

"Little Wittgenstein makes different kinds of noises," said David in the bird's defense.

"I can't believe you call him that," said Lyle.

Peter asked if the parrot said anything in English, and David said no.

"Maybe you could get him to say 'Nevermore,'" said Lyle. Atop the bookcase the parrot perched and watched them, looking every bit as nutty and fatal as Poe's raven. At last Lyle couldn't take any more and announced he had to go. On his way out the door he offered a last comment on the parrot.

"Actually, I wouldn't call that bird a pet," he said. "He's not adapting, Dave. He's making you adapt. That's called wild."

"I don't want a pet," said David.

"He's not the hostage here," said Lyle, leaving. "He's the terrorist in the embassy."

"The bird's not so bad," said Peter when Lyle had gone. "Of course most women wouldn't like it."

David said he thought that some woman might like it, a certain kind of woman. He was thinking of Gail.

"Maybe," said Peter. "But don't you think he might be just a little too aggressive for you to let him fly around the place?" David considered the matter. He knew he couldn't put the bird back in the cage.

"You think I should do something about it?" he asked Peter.

"Something," said Peter.

"What?" said David. "FedEx him back to South America?"

"Something," said Peter.

4

When Fern eventually reached Geoffrey on the phone the next morning, he had already heard about the earthquake. "It was a seven point temblor," he said. Only Geoffrey would say "temblor." "It was on the news," he said. "People were killed. I was worried about you."

"I tried to call," she said. "You weren't home. Where were you?"

"A bunch of us went to dinner," he said. "Tell me about the earthquake."

She hadn't been scared, she told him, though the bellhop looked as if he were going to have a heart attack. It had happened just after her arrival at the Hotel Rizzo, which the school in Cuenca had booked for her.

Inside, the place was unfinished. Even the reservation counter was made of pale unpainted concrete. She'd been given the key and led to the elevators by a boy in his teens wearing an old-fashioned bellhop's cap. They'd gone to the top floor, the fifth, and the boy was ahead of her, carrying her bags down the dim cool hall, when everything began to rock. The building was swaying like a ship, giving out low groans punctuated with alarming cracks and thuds. The bellhop froze, still holding the two heavy bags. The rocking went on and on—though it may have been only twenty seconds.

Still, so much had happened that day that she couldn't make it real, so she did not become afraid until later, when she was left alone in her room.

She told Geoffrey all this, as if it were just a funny story, but he was not amused. "That place is dangerous," he said. "How did you even get to the hotel? Was it a real taxi?" Before she'd left, Geoffrey had warned her, again and again, about getting into what he called fake taxis. This was how Americans were never seen again, he'd said.

At that moment she said to him only, "It *was* a real taxi." The cab had been a battered Lada, the driver an old man with pendulous features, who'd introduced himself as Vicente. They'd driven slowly through city streets jammed with orange and pink and lime-green cars and through a neighborhood of old houses, all of them crumbling, crushed, eroded, as if the place had melted. At the stoplights people had peered at her through the open window of the car, as if she were a strange sight. "Hello," she'd said to one little girl, who simply stared silently back. Finally, they'd reached the city's downtown and its main plaza, with its equestrian Bolívar and ornate bandstand.

But she related none of this to Geoffrey on the phone that morning. For the first time since she had left, she felt annoyed with him, not just for all of his warnings and his attitude of knowing everything about South America without ever having ever set foot on the continent, but also because, when she had called him the night before, to tell him that she'd made it safely to Guayaquil, he hadn't been there, though he'd said he was going to be. And he had changed the message on their answering machine.

The evening before, in her hotel room, she'd had to cry awhile, having been in an earthquake after everything else.

Then she had gone back out into the hot, smoky city air, looking for the EMETEL. It hadn't been far. The phone office was a state-run business, a stark bureaucratic place like the one in Cuenca, with armed guards, one of whom had given her a number for a booth. You went to that booth, made your call, then went to a window to pay. Ecuador was three hours ahead of Tucson, and it was about seven in Guayaquil. Geoffrey would be home from classes about three, he'd said.

But he hadn't been there. And on the answering machine had been his new message. In the old one, he had mentioned both of them, Fern and Geoffrey, but his new message just said, "This is Geoffrey. You know the drill." After the beep, she'd found she had nothing to say of this day in which so much had happened, and so simply had said, "It's Fern. I'm in Guayaquil," and had hung up, realizing just as she did that she'd even forgotten to tell him she'd been in an earthquake.

Now he was telling her about it. "The epicenter," he was saying, "was a place called Manta. Is that close to where you are?"

"Where did you go for dinner?" she asked. She wanted to ask whom he'd gone with, but she wasn't asking that. She wasn't mentioning the machine's message, either. She didn't want to appear petty or jealous or to seem to be trying to manage his life from Ecuador.

He had no such reluctance. He told her he'd eaten at Kingfisher, with Jason and some others, and asked how she was getting to the reserva. Was she planning on taking another taxi? The way he said "reserva" bothered her also. He didn't even try, she thought.

Somebody from the reserva—she said it with a Spanish accent, hoping he'd get it—was picking her up. It was too far for a taxi. Then he understood her mood better and asked how the hotel was, giving her the opening to tell him things, the way she'd done when she'd called him before.

But there wasn't much else she could think of telling him, only things she didn't want to say. The previous evening, having not reached him by phone, she'd walked to the river, just two blocks from the hotel. The river was wide and slow, and along the water were benches and pavilions. Along the shore, she saw couples embracing in the twilight. One girl giggled as a boy put his face into her neck. Fern tried not to appear to be noticing and walked to the railing and looked down. It was low tide and there were amazing things in the mud, pipes and tubs and ruined walls, an ancient and rotting museum, a whole drowned city.

"The hotel's fine," was all she said. Then, this not seeming to be enough, added that she'd gotten dinner in the dining room, for 100,000 sucres.

"My god," he said. "How much is that?" About eighteen dollars, she told him.

"Then I watched *Mad Max Beyond Thunderdome* on the tube," she said. She hadn't really watched it, though she'd had it on while she reread Alan Feduccia on the evolution of birds, a great big volume that she'd lugged all the way to South America. But the mention of the movie perked Geoffrey up, as she knew it would. He liked that movie, he said. It was easier talking to him after that.

She let herself miss him and went on to relate the events of her trip the day before, telling him about the bird on the bus even though she had just mailed the letter in which she'd told him about it. In the end he told her he loved her and said that he was glad she was okay in the earthquake.

"I didn't know what was happening," she said.

"That was probably better," he said.

She asked him once again if he had her address at the reserva and he said he did. "In fact," he said, "I've already written you something." That cheered her, and they said good-bye. She didn't know when she would talk to him again, or how, and she hung up the phone in the booth, paid the clerk, and walked out into the strange streets, feeling truly *there* again, though more alone than before. Typical of Geoffrey to say that it was probably better not to know if you were in an earthquake, she thought. For her, though, it could never be better not to know.

Rolling this grain of resistance around in her thoughts, she proceeded on her errand. It was a bright Wednesday morning and the streets were crowded. Cuenca had been a little town, really; the old part where she'd lived quaint, white-washed, with narrow cobblestone streets. But Guayaquil was a real city and it shocked her to see so much, to walk through the crowds of businessmen and schoolgirls and Indian women selling trinkets and beggars without legs. It was so dignified and dirty, so cruddy and exquisite, and it went on and on.

And she was alone in it. Here in a city of millions, she knew not a single person, and she was far, far from Geoffrey and their apartment in Tucson and her friends and her parents, back in Saint Paul. She thought of her mother, who was so afraid for her to be alone in South America. She had one piece of business, to stop by the INEVS office, to see if they had any information on her aratinga. INEVS was the Instituto Ecuadoriano de Vida Silvestre—the Ecuadorian Wildlife Institute—a government office. She found the address without too much trouble. At a desk in the small cluttered office, a young red-haired woman wearing a black blouse clacked on a computer keyboard. Fern said hello in Spanish and started to explain who she was and what she was doing, and the woman behind the desk said, "How can I help you?" in English. She didn't say it in a mean way, but Fern still felt embarrassed, though this feeling quickly gave way to gratitude.

Fern explained that she was an American researcher, there to study a certain species of parrot, *Aratinga erythrogenys.* Did they have any references for this bird and any advice about how she might find it? The woman looked in a large bird guide and told her what Fern already knew, that the bird was native to coastal Ecuador and Peru and that it had been greatly reduced in numbers in the past few years. Fern checked the references herself, verifying that there was no information there that she didn't already have, then thanked the woman and started to leave.

"I'll tell you where you might find one," said the woman, stopping Fern as she turned. "In the market. These birds are often captured by the local people and sold as pets. That's the main threat to them at this point."

On the street, Fern made her way down the crowded sidewalk, around the street stands that sold everything—toothpaste and key chains and carved wooden tops. She had a couple of hours before the car from the reserva would pick her up, and so she walked past the main plaza and several blocks farther, until she came to the square that the woman in the office had described, an open block filled with booths and tables and awnings.

This was the *mercado* and it was market day. Fern walked around, looking at everything, at piles of fruit and piles of shoes, at roast pork sliced from a whole roast pig that had a strangely delighted look on its face, at tables of melons and tables of bootleg tapes. Then she heard a squawk that she thought she recognized and turned a corner and found a sort of open-air pet store. In cages out front were doves and budgies and rabbits and mice. She asked the girl running the place, *"¿Un loro? ¿Un papagayo?"*

The girl nodded and beckoned her to the rear of the shop, where she pushed aside a curtain. From several pegs in the wall hung small cages, each about the size of a soccer ball, in which were birds of various kinds. She asked the girl to get one down. The bird looked bad. Its feathers were fluffed as if to keep warm, and it tried to hide under the piece of crumpled newspaper stuffed into the cage with it. The girl told her that the bird cost 30,000 sucres, only about five dollars. Fern wanted to buy the bird, if only to get it out of the tiny cage.

But she didn't. She was too unsure of where she herself was going to take any living thing along. She held the cage up and looked at the bird closely. It was a juvenile, and so it was hard to tell its species. Many parrots have young with mostly green feathers. It helps hide them in the leaves. The adults have fancier plumage with more identifiable colors, as well as better skills for survival. The one went with the other. Fern thought of herself in South America, suddenly more noticeable and having to be smarter.

Back in her room, Fern got out her big parrot book to check the species. There were several that shared the bird's characteristics—small green parrots with red foreheads—all of them aratinga, also known as conures. The species she'd come to Ecuador to find was known as the cherry-headed conure. Of course, the bird in the marketplace might have been imported, like Mija, from the Amazon or somewhere, though it was so cheap, it probably hadn't been expensively shipped from far off.

The mitred conure and the red-fronted conure, both mountain species from Peru and Argentina, looked quite similar to the bird in the market. Fern flipped through the pages for aratingas, making sure there wasn't some other one she had missed. There were dozens of variations on this small green bird, among them the blue-crowned and golden- and olive-throated conures, sun conures and peach-fronted conures and fiery-shouldered conures, dusky-headed and black-capped and brown-throated and slender-billed conures, all very similar, descended no doubt from some original species that had evolved into these variations all over South America, from Mexico to Tierra del Fuego.

Fern basked in the pictures and descriptions. She felt that she had begun the real work of her trip. At noon she called the desk, and the same young bellhop who'd brought her suitcases to her room came to get them. He pointed at her and said, *"Terremoto,"* recalling, as a joke now, the earthquake they had experienced together. Then he took up her suitcases and escorted her to the curb.

She'd waited awhile before a green station wagon with the name and seal of the reserva on the doors pulled up. The driver was a stocky boy of about twenty with a head of thick dark hair, and Fern got into the front seat, not wishing to appear to be chauffeured. Fern introduced herself, *"Me llamo Fern,"* and the guy looked as if he had never heard of such a name before. He said that his name was Nay-nee or something, which Fern would later understand to be Leonin, a name she had never heard before.

They went north, passing the bus station and crossing over the same bridge the bus had crossed to get into the city. On progressively diminishing roads they then traveled south, skirting the far bank of the river that she'd seen from the quay near the hotel.

Leonin said nothing until they had left the city and its traffic behind. Then he tried a little English.

"You are from chew narry stays," he said.

"Chew narry stays?" she said.

"United States," he said, more carefully.

"Yes," she said, "from America. From Arizona."

It was embarrassing to feel so restricted in what you could say, and Fern felt further embarrassed that she had said "America." Of course America was bigger than just the United States. She tried after that to speak to him in Spanish, using the phrases she'd learned in Cuenca. She was a graduate student. She studied biology and ecology. She was interested in birds—*pájaros*—especially in parrots—*loros.*

"Hay muchos loros en la reserva," Leonin said, speaking his own Spanish as slowly as she had spoken hers. Seeing that she understood, he told her about his life as he drove. He came from a small village near the reserva, a place called Puerto Alegre. As a child, he had gone often to the reserva to see the animals, and now had been working there, as an assistant to the director, for two years. He liked animals a lot.

Fern couldn't put together much of a response to this. After three months of communicating mostly in Spanish, she could more readily comprehend it than speak it herself. When she spoke she was forced to say very basic things, like *Soy de Arizona,* statements that were elemental, like primary colors. Just then she could only think to say that she liked animals, too. *Me gustan los animales, también.*

Just this comment, though, began a friendship between the two of them. She asked Leonin which animals lived in the reserva, and he immediately said there were 35 species of mammals and 207 species of birds. He went on for a while, naming them: tapir, monkey, ocelot, deer, and many other names she did not recognize. And then he stopped at the end and said, *"Y un tigre."* She knew there were no tigers in South America. But he insisted. *"Sí, un tigre,"* he said. *"Bengal."* Then he laughed to see that she still didn't believe him.

If she could have told him more, she would have said that she'd loved animals all her life, that she'd quacked back at the ducks in the park, had raised her Easter rabbits for years, until they'd grown so large and fearless that they had dug burrows in the backyard and ruled over their domain, driving the cat out of it. In high school she'd kept a dozen white lab rats, helping them learn things and recording their progress. And she'd had a series of dogs—dogs named with real names, Harry and Rose and Pearl and Jack, dogs she'd spoken to until she was quite sure they all knew English. (She had no dog in Tucson, as Geoffrey had thought it was not a good idea while they were in school.) The sight of a squirrel in a tree on campus or of a couple of crows playing in the air over the phone wires could make her happy all day.

And all her life she had loved reading about animals and birds and plants. As a child, she went almost every day to the library where her parents worked, to search the science section for something she had not seen, or to page through a great big illustrated volume, like *Parrots of the World,* which she had practically memorized in high school. At Macalester College she had delighted her professors and had pressed on into the delicious intricacies of evolutionary theory, cladistics, ecology, DNA. She graduated without ever pulling an all-nighter and without ever getting a B, *summa cum laude*. She was disgusting, Geoffrey had said.

She had her choice of universities for graduate school, but had chosen to move to Arizona for two reasons, neither of which was very powerful any longer. Geoffrey, who was still an undergrad at Macalester, wanted to transfer back home and get away from the snow. Also Arizona had been, until the twentieth century, a place where parrots lived. For a time, Fern had hoped to join a team of biologists who were reintroducing parrots to southern Arizona, taking birds from the zoo and returning them to their original habitat, where they hadn't lived for years. But that assignment hadn't worked out for her.

It wasn't the studying that made graduate school more difficult. At that she continued to excel. But in grad school the subject itself—now it was mangrove ecosystems—was often simply the excuse for the business of becoming a professional academic. She needed to care less about her subject to get through graduate school, to be political and get a committee together, a committee she could work with, never mind on what. But this she could never do. And so the love of nature and animals that had given her success in college sometimes handicapped her in grad school.

Her current dissertation chair, for instance, was not her first choice, nor she his. In her first year, she'd taken a course in evolutionary biology from a young professor, Francine Pepperbloom, who'd been so knowledgeable and enthusiastic about her subject that Fern had felt confirmed in the choice she was making to pursue the field for her career. By her second year, Fern had begun thinking of Professor Pepperbloom simply as Pepperbloom, a friend and a colleague. It was Pepperbloom who'd applied for the research grant to try to bring the thick-billed parrot back to the mountains of Arizona.

But then in Fern's third year, Pepperbloom had been denied tenure and had taken another job at a college in Boston. That year Fern's application for a fellowship had been rejected as well. Fern and Pepperbloom still talked on the phone and wrote letters on e-mail, and Pepperbloom was still Fern's counselor when it came to matters of graduate school, but she was no longer there to direct Fern's dissertation.

So she'd had to ask Ron. Ron, whom she'd never been able to think of as Professor Hudson, hadn't wanted to chair any dissertations. He hadn't wanted to be there at all. He never showed up for anything he didn't absolutely have to do. He slept all day and stayed up all night, doing god knows what. If she had to call him about her work, she set the clock for one A.M., and he would answer as if nothing were amiss. But Ron was it for tropical ecology—if she wanted to do tropical ecology, she had to work with Ron. So she persisted. Ron was the main reason Fern never wanted tenure, anywhere.

As Leonin drove, a white ridge forested with strange elephantine trees rose east of the road. Just the sight of the trees thrilled Fern. They were ceibas, pale green, thorny-barked giants with huge bare limbs that began sixty feet up the thick trunks. They looked like trees from a child's book about castaways.

Then on the west side of the road, the mangroves began. *"Los manglares,"* said Leonin, who knew that she would be excited to see them. Pools and streams opened momentarily in gaps among the low trees, and beyond these lay patches of water and banks of mangrove trees, standing on their stilt-like prop roots, their trunks dense as hair, making a single reddish texture. She'd studied them for years, but had seen them only once before, on a class field trip to Key West. These trees lived on seawater, exuding the salt through a complex root system. They existed around the world in tropical lowlands, sheltering and feeding a huge number of other species. The mangroves were magical, Fern thought. They were the cradle of all life in the world.

"Alto, por favor, alto," she said, and he did stop, and she got out of the car. It was quite hot already, the tropical sun potent on her face. She walked to the edge of a tide-slicked bank and looked into the mangrove swamp. The air pulsed and hummed with insect sound, and a dozen different kinds of butterflies fluttered and dipped close to the surface of the water. The stream curled and diverged around islands of mangroves, a living maze, beginning there and winding for thousands of miles, down to the sea.

At that moment, grad school, Geoffrey, Tucson, even Cuenca and the three months she'd already been in South America, left her thoughts. All she wanted to do was find a boat and paddle out into the swamp. Leonin called her from the car. Though she didn't know it then, it would be the last time she'd see the mangroves for weeks.

5

Peter's suggestion—that "something" would have to be done about the parrot—echoed in David's ears, even as he was enjoying the company of the bird, feeding him and trying to get him to speak. *Hello hello hello hello hello,* David said every morning, as the bird stared bellicosely and eventually squawked, not helloing. The parrot resembled Elvis, David thought. His crooked upper beak seemed to give him a wry sneer. He pushed his chest forward and rocked on his feet when he strode around the apartment. He was a tough little sailor. Little Witt wasn't bad; he was just not at home in the human environment where he found himself. David felt the same way.

But David began to fear that Peter was right. To anyone else Little Witt would not make an acceptable pet. The parrot had begun to wake David up at night, for one thing. Every night, whenever one of the residents hit the call button, there was a clank and a rattle and a long loud buzz that ended with another clank and rattle as the elevator started, descended, and stopped, heaving its gate open and shut. The whole noisy process was repeated when it climbed to the desired floor and stopped again. David had his earplugs, but Little Wittgenstein, who by now liked to perch on the gooseneck of David's desk lamp during the night, heard this repetitive intrusion clearly and unfailingly responded to each stage of the elevator's progress with a sharp, earplug-defying cry of alarm.

Plus, the parrot crowed at dawn like a rooster. As soon as the sky beyond the windows of the apartment showed any light, he let forth this crow several times. It was a particularly piercing variation on his usual theme, the short blast loud and the longer one louder. The scream was right out of the jungle.

One morning after it happened the phone rang, "What was that?" said a woman in sleepy voice.

"Who is this?" said David.

"It's Gwen, in 201. Are you blowing a whistle? Please stop." She hung up then, and David could imagine her heaving her head back into her pillow.

These signs and premonitions David put aside as best he could, still hoping he could both keep the bird and find someone else, a human being like himself. Was that too much to ask? he thought. It was too much to ask. One morning this became obvious, when at their regular table at Savor, David pushed through the ongoing witty repartee with Gail and asked if she'd like to see his place. "Sure," she said, and they left the table. David's heart pounded as he walked beside her the few blocks down the hill to his street. It seemed as if it was going to work. She was cheerful, she was chipper, and she seemed to understand that more was intended by his invitation than a simple tour of his apartment. David was so hopeful and excited that he didn't even think about Little Wittgenstein until they had entered the small lobby of his building, passed over the red floral carpet that his landlord Bozuki seemed to think enhanced the place, and pressed the button for the elevator. Two floors above, through several layers of wood and plaster, the bird screamed back at its mechanical enemy. David grimaced, fearing what would happen next.

When they opened the door, there he was, standing alertly in the middle of the hall. Gail eyed the bird warily the instant she saw him. David ushered her into the living room and, he hoped, out of range. No such luck. In an instant the parrot came hopping in, taking an extreme interest in this attractive visitor.

"Does he have a cage?" was all she'd said.

He did, said David. He looked into Gail's face to see if there might be any chance they could just get past the presence of the bird, who hopped even closer. But he saw there only her fear. Putting aside his reluctance to cage Little Wittgenstein, he added, "Shall I put him in it?"

"Yes," said Gail, with real relief in her voice. "Please."

LW's cage had been stored away for months, and David first had to dig through the hall closet. He pushed aside boxes, wrestled with the big cage, and knocked over things in the dark, calling out as he did so, in his most pleasant voice, "I'll be just a second with this."

None of this went unnoticed, of course, by the parrot himself. The sight of the cage emerging from the closet alarmed him greatly. He shrieked and flew up to his bookshelf perch and shrieked again. David took an afghan from the back of one of the chairs and tried to catch the parrot with it, but the bird evaded him handily, several times, jumping away, flapping and screaming, and finally getting too close to Gail for her comfort.

"Never mind!" she shouted, leaping from the couch.

"Just never mind." They could go back to the café, she said. It was okay. Don't worry about it. Just never mind.

So he dropped the afghan and they retreated out of the door of his apartment. Nevermore, David was thinking as they walked up the hill in awkward silence to the café, where they sat until she said she had to go. Then he went back to the apartment. The big cage stood empty in the middle of the living room and the bird himself stood undaunted on his bookshelf. David glared at Little Wittgenstein. Little Witt glared right back.

A couple of days later David called his father at the office. "Dad, it's me, David," he began. "Listen, I need you to take this parrot back."

"Take the parrot back?" said his father. "You must be joking. You love parrots."

"Dad, I don't love parrots. I've never loved parrots. When did I ever love parrots?"

David had loved parrots all the time when he was a kid, his father said. Did David remember that fancy party in Hillsborough, where there was that great parrot, who walked around and sang?

David did. He had been about twelve at the time. David's mother had been an amateur singer. David's mother's singing was torture to David. She would sing at parties, at *his* parties, and he would cringe and hide. On the occasion his father referred to, he had been taken to a party for the cast of *Pirates of Penzance,* in which his mother was appearing. And though there was lots of awful singing, the event was saved for David by a parrot, a big golden-headed bird that had captivated the guests. He'd perched on an oak limb and had sung scales and trills, even bits of Italian opera. Spoken to, he uttered, in an urbane, Leo G. Carrollish way, only the word "Pardon?" In this way, he made his audience repeat their own silly utterances again and again, they for once the parrots. David did remember that bird. It had flown freely around the house and gardens and had walked bowlegged on the trim lawn, chortling like a burgher.

"Now that was a great bird," said Ben on the phone.

David had to agree. Yes, it was a great bird. But it was nothing like this one, which was not a charmer, was never going to entertain people at parties.

"Oh, that bird's okay," said Ben. "Has it spoken to you yet? Has it said anything? Did it call you a *cabrón*?"

"No, Dad," said David. "It hasn't said anything. Dad, I really need you to take this bird back"

Ben let out a sigh. "No can do," he said. "The girlfriend doesn't like the bird. I don't know what's the matter with her. But she said either the bird goes or I do. So you got him now, kiddo. Can't help you."

David knew better than to try to convince his father, so he gave up, got off the phone, and turned back to his apartment, suddenly aware of a sour smell, the smell of a guano cave. And there was Little Wittgenstein, still atop his bookshelf, not about to sing arias, ever.

David considered the matter for a few days and then called Lyle and asked him to come over. He said he wanted Lyle's advice about Little Wittgenstein.

"I don't like that parrot," said Lyle suspiciously.

"I know," said David.

Lyle showed up more quickly than David expected. He rang the bell within twenty minutes, and David realized he had never called Lyle before to ask for help or advice about anything. And Lyle had rushed over, only too happy to advise him. This in itself made David regret asking.

Readiness in others had always made David nervous. This was the legacy of having Ben as a father. If Ben were ready to help or advise or participate, you could be sure there was something in it for Ben. In any case, when Lyle came up, ready to help, David was no longer in a mood to ask him about anything. He acted as if Lyle had just dropped by, and offered him a beer, an Old Milwaukee. The X poetry crowd was anti-chic when it came to beer. None of them had any use for fancy brews. If you went into an X poetry hangout and ordered an Amstel Light, you might be openly laughed at.

They sat in the kitchen, saying nothing and looking at the *Chronicle,* which David had spread out on the table. Not that it was quiet, of course. The parrot, alert to the presence of his old nemesis, had stepped up his regular screeching, this time from his perch in the living room, which was why Lyle had settled in the kitchen. The noise belied the studied casualness of David's demeanor. Every time Little Wittgenstein piped up, it reminded him of the reason for Lyle's visit. Finally, Lyle, who'd been making a pretense of reading Adair Lara's column, something he would never do, just stopped, endured one more shriek from the bird, and said, "Why don't you let him go?"

This was the equivalent of a call in poker, and David held out a moment longer, looking at the sports page as if he found it absolutely fascinating, but then he gave up, folding his hand.

"I'd like to," said David, "but I'm afraid he'll die out there." He gestured out the kitchen window at the cityscape that presented itself. They looked north, into the middle of the block, an area cluttered with high fences and garages. Beyond the apartments and houses was the palisade of downtown high-rises. Just then the fog was coming in, breaking, like the huge cold slow wave it was, over the hills of the Haight and engulfing the taller buildings.

"I mean," said David, "he's a tropical bird."

"You never know," said Lyle. "Maybe he'll fly back to the rain forest, or wherever it is he came from."

"He doesn't seem like a long-distance flyer," said David. "More of a flapper, like a pigeon."

"Did you know that pigeons are actually Moroccan rock doves?" said Lyle. "They're like exotic. Like nonnative. Somebody brought them here, and they did great. They're everywhere now."

"Moroccan rock doves?" said David. "How do you know about Moroccan rock doves?"

"I know stuff," said Lyle. "Anyway, think about it. It's the humane option." The parrot shrieked twice in the ensuing pause. "Whatever he has to deal with out there in the larger world," Lyle added, gesturing again at the chilly panorama of downtown San Francisco, "it can't be any worse than his current fate."

"It's not so bad here," said David.

"It's bad," said Lyle.

David considered this a moment. "It's bad?"

"It's bad," said Lyle.

"But you can't just let a wild animal loose in the city," David argued. "There are restrictions on that kind of thing." He was grasping at straws, and he knew it.

"That's my point exactly," said Lyle. "Little Wittgenstein *is* wild. Listen to him." The bird shrieked again, right on cue.

"Look," said Lyle, hammering his point, "this is one tough little parrot. If any bird could make it out there"—again that specter of downtown with the fog closing in—"it's Little freaking Wittgenstein. Who's going to mess with him? Pigeons? Moroccan rock doves. Shit, he'll have Moroccan rock doves for breakfast."

Cats, David was thinking. Cats would attack the bird if he were out on his own. But then he tried to imagine a cat attacking Little Wittgenstein and couldn't. Little Witt himself was like an alley cat, with wings.

"And you have to admit," said Lyle, "this bird is not going to be your pet. It's not going to say good morning to you when you get up. It's not going to be nice."

"No," said David, giving in. "Nice is probably out."

David talked about it a little more, without admitting that he had already decided. Then they went to the living room—David first—ostensibly just to look at the bird, to see what kind of shape he was in. Lyle moved cautiously into the parrot's domain.

The bird looked good. He had completely regained the ability to fly by then and could soar around the apartment, making quick and surprising evasions of the arches and the lamps. He was preening himself, chewing into his thick green wing feathers. He looked strong and healthy.

The living room, on the other hand, looked bad. It testified in many details to Lyle's argument. Working and sleeping in the bedroom, eating in the kitchen, David had left the living room to the bird, especially after the fiasco with Gail. Now the air in there was fetid and tangy. The parrot had shredded the place, had torn up David's papers, had chewed up the bookcases and the molding and the windowsills. The woodwork bore dozens of beak marks. The parrot paused in his preening to look, first with one eye and then with the other, at the two men who were looking at him.

"Bright plumage," said Lyle, like some vet or something. And then, meaningfully, he added, "Let's get some air in here." With some difficulty he slid the casement window up. There was no screen. Fresh cool air poured into the sour space.

"What do you think, Witt?" said David. "Look, freedom."

If Little Wittgenstein was tempted at all by the prospect, he didn't show it. The two men stood back and waited awhile, but the bird made no move for the window. David retrieved the wooden ruler he had used previously to move the bird, and lifted it toward him. The parrot bit the ruler twice, ripping chunks off it with a twisting motion of his head. Then he calmly stepped aboard. David, looking like an unbiased experimenter, walked over to the window and put the stick with the bird on it out into the open air. The parrot lifted his wings but didn't leave the ruler.

So David gave it a decisive shake, and the parrot flew off. He flapped his green wings twice and was gone, over the fences of the back lots, the little territories of the city dwellers, over the rooftops of the houses on the far side of the block. He rose high into the white space of the foggy sky beyond, then dipping once, barely visible, shot away, flying strongly in a straight line, flapping regularly and purposefully toward the distant façade of downtown, and at last vanishing from sight.

David and Lyle watched him go, standing there a moment when they could no longer see him. "Well, he sure could fly," said Lyle.

"Do me a favor, Lyle," said David. "Shut up. And get out of here, would you? Would you leave?"

"Sure," said Lyle, good-naturedly. "Whatever." There was no alienating anyone after the Wadsworth, David thought, especially Lyle. So Lyle gathered up his book bag and left. David could hear the elevator taking Lyle down, and when its buzz and clank ceased, he sat for a time in the odd silence, such as he had not known for months. It was good, the silence, David thought, though in his heart he did not really enjoy it.

David left the window in the living room open for a couple of days, in case Little Wittgenstein came back, but he didn't. So David shut the window and cleaned the living room, not just the living room but the whole apartment. When he got to the bedroom he cleaned up all his papers and picked the books up off the floor and returned them to their shelf. Mentally David still heard the bird's cry, that two-toned rasp that had been so constant in the place for months.

And when he was done cleaning, the apartment looked so orderly that it might have been ready for someone new to move into it. This feeling persisted, a presentiment that David could not shrug off. Somehow, now that the bird was gone, so was he. And with each day that passed came the absurd sensation that he, too, should acknowledge his departure and leave. He pushed it away every time, reminding himself that he'd been in the apartment forever. Still, there was undeniably this call, this sense of belonging elsewhere.

6

By the time Fern and Leonin arrived at the reserva, it was nearly dark. A storm had begun at sunset, exploding from the clouds that had built up through the afternoon, and the water had poured over the windshield as they drove on. The hillsides along the road to the reserva had been cleared in large patches, exposing the pale earth, and though the land above was still thickly forested, the rivulets that ran down to the road out of the trees were frothy and muddy, the color of chocolate milk.

They drove up to a high cement wall and a railed gate, which bore a sign with a macaw—a scarlet macaw, which Fern thought was odd, as that species did not live in the region—and the words BOSQUE PRIVADO, Private Forest. Leonin stopped the car, and they waited. She pointed at the macaw on the sign and said to Leonin, *"¿Aquí?"* meaning did one live here? He answered, *"Sí, hay cuatro."* Yes, there are four of them. The gate swung open and they proceeded up the drive to a small guardhouse, where a man clad in the same khaki and brown uniform as Leonin consulted his clipboard, gave her a key, and let them pass.

They drove up a narrow lane, arched over by dripping trees, which blocked the last of the light from the cloudy sky. Fern felt uneasy about the place. It was not quite what she had had in mind. She had expected something more like a National Park in the States, or a university field facility like the one she had visited in the Chiricahua Mountains in Arizona. But the reserva was more like somebody's estate, enclosed, *privado.* And they'd left the mangroves behind, miles back.

She'd researched the region and had found the reserva on the Internet, then had written a letter to the director, one Dr. Leonard Qualles, who had written back to her in English. "Congratulations," the letter had begun. "You have been accepted by the Reserva for a period of work/study here." Fern thought it was odd that his letter implied that she'd won some competition. She had simply written for information. Qualles had offered to give her room and board and time to pursue her own studies in exchange for a few hours per week when she would attend to some duties. Fern had shown the letter to Ron, and he'd said it sounded like a great deal, and so she'd written back, accepting the offer, and letting Dr. Qualles know when she'd be arriving. Ron hadn't ever actually been to Ecuador, she recalled now—he'd studied his tropical ecology scuba diving in Belize.

Leonin informed her that she was to meet with *el director* in the morning, and that he would take her to her *casita.* They drove past a cluster of buildings and continued farther up a slope, along a swollen stream. He stopped by a cottage, helped her get her bags up the stone steps to the door, and said *hasta mañana.* He pulled away as she tried the key the guard had given her in the lock. It stuck, didn't seem to work, and then gave.

Inside, the place was dim and rustic, the wood of the walls unpainted. The windows were open and through the screens came the sound of the rain in the leaves. The front room was part kitchen, part living area, and there were dishes in the sink, change and pencils and other things spread out on the table, and a woman's flowered blouse on the floor by the couch. The cabin seemed to have a tenant already, though at the moment no one was home. At the back of the room were two doors. Behind one was a mess of clothing and an unmade bed. Behind the other was a small, mostly empty room that she took to be hers—in it was a lamp, a small wooden dresser, and a single bed, bare of covers.

She brought in her luggage and was unpacking a little, setting up her books on the top of the dresser, when she had the spooky sense that she was being watched. She turned back to the window to see a face there, a wet, weird, tiny, pale, naked, semihuman face, like nothing she'd ever seen. Fern jumped and let out a scream, and it disappeared.

"Sheesh, you scared me," she said to the empty screen. Her heart was pounding and she had to take a moment to recover. She calmed herself by beginning to wonder what kind of animal it had been. It hadn't been a monkey. She wished she'd brought her tropical mammals book. In a moment the creature was back, clinging to the screen. It had round ears and tiny, weirdly human, hands, a curly tail, and a penis and balls. It looked a little like a lemur. Kinkajou maybe, she thought. Family Procyonidae, like raccoons. With an amazed expression on its eerily recognizable face, it watched her.

At that point she felt suddenly exhausted, more tired than she'd been the whole trip. She was finally aware of all the work it had taken to get there. And just then it was too much. She could no longer revel in being so present. That, too, was labor. She rolled up a T-shirt for a pillow, turned off the lamp, and lay down, curling up on the dusty bed in her clothes. In the dark, the creature on the screen—the kinkajou or whatever it was—continued to watch her for a time, silhouetted now against the dim outside light. Then, with the same weird humanlike purposefulness of movement, he climbed slowly down. After a time the sound of the rain, the billion-tongued licking of raindrops on leaves died down, and the underlying whir of insects rose.

The birds woke her early, and Fern lay there, trying to count the different calls, the hoots and groans, cries and squawks, squeaks and twitters, some so beautiful, some grotesque. She'd never heard anything like it. She'd known abstractly that diversity increased as latitude decreased, that the number of species was vastly larger in the equatorial regions than in northern places. A dozen kinds of birds might live in Labrador. In Ecuador there would be thousands. She'd memorized the numbers for her exams. But none of these generalizations could have conveyed what one minute listening to the dense symphony that these birds created brought to her, this feeling of the almost crazy abundance of the tropics.

The early light glowed through the windows and the breeze brought in the smell of wet deciduous forest, the acid smell of tannin, of olives and acorns, of leaves decomposed on the forest floor. All her life she had associated this smell with camping. With all the work and excitement of the trip, she'd let go of what it would really be like to be there, back in the woods she loved, but with those woods intensified a hundred times.

She got up, still in her jeans, pulled her hiking boots out of her bag, and, leaving the cabin unlocked, went out into the rosy light. Across the road was the small stream, which she crossed, stepping on dry stones. On the far side, a path ran beside the water. It led into the trees, where it steepened and narrowed. Grasses soaked the legs of her jeans as she climbed.

Everything interested her, and almost everything baffled her. The diversity of the birds, whose cries still rang out all around her, had its equal in the trees and plants. She'd grown up walking in northern forests that were often dominated by one or two species of tree. But this place was a riot. Everywhere she looked was some new species of flora. The trees formed three canopies above her head, a level for saplings and the taller bushes, a level for other mature trees, and the ultimate canopy, where the soaring branches of the ciebas crisscrossed, seventy feet above.

By the time she'd hiked even a quarter mile up the trail, she was giggling, elated at the richness of it. The path crossed the stream several times, switchbacking up the steep bank on either side. This was it, she thought, the reason she had studied so long, had worked to put herself through school, had persisted with Geoffrey when he had opposed the trip. She thought several times that she should go back for her binoculars and her notebook, but each time she saw something new and had to go on.

After she had hiked up for about a mile, she reached a point where the trail again descended to the stream, which it crossed by a bridge. There, sitting in the middle of the span and looking up at her, was Leonin. Saying nothing, he put a finger to his lips and pointed upstream into the undergrowth. She understood that he was watching something, and she approached him slowly and silently, sitting down beside him on the bridge when she reached the center. He was looking intently into the dense cover of the stream bank, and she looked there, too, but saw nothing. She continued to stare, for one, two, minutes, as Leonin remained absolutely still. Finally, something moved in the leaves. She drew in her breath when she saw it—dark eyes, spotted fur—and whatever it was instantly, silently, disappeared.

"Ocelote," said Leonin. It had been an ocelot, a small cat, which had come down to drink. It was very good to see such an animal on her first day, he said in careful Spanish, very lucky. The bridge was a good place to watch for animals, he explained. He came here before work and after work to sit and watch. He'd seen many animals here. Fern felt clumsy. Leonin had taught her something about patience and something about animals just by the calm with which he'd watched and waited. It was as if he had conjured the ocelot with his stillness.

Leonin got up then, saying he had to go to work, and Fern walked back down the trail with him. There were times to see the animals, he said, just before the sun and just after it. Now it was the time of the birds, he added. Later it will be the time of the insects.

And also the time of the director, he said. She was to see the director that morning, was she not? *"Buena suerte,"* he said, with a knowing smile. Good luck, as if she were going to need it.

When they reached the cabin, she remembered that she had questions. Who else was living there? What was the animal she'd seen the night before? But Leonin continued on his way, saying *hasta luego* before she could think of how to ask. She went inside and washed her face at the sink in the bathroom. She would have loved a shower, but the cabin had neither shower nor bath.

She unpacked the rest of her things then. In the three months she'd been in Ecuador, she hadn't taken some items out of her bags—her fieldwork clothes, the long lens and tripod for the camera, all of her books and papers. She set these things out in the room, moving in and taking possession. She was full of happiness as she ordered and arranged. She'd made it; everything would be perfect now, she thought.

Wrongly, as it turned out. First it was the cages. As she walked down the main compound to meet the director, she saw what she had not seen the night before. On its main grounds the reserva housed a kind of zoo, with dozens of big cages for animals. Fern hated seeing animals in cages. The monkeys she noticed first. They were being fed and they screamed at the bars and hopped and swung around inside. At a distance, she couldn't tell what was in the other cages, but as she drew near the main building, which was landscaped with flowers and a gravel drive, she saw the reason for the sign on the gate.

The cage next to the main building housed macaws, four of them. Fern stopped, put her hands on the bars, and looked at the birds as they looked at her. The cage was bare, except for a tree that had been trimmed of its smaller branches and installed as a perch. All four birds sat on the limbs of this tree, looking astonishingly large. They were bigger than cats, she thought, bigger than a lot of dogs.

Two of the parrots she recognized. They were scarlet macaws, their plumage a deep red except for their wing feathers, which were yellow and blue. She examined the nearer bird, the larger of the pair. Around its cheeks and eyes, it bore red tigerlike stripes. Its yellow bill was outsized, almost comically large, and it gripped the branch with thick black reptilian claws, the middle two facing forward and the outer two facing back: zygodactylism, she recalled. Never try to pry open a parrot's foot, she'd read. Its grip was so strong that its toes might break before it would let go.

The other scarlet sat midlevel in the tree. Higher up perched the other two birds, a different species of macaw and, at first glance, plainer. They were mostly green birds, though some of their tail feathers and the edges of their wings were a beautiful pale blue. They were smaller overall than the scarlets and had narrower, more delicate, black bills. These two were shyer. They stayed on their higher perches and did not watch her as obviously. They peered intermittently over their shoulders.

The big scarlet macaw evidently decided that Fern was approachable. It gave a squawk and flapped clumsily to the floor of the cage. Then it waddled over in her direction. When it reached the bars, it ducked its head three times and said very clearly, in a deep voice that startled her, "Don't give me any crap."

It turned out to be the voice of Leonard Qualles. When Fern arrived at the main building, she was ushered into the office by the director's secretary, a young woman called Sonia, who gave Fern a penetrating look, as if to test her credentials and her seriousness. Sonia escorted her into the inner office, which was carpeted and lined with books. It was cool and shaded inside, the windows hooded with metal awnings. Qualles sat behind a broad desk, which was covered with a sheet of beveled glass and nearly empty. He was a small man with tight curly hair and a beard, both red. These and the ruddy appearance of his face gave him an inflamed look. He said nothing as Fern came in and took a chair in front of the desk. On the glass before Qualles lay an open folder that held her letter and her CV, the academic's résumé. Qualles put his fingertips together in a delicate little tent or cage and let another moment of silence pass before he began. When he did, he spoke quickly in English, as if he did not have much time to take up with her.

He reviewed her experience, noting what she had not done. "I see you have no training in avian care," he began. Also that she had not worked outside the United States and that she did not yet have her Ph.D.

"Well, we need someone," he said, "so you'll have to do." Qualles then gave her his own experience. He had been in Ecuador for fifteen years, he told her, having come down after graduate school at Kent State, back in Ohio. "You know," he said, "where the shootings were."

"You'll be working with the finest collection of wildlife in this part of South America," he said. "All our animals are very valuable. Some of them are quite rare. You understand?"

"Yes," said Fern. It was the first thing she had said.

"Let me be clear," said Qualles. "It's a big responsibility. Do you think you are up to it?"

She hoped to be, said Fern. Qualles answered this with a doubtful look. Fern expected to discuss her research project, but he shut the folder containing her letter and got up. They would tour the collection now, he told her. Fern followed him back through the front office and into the tropical sun.

Among the cages, he launched into what seemed to be his routine introductory speech. The reserva had been established in 1957 by a consortium of foreign corporations doing business in Ecuador. These companies had wanted to give something back to the Ecuadorian people and to preserve this extraordinary environment. His tour started with the monkey cage, inside of which several species leaped and chattered as they saw Qualles approach.

Fern recognized some of them, from the white rings around their eyes, as capuchins. They were small animals with vivid facial expressions. Fern knew that as a scientist she was supposed to refrain from interpreting animal behavior in terms of human emotions, anthropomorphizing, as it was called. But she'd always found this difficult. And she found it impossible not to read feelings on the faces of these monkeys. For one thing, they didn't like Qualles. They jumped into the branches, agitated by his presence.

They walked next to the cage with the macaws in it. The big scarlet macaw had returned to his perch, but hopped down again and waddled over to the bars. Qualles took a single sunflower seed from his pocket and held it before the macaw's bill. "Hello," he said, and then more emphatically repeated it. "Hello!" The macaw croaked back, "Hello," in a clipped way, though the tone was unmistakable. The macaw spoke back to Qualles in Qualles's own voice. It crossed Fern's mind to tell Qualles what the bird had said to her earlier, but she decided not to mention it. Qualles held out the sunflower seed. The bird turned his head sideways and took the seed with his squarish black tongue.

"This one is Hoover," Qualles told Fern. "I name all my parrots after U.S. presidents. That one"—he pointed to other scarlet—"is Roosevelt. Truman and Eisenhower are up there."

"What kind of macaws are those?" asked Fern, referring to the smaller pair.

Qualles looked at her a moment before answering. "They're a local subspecies," he said finally. Then seeming not to want to denigrate the birds, he added that any one of these birds would fetch $25,000 on the black market. At least, he said.

"Not that we'd ever consider selling them," he added.

"They're protected, aren't they?" asked Fern.

"Of course, they're protected," said Qualles rather testily. "We're protecting them."

Qualles informed her that these birds had been confiscated as they were being smuggled out of the country. "Eisenhower there had been chloroformed and stuffed into a box of bananas," said Qualles, smiling at the notion. "He was on his way to the U.S. on a freighter." The birds in the collection were being rehabilitated, he said. Eventually they'd be released into the wilds again.

"When?" asked Fern.

"Eventually," said Qualles. "When they're ready."

Inside the cage, Hoover stretched his wings impatiently, waiting for another sunflower seed.

"Are these scarlets native here in Ecuador?" Fern asked.

"Oh yes, quite native," said Qualles.

Fern didn't think so, and she said so, explaining that she recalled from her book that the scarlet macaw had not been observed west of the Andes.

"It's not all in the books, you know," Qualles said. And that was all. He gave Hoover another seed, saying hello first and getting his own hello from the bird in return.

"These birds will be your responsibility," said Qualles. "You're to keep the cage clean and the birds fed. Leonin will train you on how it's done. It's good that you're here. The other girl who was supposed to do this just left."

Fern said nothing to this, and Qualles resumed the tour of the cages, describing the items in his collection. She saw anteaters, sloths, peccaries, tapir, and a second aviary, this one holding dozens of different kinds of birds.

"Maybe you can help out here, too," said Qualles. He

had one last thing to show her, he said. The last set of cages stood amid the trees, the forest floor extending beneath the bars. The cats. First were ocelots, beautiful spotted animals with big limpid eyes. Seeing them, Fern wished she had gotten a better look at the wild one drinking by the stream that morning. In a nearby cage was an old jaguar, who peered at them from his rock den. In the last and biggest enclosure was a tiger, a Bengal tiger, just as Leonin had said in the car. Fern's heart pounded when she saw this huge cat. It was called Kaiser, said Qualles in a confidential tone. Kaiser had been owned by a drug dealer who'd been arrested. The bars of Kaiser's cage had been set into concrete, but the forest floor inside the cage was the same as it was outside. The big cat padded through the undergrowth toward them. It drew near the bars and then, as Fern stepped back, turned away, pacing and not looking at them, as if never having seen them at all.

Fern and Qualles walked back to the offices, and Qualles resumed his official manner. "We're offering room and board," he said. "And we do need someone to take care of the macaws. Are you interested or not?"

She was interested, she said.

"Good, then," he said. "You can start in the morning. Now you seem to need a shower. The bathhouse is there"—he pointed to a low building up the road from the offices. And with that he went back into his office.

Left alone on the gravel walk by the flowerbeds, Fern felt exhausted. Qualles was such an odd man, curt and quick to take offense. He had not even raised the matter of her own work. She started back up the road to the cabin. By then it was hot out, and the birds had stopped their singing. This was the time of the insects, as Leonin had said. They hummed audibly about her on all sides. Among them dragonflies, several huge iridescent blue butterflies—morphas, she thought—fluttered above the puddles on the road. As Fern walked away from the compound, she felt the power of the place itself again and reconsidered her situation. She had no choice, really. She was there. Maybe she could still find a way to do what she needed to do.

When she reached the cabin, she retrieved her towel and bath things and walked to the building Qualles had pointed out, which had one room divided for men and women by a wall, with curtains for the showers. The place was empty, and she took a long hot shower, letting herself soak and relax for the first time in days. When she had dried and dressed and brushed her short wet hair, she felt reconciled to being there—at least for a while. She would not, though, give up on the mangroves.

She walked back to the cabin and lay down, still tired from traveling. She got out her parrot book and looked up macaws. She'd been right: Scarlet macaws were not native to western Ecuador. "Generally East of the Andes," the book said. Of course, there could be exceptions, but it was strange that Qualles had been so insistent about it. She paged through the book, looking for the other species of macaw that she had seen in the cage. The only birds that fit the description were Buffon's macaws, which the book noted were vary rare, almost extinct in that part of South America

She began a short letter to her parents, but in the midst of telling them how wonderful things were there, grew too sleepy to finish. When she woke, the room was dim. The day was already over, and someone was knocking on her door. She was very surprised upon opening it to find Qualles standing there in the twilight with a bottle of wine in his hand.

"You had your shower. Good," he said. "I thought maybe you'd like a little drink." He held up the bottle of red wine. "Sun's over the yardarm."

"Uh," said Fern, as Qualles came in. He moved to the sink and opened a drawer, finding in it a bottle opener. He was a little man, his red hair gray at the temples, and now that he wasn't being stern, he was smarmy. What was he doing here? she managed to think, as he poured a glass of wine and handed it to her. He poured one for himself, and with the same familiar air carried the glass and the bottle across the room and sat on the couch.

"To the animals," he said, raising his glass. Fern raised her glass and sipped. The wine was sweet, too sweet, sticky. She didn't like Qualles, and she especially didn't like the liberties he was taking with the place where she lived. He'd made this visit before, it seemed.

"There's one thing I've been wondering about," said Fern. "Is there someone else living here?"

"She had to leave," said Qualles. "It didn't work out for her here. She was an American graduate student. Like yourself," he added.

"It's just that she left some things," said Fern.

"Oh, throw them out," said Qualles, "or keep them, if you like. She won't be back. She got a plane back to Cincinnati, or wherever it was." He finished his wine and poured another. "Any other questions?" he said.

"Yes, actually," said Fern. "I was wondering how I could do my own research here. I need to get into the mangroves."

"Really?" said Qualles. "I don't think that's such a good idea. What would you want to do in the mangroves?"

Fern said, "I'm down here to observe a certain species of aratinga. I thought I made that clear in my letter."

Qualles trained his eyes on her then, seeming to see her in a way he hadn't since her arrival. "Well, I don't know what you thought you were doing in coming here," he said, "but there are no aratinga in the collection"—he said the Latin to let her know he knew it as well. "They're parakeets, trash birds. They're all over the place."

"Well, that's my dissertation topic," said Fern. "I plan to study them in their habitat. In the mangroves."

"First of all," said Qualles, "they don't live in the mangroves." Then, after a slight pause, he added, "You need to know that the mangroves are very dangerous. For all kinds of reasons."

Fern said nothing to this, and Qualles said nothing either for a moment, then relented. "Oh, don't worry about it," he said. "There's a library here for you to study in, and I'm sure we can find something worthwhile for your project. There's certainly plenty to do here!" His false joviality was intended to put the matter aside. He offered her another glass of wine, not noticing that she had not taken a second sip from the glass she had.

She said she didn't want any more. In fact, she was really very tired.

"I see," said Qualles. "Well, I'll go then. There was one thing I wanted to mention, but we can leave it for another time."

"What was that?" said Fern.

"Nothing, really," he said. "It's just that this place is so"—he looked around at the cabin—"so cheerless. I have a guestroom in my quarters near the office. Sometimes the girls we bring here stay there. It's quite a lot more comfortable." As he said this, his eyes took on a greedy look that made Fern recoil, though she tried not to show it.

"Oh no," she said, "that's fine. I mean I'm just fine. Just fine here." She said it coldly and conclusively, in a tone she'd learned to use with men whose advances she didn't want to encourage.

Qualles understood. He drank the rest of the wine in his glass. "Good then," he said flatly. Then he stood up and walked back over to the sink, where he unscrewed the cork from the opener and put it back in the bottle. Taking the bottle with him, he said, "Good-night," and went out. He seemed to be concealing his anger as he closed the door firmly behind him, not slamming it.

Fern got up and poured the rest of her wine into the sink, shaking slightly. She might have been more charming and still not have encouraged him. But he'd called her aratinga trash birds. There were no trash birds. How could anyone with any training in biology or zoology say something like that?

She locked the door to the cabin. When she turned back, there was the kinkajou, clinging to the screen with its needy eyes and its little penis. With a wave of revulsion, she shut off the lights and went to bed, sleeping for a second night in a row fully dressed.

7

In his clean apartment, David waited. He couldn't shake off the unnerving sense that he was not at the end anymore, but at the beginning. The new quiet of the place, the sounds now domesticated, the humming of the refrigerator, the gurgling of the pipes, the lumbering of the elevator—all of it was subtle and continuous and poised, waiting to be broken by some sharp wild cry that did not come. David felt with growing dread that he himself would be the one to break it.

He remembered "The Rime of the Ancient Mariner," in which the killing of an albatross brings terrible luck to the ship's crew. David pulled Coleridge's poem from the shelf in the weeks following Little Wittgenstein's ejection. "And they all dead did lie," read the poem, "And a thousand thousand slimy things/Lived on; and so did I."

There was no going back. At the time of Little Wittgenstein's ejection, David had assumed that he would simply clean up the apartment, find Gail, and take up where they had left off, sans insane parrot. But then—of course—he couldn't find Gail at the café, the only place he'd ever seen her. Apparently the incident had been sufficient to convince her to get her coffee somewhere else. Maybe her brush with David and the parrot had forever cemented her relationship with Brian, who, boring though he might have been, did not have a mad bird in his house.

David could not return to his old life. Maybe nobody ever did, he thought. And he didn't really want to, either. Some part of him was glad it was no longer possible to go on living like that, locked in and isolated. Still, the larger part of him quailed before the change and clung to the things that remained—his apartment, for instance.

Almost concurrent with the thought came the landlord, that harbinger of doom. David's apartment, which he'd rented for years, had grown a bit more expensive every year, at a rate controlled by law. When he had started renting it, in the early '80s, the place had been $350 a month. Over the years the rent had more than doubled, though rents in the other apartments in the building had gone up much more. Unlike David, other people moved in and moved out, and when they left, the landlord, Bozuki, a rich Greek who lived down the Peninsula and seldom came to the city, could charge more. For this reason, Bozuki didn't like David. David was the holdout in the place, who had, moreover, one of the nicer apartments in the building—on the top floor, with a view of downtown out the big bay windows. David was costing him money every month.

Nobody ever knocked on the apartment door (they buzzed from the street), so the very sound of it aroused David's dread. He left the work he was not doing to get the door, and there stood Bozuki, a squat hairy man with a mustache from the '70s. Bozuki didn't say hello, only that he was sorry. David had to go. He was being evicted.

"My son needs a place in the city," Bozuki said, citing one of the few legal grounds for eviction—replacing a tenant with a family member. "I want to give him this place."

"What do you mean?" said David.

"What do I mean? I mean it's simple. I mean you gotta go," said Bozuki. "September one."

The news made David frantic. For years he had been spared many of the fiscal difficulties of life in San Francisco, and he had really come to believe that he would never have to address them, especially now that he had the Wadsworth.

"What if I just paid you more," he proposed, "for the rent?"

"My son really wants that place," said Bozuki. "Besides, it would be a lot more. You're only paying $750 now. I could get $1,500 a month on the open market for the place. But like I said, my son wants it."

"Maybe your son can find another place," David suggested. "I can pay you the $1,500." This was a rash thing to say, but David really did not want to think about moving. Besides, the Wadsworth would take care of it.

Surprisingly—or not—Bozuki agreed, trying to seem like a nice guy for letting David continue in his apartment at double the rent. He was going to ask for a further damage deposit also, he said, as he'd heard that David had a parrot in the place, but he would forgo that. The whole business was disagreeable and economic, not interesting to David, and when he shut the door, he tried to forget it. He had his work to do, for one thing, his book.

But when he got back to his desk, he sat poised at the keyboard and nothing happened. Or, rather, the nothing that had happened for weeks continued to happen. Jolted by Bozuki's visit, David let himself have a further taste of the truth. The writing he had been doing no longer appealed to him. He didn't want to be difficult and disjunctive anymore.

The parrot's last lesson—that whatever was positive about difficulty, finally difficulty was simply difficult—this had stayed with him. In the weeks after he had thrown the parrot out the window, David had held off the implications of this lesson with the considerable might of his repressive faculties.

But now it occurred to him. The difficulty of his poetry and the difficulty of himself, were, in fact, simply difficult. And he didn't want to be difficult anymore. He lifted his hands from the plastic keys. He, too, had screeched. He, too, had been ejected. He, too, had, however little he wanted to admit it, already entered the larger world. The words of the Ancient Mariner echoed in his ears. "Is this the hill? is this the kirk?/Is this mine own countree?"

David's energies turned to the question of what had happened to the bird. The lost parrot seemed to be a key to his own fate. Part of it was guilt. Even though Lyle had encouraged him, he had maybe killed a parrot. He felt responsible for sending this tropical bird out into San Francisco, this reputedly Californian city that was actually more like Scotland, most days pale and chilly. What kind of parrot had this one—Little Wittgenstein or Pepito or whatever—been, anyway? David wondered. And where had he come from?

One of David's familiar channels through the city took him to the downtown branch of the public library, then housed in a cramped and smelly neoclassical building. For years David had gone there, to wander the stacks. He had a secret and, for him, highly adventurous routine. He liked to slip past the barricades put up after the place had been damaged by the 1989 earthquake and to climb into the condemned stacks, stepping over the cracks in the floor. There, he searched the dusty, tilting shelves for some obscure volume, often chosen at random, from which he might take obscure language and then obscure it even further in the process of his art. Nobody had ever reprimanded David for occupying the condemned part of the library; in fact, nobody had ever noticed him, and he spent whole days up there, at a tiny table, reading in the light from a dim window.

Now he put this routine at the service of his new interest. One June day David went to the library, but deliberately sought out the zoology section first and found a big book, which he took up to his secret aerie. The book was *Parrots of the World,* written by Joseph M. Forshaw, illustrated by William T. Cooper, and dedicated, David noticed with a twinge, "to our wives and families."

The book showed hundreds of pictures of psittacines, a term from the scientific Latin for the family of parrots and a word that to David's ear chimed with "citizens." David leafed through the big text—absorbing the pictures and data on the glossy cockatoo, the yellow-capped pygmy parrot, the red-rumped rosella, the Fisher's lovebird, and dozens of others—until he found a picture of the cherry-headed conure. Although Little Wittgenstein's head was just flecked with scarlet, the identification seemed right. At birth, cherry-headed conures had entirely green heads, the book said. They got more red feathers as they grew older. The description of the bird's call, "rasping and disyllabic," was what convinced David. He'd heard that hammering cry a thousand times. Cherry-headed conures came from western Ecuador. The page bore a small black-and-white map illustrating their range, with a shaded area surrounding the lips of some estuary or bay. The place was right on the equator and no doubt very warm.

When David left the library that day, he walked back out into the rather desolate open space called Civic Center. Even in June the cold wind off the Pacific always blasted through the place, focused by the high-rises into the plaza between City Hall and the library. There were some pigeons around, Moroccan rock doves, David recalled. They didn't seem to mind the chill. David scanned the sky for other birds. This was new for him. He stopped on the street with the cold wind stirring his hair and flapping his jacket, looking skyward, wondering about the climate of Ecuador.

Once he knew a little, he needed to know more. In other things he read, he noticed bird references. He began to look for news from Ecuador and Peru in the newspaper he read at the café. He called the Audubon Society. He didn't want to call the Humane Society, as he had thrown a bird out the window and he didn't think they would appreciate it. But he needed to find out more about what might happen to such a bird, and he thought the Audubon Society would have a clue. They didn't. The guy who answered the phone explained that they were interested in native species, not in exotics like feral parrots. There was some disdain in his voice, as if David had asked a lion specialist about stray cats.

It was an attitude that David recognized from the world of poetry. Among poetry critics there were connoisseurs who felt that no real poetry had been written for the past fifty years. If it didn't rhyme or clank along like Robert Frost, it didn't count. These loose conures were like contemporary poems, which in this view didn't deserve the term. There were evidently levels of snobbery in the bird-watching world that David had never imagined.

The term *feral* was also derogatory, as if the fact that Little

Wittgenstein had passed—involuntarily—through human hands had spoiled him forever, making him unfit for study. This also seemed unfair to David. Besides, wasn't a "feral" animal one that had once been tame? Nobody who knew the bird would ever have claimed this about Little Wittgenstein.

Now that David had started noticing birds in the sky, he saw them all the time. It amazed him that there existed this class of wild animal, right in the midst of the most intense human culture, occupying the spaces human beings couldn't get to, the air, the high perches under eaves, the branches of trees. In the mornings David had continued to go uphill to Savor, in hopes of running into Gail again, and one morning at the café he noticed a different bird among the others around the sidewalk tables. It was pigeonlike, but slender, a dusky twilight color, with iridescent violet spots on its back. A man at a nearby table watched him as he watched the bird.

"That's a mourning dove," said the man, as if he could read David's mind. The guy was small and birdlike himself, with dark eyes and pointed features. He wore a strange cap that made David wonder if he might be European. David thanked the man for the information and they said nothing else.

On the way home David stopped in the bookstore and bought a field guide to birds. He read it on the sidewalk, heading home, charmed by the elaborate descriptions of each bird's song. The golden eagle produced a "rather weak high yelping, a two syllable kee-yep in a slow measured series." Rounding the corner on Guerrero Street, David used the book to identify three small birds in a stunted purplish tree outside his building: house finches.

The next day, David bought a travel guide to Ecuador, though he had no intention of going there. He'd never owned a travel guide to anywhere before, and he used it oddly, reading it from cover to cover late into the night, as if it were a novel. Reading the guide was like traveling without having to. The book proceeded in an orderly fashion that pleased David, beginning with a list of what to bring—water bottle, paperback book (easily exchanged with other travelers once you've finished it), sunglasses, a few meters of cord (useful for clothesline and spare shoelaces), etc. The simplicity of this list appealed to David, the self-contained and self-reliant aspects of this kind of travel. The author recommended just two changes of clothes—one to wash, one to wear. This, too, was Waldenesque. Then there was the list of difficulties and dangers—dengue fever, altitude sickness, reptiles, theft—that in reading he could experience vicariously and safely.

The description of the country itself was related not in exciting narrative or colorful description, but in listlike paragraphs of rather dull detail, David's favorite kind of reading. He liked learning that an *hospedaje* was an inexpensive boardinghouse, that the bullfighting season in Quito was the first week of December, that people sometimes entered the public baths at Banos fully dressed, especially on Fridays.

David read on, more transported than he had been by any book in a long time. He read about snowy volcanoes and statues of the Virgin. He read about admissions charges for the museums of Otavalo, about the rain forest and the Galápagos. And he read about the birds of Ecuador. It was truly an extraordinary place for birds, more than 1,500 species of them, twice as many as in North America. In Ecuador were 120 kinds of hummingbirds alone. Reading about the amethyst-throated sunangel, the spangled coquette, the fawn-breasted brilliant, he could feel in these extraordinary names the old tug he once felt for poetry.

When he finally closed the book, David lay in his bed in the dark and felt quite palpably the country of Ecuador as an intimate geographical presence. It reminded him of a feeling he'd known years before, of sensing the woman lying asleep near him in a dark room, that awareness of her being seeming to arise from something more than the dim sight of her form or the soft sound of her breathing.

But this was a whole country, Ecuador, warm and silent, as if nearby, not a story in a book or a body of information but actual, physical, and just there, beyond the walls of his apartment, over the intervening land and sea. He knew it. The night that lay around him lay there, too, cloaking the mountains and the coast, the towns and the cities he'd been reading about. He could feel the tingle of the waves fringing its beaches, the grip of the glaciers in its highest passes. He roamed the airy spaces above the streets, moving between its tallest buildings, along the leafy corridors of the roads passing through its jungles. He was flying over the landscape and embodying it himself, becoming the valleys and churches and waterfalls he'd read about. Perhaps already dreaming, he grasped with certainty and wonder this sensuous presence, which was also his own, and for the first time in many years, he felt no fear.

8

In the weeks that followed, Fern tried to avoid Qualles and looked for the chance to do her work at the reserva. None came, though, and she began to hold out against the thought that she had made a terrible mistake. Later this thought would break in with its full force and make her long to be back home. But by then she wouldn't even be sure where home was.

The sky boiled with low clouds that spat rain almost every day, though it rarely amounted to a downpour. Every morning Fern walked down the hill to do the job she had been assigned. The macaw cage had a peaked roof that made it look like a small skeletal house, though it offered no shelter. Water fell right through the bars.

The first day when she'd brought their food tray, the birds watched her knowingly, impassively. In the kitchen of the long building by the main house three local women prepared the food for the animals in the reserva. They cut up bananas, apples, mangoes, and other fruit and placed it on aluminum trays. The first time Leonin helped her unlock the cage door. He stayed outside as she stepped in.

In an instant, she knew why. The big scarlet called Hoover came flapping off his perch and charged at her, his wings outstretched. Fern held out the aluminum tray to fend him off, then dropped it and retreated. *"Está muy bravo,"* said Leonin, raising his brows. Hoover was the dominant creature in the cage. He chased the other macaws away from the food tray until he had his fill. They waited until he had finished, then fluttered down to the spilled food. The other scarlet macaw, Roosevelt, was Hoover's mate. Macaws mate for life, and the other two, the Buffon's macaws, were mates as well.

Fern had tried to placate this alpha parrot, Hoover, by feeding him by hand from outside the bars after that, offering him a chunk of apple to make friends, to familiarize him with her presence. But the big bird had taken his first opportunity to give her a hard bite on the hand, a sharp quick chomp that communicated that he could bite harder and longer if he liked. She dropped the apple and he snapped it up. He was going to be a challenge, she thought. After that, she would continue, carefully, to feed the bird by hand until he began to seem less fierce.

The scarlet called Roosevelt always allowed Fern to feed her. Fern thought of Roosevelt as the female, though she couldn't tell by looking. That first day, as Hoover ate, Fern offered Roosevelt a piece of mango, and the macaw took it delicately, pulling it gently from Fern's fingers. This favor did not escape Hoover, who became enraged and chased the other bird around the cage, screeching and flapping his wings, as Fern shouted "Hey! Hey!" to no avail. Roosevelt did not forget this hand-feeding, and whenever Hoover was otherwise engaged—hogging the food tray, usually—Fern slipped a little mango to her, until she began to adore her new keeper. Roosevelt was sweet, even demure when she came near Fern, ducking her head coyly and looking at Fern first with one eye and then with the other.

The other two macaws, Truman and Eisenhower, were quite standoffish. They stayed in the tree, coming down to the food tray after both the scarlets had eaten and Fern had left the cage. They were beautiful birds, too, though in a subtler way than the scarlets. The blue on their wings shone with a deep iridescence and the lighter blue on their upper tail feathers looked like the sky after a spring rain, Fern thought. Their long tails were almost golden underneath, as were their irises.

All four birds got very agitated when Fern had to hose down the concrete pad beneath their cage. This was the chore that accompanied their afternoon feeding. When she entered the cage with the hose, the macaws screamed bloody murder and flew to the highest branches of the tree. Leonin told Fern to spray them with the hose if they bothered her—*"Lo odian,"* he said, they hate it—but Fern wouldn't do that. So each day the birds let her have it, screaming until they hurt her ears. Fern never became angry at the macaws, though. Privately she believed their bad behavior was justified by the conditions of their captivity.

One day, about two weeks into the job, she had been spraying down the pad when she noticed Qualles and two other men in business suits standing outside the cage. Qualles had a sneering smile on his face, as if he had just said something to his companions about her. It gave her the creeps. Who knew how long these three had been standing outside the bars, looking in at her. When she turned off the hose, he said hello to her and she answered him curtly.

"Found any time for your research yet?" he asked. His question had the edge of a taunt.

"A bit," she said. Qualles said nothing. He turned to the two men in the suits and began speaking low, in Spanish.

In fact, she had proceeded nowhere with her fieldwork. It hadn't simply been that her time was otherwise engaged. She felt paralyzed. The place discouraged her. It was a zoo, pure and simple. The animals were held for display and came from anywhere and everywhere, simply exotic specimens in a private collection. There was no attempt made to represent local wildlife or to educate the public. She'd never seen schoolchildren visit the place.

Fern had always had a problem with zoos. They'd upset her, even as a child. Her enduring memory of a visit to the zoo was the image of a grizzly bear with marshmallows stuck to its back. Even pigeons in a city park gave her more of a thrill, more of a sense of the life of animals, than the sight of any caged zoo creature. As she'd studied the field, she'd come to see that there could be good work done in zoos—last-ditch rescues of endangered species, biological and environmental education—but nonetheless she would never have gone to a zoo voluntarily, and she'd always entertained the fantasy that society would come to its senses in the distant future, when people would look at zoos as we look at the bear-baiting of the Middle Ages, with disgust and amazement that such casual cruelty could be generally accepted.

And now she found herself working in one. The monkey cage disturbed her the most. Fern found it difficult even to watch them. Their behavior stopped short of speech, but in every other respect their actions were intelligible and clear. Their eyes spoke to her. The monkeys seemed especially aware of the limitations of their lives. Part of it was that these monkeys were caged in the midst of the jungle and were constantly reminded of that larger life. Indeed, wild monkeys sometimes came to the bars to examine their captive kin, an event that caused a great commotion inside the enclosure.

Had she felt able to do her own work, she might have made her peace with the place. The reserva was within an hour's drive of the mangroves, and this tormented her, to be so close and yet still unable to see them. She had no access to a car. On the first Sunday, her day off, she had attempted to walk to them. After a hike of two hours in the heat she came to a few straggling mangroves at the edge of a patch of water, these the only ones left when a field had been cleared. Across the water, more grew, though those were out of reach. She'd hiked back, returning to her cabin exhausted.

She had determined, after that, to make what use she could of the reserva, though this, too, was difficult. By mid-morning, when she usually finished the first feeding, it was too hot to hike the forest. Here on the equator, the moisture in the air carried the heat into the shade, and so shadow and cloud gave no relief. The cabin was stifling by noon, when she walked back to the main building to go to her midday meal.

This meal offered her the one glimpse she got of the world beyond the walls of the reserva. Every day except Sunday, when she was expected to fare for herself, Fern rode in an open truck with the rest of the workers some five miles, to get lunch in the company cafeteria of a cement plant. Qualles himself drove the truck. The U.S. cement company was one of the reserva's sponsors, and the plant was huge and gleaming and new, a city of silos and pipelines and conveyors cut into the limestone ridge and fenced from the forest that surrounded it.

Qualles had contracted this meal, the only one provided in the day, and the reserva's workers made the most of it. The first time Fern had no appetite as she watched the men who kept the grounds and the women who worked in the offices pile their plates with rice and beans and plantains and some kind of pork stew. *"Tendrás hambre,"* said Leonin, when he saw Fern's meager plate. You'll be hungry. She didn't believe him, but the next day she took more food, stowing some fruit in her bag to eat in the evening.

Returning to the reserva after lunch, she always felt groggy from the heat and from eating so much, and though she tried to read, she usually fell asleep for a couple of hours, until she had to get up and do the afternoon feeding. No matter how tired she was, she looked for wild parrots at the end of the day, walking out under the trees with her binoculars and camera at ready, but she'd had no luck spotting them. In the high leafy canopy of the ciebas, birds simply disappeared. One evening when she was taking a walk around the grounds, she heard a brief squawking overhead, a sound that might have been parrots in flight, but she saw nothing.

Qualles had mentioned a library, but Leonin had not heard of it. Sonia insisted at first that there was no library and then, when Fern said that Qualles had told her about it, Sonia replied that she had no time to search for the key. Then, one afternoon several days later, Leonin had brought her the key, and together they had gone to discover the place, at the end of a corridor in the building where the stores were. Unlocking it, they found a dusty room lined with shelves and file cases, and they pulled down a few of the old books, most of which were accounts by European explorers of the birds and animals of South America.

One volume interested them, a dissertation from 1954, typed in Spanish with illustrations drawn by hand, describing the animals of the region. Looking at it, Fern and Leonin were able to exchange the names they knew for the various creatures, *zorro* for fox, *chucha mantequera* for opossum, *cusumbo* for raccoon. One of the illustrations showed a kinkajou, and Fern was finally able to talk to Leonin about her nightly visitor, called in Spanish a *perro de monte*—dog of the mountain. Leonin knew the animal. One of Fern's predecessors had begun feeding it, and now it hung around the cabin, looking for a handout. Still, they found nothing on local birds, and the rest of the little library did not seem likely to be of any more help with her dissertation.

After this visit to the library, Fern decided that she had to try again to enlist Qualles's help. But her second interview with him was even more discouraging than her first. He sat behind his shiny desk with his hands tented in that supercilious way and dismissed her every word. She had tried to break the ice by asking him about the Buffon's macaws, though this alarmed him. Were they an endangered species? she'd wanted to know. Qualles said he didn't really agree with that classification, and besides they weren't that rare.

Fern had also asked if she might pay to use one of the cars, so that she could at least begin to explore the mangroves. But he'd simply asserted again that a car was not possible and had said again that going into the mangroves was dangerous, especially at this time of year. The real threat, he said, was the danger of armed guards employed by the shrimp farms.

"They'll shoot you as soon as look at you," he said, "and nobody will ever find you in there." Plus the reserva had no boat, and a boat was the only way to travel in the mangroves. She had better just buckle down and do her job, he said.

She left angry, but by the time she had reached the cabin, she felt depressed. She had cleaned her living quarters, getting bed linens and a small electric fan from the main building. She'd put the items that belonged to the vanished roommate in the other room. But there had been only so much she could do with the place, which was rotting in the jungle, and at that moment she longed even for the stark concrete hotel room where she'd stayed in Guayaquil. The dim, cool hacienda in Cuenca, with its fountains and wonderful smells from the kitchen, now seemed like a paradise.

Then she'd gotten sick. She started out on her evening hike, but had gone only a few hundred yards into the trees when she felt the tug of nausea. Whatever it was came on violently, and she stumbled back to her cabin and inside she threw up again and again, then lay with fever and cramps on the couch as night fell.

Even in her illness, she was angry with herself. She reproached herself bitterly for not checking out the reserva more fully before she'd committed herself to it. It was unlike her. What had she been thinking? She wished she could call Geoffrey, but there was only one phone, in the main office, and Qualles had said expressly that it was not to be used for personal calls without his authorization. She was too sick to start a letter. So she lay on the couch, ill and miserable in the depths of Ecuador, feeling cut off from everything and everyone.

This was the moment when the thought she had been holding back since her arrival at the reserva broke through. It *had* all been a terrible mistake. She should never have come there. As soon as she felt better, she would go home. She would give up on the fieldwork, go back to Tucson, marry Geoffrey, quit grad school, and work in the nursery. Just then, all that seemed like a wonderful life.

The next day she was sicker, so much so that it frightened her, and she imagined she had contracted some fatal illness from the macaws. She lay shaking with fever, doubled up with stomach cramps, and so afflicted by nausea that she could not stand. Leonin came by to check on her and said that he would tell *el director* that she was not able to work. Later that afternoon he reappeared, bringing her broth and fruit juices from the cement-plant cafeteria.

The macaws, all four of them, appeared in her fevered dreams, commingled with other distinct aspects of her life and various people she knew. Geoffrey was there, in the macaw cage, still telling her not to go to Ecuador. Her parents chatted with Qualles about gunmen in the mangroves. Even Ron Hudson was there, feeding the macaws. She still had not fulfilled her scuba-diving requirement, he told her. In another dream she walked and walked through the forest as parrots she could not see screamed and sang from the upper branches. *Aratinga erythrogenys,* she said to Leonin, when he visited her in the cabin. She had to find them. Leonin listened to her seriously and quietly, in the same patient way he had waited on the bridge for the animals.

On the third morning, Leonin brought her a letter, thinking that some news from home would help her feel better. It was from Geoffrey, the first letter she had received from him at the reserva, but even in her illness, she got a sense of dread looking at it. There was something plain and businesslike about it, his block-print handwriting looking dutiful and serious. When she opened it, she knew at a glance it was not good news. It was far too short, just a paragraph.

"Dear Fern," it read, "I probably should have written this sooner, but I didn't have your address. I've met someone, and I have decided to be with her. She's moving in, I mean.

She is a wonderful woman and we're very happy. I bet you had a feeling that something like this was happening. You always were so sensitive. Anyway, I'm sorry and I hope you are not too upset. I told you not to go to South America. We will hold on to your things until you get back to Tucson. I hope you are having a wonderful time down there. I know you'll probably want to talk about this, and I am open to that. Take care of yourself, Geoffrey."

Fern was breathless, astonished, as she read. The letter said nothing and everything. Geoffrey had included no details that might have made his decision more real—the woman's name, how they had met, his feelings, whatever—just the bald facts and his idiotic summary. Every short sentence in his note left her gasping. He had cheated on her, then blamed her for it. She always was so sensitive! He'd told her not to go to South America!

Furious and sick, then grief-stricken and sick, Fern screamed and cried and threw up until she was exhausted. Poor Leonin stood by, dumbfounded at the desperation and pain that this letter, so innocently delivered, had caused. Finally she asked him to leave, and when he did, she just lay there, feeling as low as she had ever felt. She got out her notebook to write Geoffrey, but then was too ill and exhausted and too full of feeling to know where to start.

After an hour of picking the note up and putting it down, she saw the date, and realized that Geoffrey had written it before she'd spoken to him last from the EMETEL booth in Guayaquil. All of this had been true then, and she had yammered on about *Mad Max Beyond Thunderdome*, just to please him. And he'd said he had been out to dinner, with some people and Jason at Kingfisher. The little liar, she thought. She remembered getting his phone machine—"you know the drill" —and she remembered him saying, all the while knowing he was cheating on her, that it would be better not to know if you were in an earthquake. And this was the letter he'd said he'd written her! She hadn't suspected a thing. She'd been so stupid. Fern raged around the dim cabin, furious, hating Geoffrey, hating herself, hating the United States, hating South America.

She remembered walking down to the wide, slow Guayas river in Guayaquil, seeing the couples making out, and feeling so wistful and missing him. And with that, her strength gave out and she threw herself on the bed and let herself cry without limit. She had loved him. She had worked to make it work. Now where would she go? What would she do? She cried for an hour and then thrashed and lay still and got up and threw up and lay down and cried again, until it was too dark to see and she fell into a half sleep, her head full of phantasms. Each time she looked up, there was the strange, tiny, semihuman face staring in at her through the screen. It was a bad and long night, and she did not sleep until nearly dawn.

When she awoke in the morning, the letter from Geoffrey was still there, seeming stupider and crueler than ever, making her wonder how she could ever have cared for him in the first place. How could she have loved a man who could write such a thing, somebody so inarticulate, so amazingly capable of blaming her for his own weakness? And then to speak to her on the phone, knowing the letter was on its way, like a bullet having left the gun, without saying anything, acting normal, telling her he loved her, even.

She felt shaky and weak, drained empty but her nausea

was gone, and so was her rage. The thought that she would abandon her fieldwork and go home was stupid to her then.

In the night she'd had moments of real panic, when she'd felt abandoned and deathly ill and far, too far, from a home or for that matter from a hospital. But the morning had come. She'd lived—no thanks to Geoffrey or to Qualles or to anyone, except Leonin. She had not come this far and felt this bad to go back. Never mind Geoffrey, never mind anything.

Even that morning she got an indication that she might succeed. She was still too weak to do her job, but she managed to dress and walk—slowly, evenly, trying not to jostle herself—down to the main compound, where she sat in the library until she felt well enough to read. She scanned the shelves. Most of the books dated from the '20s, and she found no references in their indexes to the species she sought. Exasperated, she went to a large file cabinet that stood in an alcove layered with dust. In the top drawer she found piles of newspapers and magazines, in no particular order. The pages were yellow and chewed by mice, who had made a nest in one corner of the drawer and had left their droppings in it.

In a middle drawer, however, she found a few intact files, marked only by year, 1959 through 1967, and in these she found handwritten notes in Spanish—field notes, she thought, though she could not understand them. She took the files back to her table and leafed through them anyway. One page in the file marked 1963 attracted her attention. Unlike the others, it was not a page of script but a list of several dozen Latin names in small neat handwriting. Two columns opposite the list were marked LM and CA. She read down the list: *Larus atricilla, Sterna maxima, Leptotila ochraceiventris, Aratinga erythrogenys.*

There it was. There they were. The birds she had come to find. In the column opposite the name there was a check under the letters LM. She hoped that she had come across a checklist of birds—and she was fairly sure they were all birds—that had been observed in the field. But whether they had been seen in the reserva itself, or whether any notes so old would be useful at all, she couldn't know. She took the whole file and went, still feeling shaky, to find Leonin.

She found him at the cat cages, talking to the ocelots. Leonin had told her that someone had captured this pair of cats and had attempted to make them into pets. But they had grown too large and in their play had begun wounding their owners, who had brought them to the reserva. They were Leonin's favorites, spotted cats as big as beagles with enormous eyes. Leonin was crouching by the bars, talking to them, and inside, they rolled on their backs like housecats, happy to be praised. When Leonin looked up, he was surprised to see her, grim and determined, holding out her papers.

"¿Qué son ésas?" she said, pointing to the letters LM and CA on the page with the list. Leonin looked, but did not know. He glanced at the other pages in the file, but only said *"Muy antiguas."* Yes, she said, they were very old.

The air had begun to grow heavy and hot by then, as the noon hour approached, and suddenly Fern felt she had to go back to her cabin and lie down. She felt the last of her strength dwindle and her nausea return as she went up the path. Once inside the cabin, she fell on her bed and tried to sleep. A couple of hours later, she awoke, covered with sweat. Leonin stood at the cabin door, holding a cardboard tube. When she let him in, he drew a sheet of paper from the tube and unrolled it on the table. *"Mira,"* he said. Look.

It was a map of the reserva, almost as yellow and faded as the notes she had found. Leonin put his finger on one point of the map. *"Cerro Alto,"* he read. He put his finger at another point. *"Las Manos."* CA and LM. Fern was elated. Here at least was a place to start, a place someone, sometime, had recorded the species she was looking for, a place called Las Manos on the ridge above the cabin.

Leonin asked her if she planned to go to this place. Tomorrow morning, she said. She tried to explain, in her Spanish, that she might find her parrots at this place, Las Manos. Leonin, to her delight, asked if he might go with her. They agreed to go before work. They would meet before dawn, at five in the morning.

9

The stairwell in David's building continued past the floor where he lived, leading upward into the unknown. When he was by himself, David used the stairs—he didn't really trust the elevator—but in all his years in the building he had never proceeded past his floor, until one day when, without making a big decision, he went up. The staircase climbed toward a skylight—executing another squared spiral of the red-flowered carpet that began in the lobby—and ended at a narrow door. David pushed it open and stepped out onto the roof.

He was outside, in a cool pale summer day in San Francisco. The roof's flat expanse of white gravel erupted with vents and pipes. The ladder of the fire escape looped up over the edge, and a squat little house capped the elevator shaft, housing its motor and winch, David assumed. The apartment building was taller than those nearby, and David had an unobstructed view. To the east lay Potrero Hill and, beyond it, the bay and the distant ridges of Oakland and Berkeley. Elsewhere each urban hill and canyon bore rows and columns of pale structures, thousands of dwellings. In the north rose downtown, where Little Wittgenstein had gone.

The sky sprawled overhead, not the strip of sky he could glimpse from the sidewalk, but the whole sky, which was blank, white, void that June day. The night fog had only partially retracted, pulling back toward the ocean along the ground but seeming to hang overhead. In an hour it would begin pouring back in, a towering, slow-motion avalanche.

David had never minded the fog. For years it had helped him to conceive of the whole town as a single interior, lit as if by cool fluorescent tubes. But that day, as he stood on the gravelly roof, he wished it were sunnier. There was a tropical parrot out there somewhere. So sun would be good. Over there in Berkeley, he noticed, it was sunny. Far off to the east stood the campanile on the UC campus, shining like a needle. Maybe Little Wittgenstein, like so many others before him, had taken refuge in the East Bay.

David began making this trip to the roof every day, even two or three times a day. He took his new bird guide, though most of the birds he saw on the roof were high above him on the wing. On his trips to the library David concentrated on ornithology and Latin America. In these studies, too, he had not made a momentous decision, but had just slipped in that direction. He was not quite in control. On the roof, he let himself feel that the sky, the day, the weather, and especially the birds were acting on him for some outcome, using him to express something. For so long, David had been responsible, not to other people, but to himself, for composing his day, for giving meaning to things or more precisely for giving things the meaning of no meaning, which is the most stringent meaning of all, requiring constant vigilance lest some sneaky significance slip in. But now David was letting himself be subject to the sky and the birds, and it thrilled him. It made him tremble sometimes.

The semisurrender gave him tremendous energies. In his dingy hideout in the public library, he reread the whole of *Parrots of the World*, absorbing its delicious detail in the way he'd read the Ecuador guide, letting himself be subject to all 616 pages of it, at the end even savoring the index, letting each entry bring back its whole reference: Newton's Parakeet, 342; Niam-Niam Parrot, 304; Night Parrot, 276; Norfolk Island Kaka, 140; Northern Rosella, 242.

Then he began to look for parrots in human history, learning, for instance, that the first parrots to arrive in Europe had been introduced from India. One of the first was called the Alexandrine parrot after Alexander the Great, whose exploits had opened the trade routes by which these birds were imported to the West in the Middle Ages. Alexandrine parrots still lived in the wilds, it turned out, in the Himalayan foothills. To David the list of the colors on the birds' feathers was the sheerest poetry. He read several times Forshaw's description of the Alexandrine, relishing the guilty pleasure that arose from knowing that he would never have admitted to admiring anything so poetic in other literature: "general plumage green; cheeks suffused with bluish-grey; faint blackish stripe from cere to eyes; wide rose-pink collar; dark purple-red patch on secondary coverts; tail green tipped with yellow, bill red, iris pale yellow."

When David learned that a parrot identified by some scholars as an Alexandrine had appeared as part of an intricate illustration in the Book of Kells, he tracked down a facsimile of that enormous and venerable tome in the library's rare-book room. The clerk there took David's pen and gave him a pencil and a pair of white gloves, then served him the book at one of the reading tables. There was no index, so

David had to go through every page, looking for the parrot, leafing through what seemed like acres of Latin script and illuminations, feeling as if he were on some wild Celtic safari. Then he found it, his eyes drawn to the spot, the bird instantly leaping from all that detail, a parrot for sure, peering out of the Celtic knots composing the *Z* of the name Zachariah. It looked familiar. There was that beak and that goofy wide-eyed half-ironic look he'd seen so many times. This ancient bird, drawn by monks in the eighth century and in its time a fantastic emblem for the most exotic life, could have been the bird known as Little Wittgenstein. It was as if, having flown out of the kitchen window, Little Witt had magically taken up residence in the forest on the pages of a thousand-year-old book.

On the subway going home, David wondered what the Wadsworth people would think if they knew that, instead of pursuing the lifelong work that had won him the honor, David, with nothing, no goal, in mind, was studying the minutiae of parrots. Having to have nothing in mind had always been a big part of the attraction of his poetry. Nobody had required anything of him. Had he wanted, all along, simply to escape from requirements, including the requirement that he have something in mind?

He couldn't resolve this, but as the train drew up to the Twenty-fourth Street Station, he suddenly felt free and alive, as if he had his mind back. And in the same moment he knew that he no longer knew who he was. Before he had possessed at least the term *poet,* however unhelpful that had been when others had offered themselves as professor, director, editor, lawyer. It had been something, anyway. What was this? He climbed out of the station. The escalator was broken again, the opening of the tunnel framed the white sky, and David felt as if he were ascending into this namelessness and realized it wasn't a bad feeling.

At home, he found that Lyle had left a message on his answering machine. A long message. He knew it was from Lyle as soon as he rewound the tape. Even the skipping chirp that was Lyle speaking fast in reverse took too long for it to be anyone but Lyle. He talked forever. In forward and at normal speed, Lyle yacked on about this and that, about Keats, who actually dared to show his face at Babar after that review, about the disgusting new issue of *This,* which had appeared without a poem of Lyle's, even though he had been promised.

Mainly, Lyle was trying to act as if nothing had happened. "So what are you up to?" said Lyle, as if innocently, at the end of his message. "How's tricks? Haven't seen you. Gimme a call." That was it. Then David had to decide whether not calling Lyle back would be more significant than actually calling him. He decided that it would and called. David was hoping that he, too, could leave a message, but Lyle answered. So David had to talk to him, but he just shined Lyle on, saying all the things he could think of that sounded positive and meant nothing. He was fine, he said. He was doing good. The book was going well. Lyle sensed that he was being shined on.

"You're not still mad about that parrot, are you?" he said. "I'm telling you, Dave, getting that bird out of your house was a good thing, a regular boon to mankind."

David said he didn't know about that, but that no, he was not still mad at Lyle. This was true. It was part of something that had to happen, he felt. Now that the parrots of his reading were compensating for the loss of his own bird, it was almost as if he had a parrot in the house again.

On his next trip to the library David plunged into some particularly poignant reading on extinct parrots. He'd been intrigued by Forshaw's supposition that there had once existed on the island of Guadeloupe in the Lesser Antilles a magnificent, large, long-tailed purple parrot, called in retrospect *Anodorhynchus purpurascens*. Forshaw assumed that this bird had belonged to the same genus as the largest and most impressive parrots on the South American continent: the hyacinth macaw, which had as its dominant color a rich cobalt blue, and the Lear's macaw, an aquamarine variation.

David's awakening imagination stirred at the thought of this lost creature, which Forshaw had based only on a single report by a European sailor, who had been so astonished by the beauty of the bird that he had written something down. David could picture the scene: the anodorhynchus, big and imposing, its long tail streaming, its feathers the violet blue of dawn, flying over this openmouthed sailor and into extinction. The early European explorers of the Caribbean often killed, cooked, and ate macaws, and Forshaw considered this the main reason for the bird's demise. Somebody had turned it into food.

David left the library that day acutely alert to the physical space of the city, as if he, too, might be about to glimpse something extraordinary and gorgeous and about to be gone forever. On the street, he had an almost physical impression of the hills insisting that the streets rise and fall over them in just that way. He noticed the water beyond them and he noticed the air, the high bright space above everything, which previous to this had been to him—what?—a blank, a negative, a not, and now was this thick fluid medium, on which the seagulls could linger.

The next day he discovered the Carolina parakeet, the

only parrot native to the United States. These yellow-headed birds had ranged from Florida to Michigan in the colonial period. Lewis and Clark had noticed them on a tributary of the Kansas River. They lived in large flocks, of three hundred birds sometimes, and their seemingly tropical appearance had startled people in Conestoga wagons. One report described a flock of Carolina parakeets on a bayou in southern Louisiana in the summer of 1895. In the light of dawn, they had raised a clamor in a stand of black mulberries.

In his dusty carrel in the library, David felt moved by the description of these birds. They were conures, too, he noted, their Latin name *Conuropsis carolinensis.* They'd been too smart for their own good, seeking out the most delicious fruits—those most highly prized by that other too-smart-for-its-own-good species, human beings, who had rid the planet of this competitor. Farmers with firearms had killed great numbers of the birds in their fields. The birds had no fear of guns and so were slaughtered by the hundreds, "eight, ten, twenty at a shot," wrote John James Audubon, who shot dozens of them himself, collecting a bushel basket of dead parakeets for his sketches.

The gregarious nature of these birds, noted Audubon, had contributed to their extinction as a species. They could not leave their wounded companions behind. As the farmers shot at them, the living birds, "as if conscious of the deaths of their companions," swept over the bodies, screaming as loud as ever, until so few remained alive that the farmer didn't consider it worth his while to spend more of his ammunition. The final representative of the species, the last Carolina parakeet, named Uncas after James Fenimore Cooper's Indian in *The Last of the Mohicans,* died in the Cincinnati Zoo in 1918.

David had to pause there, astonished to find his sight smeared with tears. He, who had not really even looked at a bird until the parrot in his apartment had driven its call into his consciousness, he who had not wept a single tear during his divorce, cried in his alcove in the ruined library, baffled even as his crying shook him, but giving in and blubbering into his hands over the desk. For the bitter fate of these long-dead birds? Yes, partly, but it was mostly for the species' overwhelming wish to live, that screeching, stubborn attachment that had proved so fatal, and for this colorful vital possibility lost to the world, gone out the window.

He left the library feeling shaken, wondering if it wasn't a bit crazy, having reached such heights from reading odd and ancient bird lore. He rode the subway—starkly now a train in a tunnel someone had dug through the stone and dirt of the earth—back into the Mission District and walked up Twenty-fourth Street, heading for home. He could not manage to direct himself into his building and into the solitude of his apartment. He turned back, deciding to continue up the hill and find something for dinner in Noe Valley. The sun was setting behind Twin Peaks as he walked west up the silhouetted hill toward the conflagration.

And then, as if he had readied himself for a vision in the ancient fashion, David heard an odd yet familiar sound, a steely twittering. It came from the crown of a palm tree in the middle of the traffic island on Dolores Street, and it sounded like a gang of Little Wittgensteins. He couldn't see anything in the tree, though he walked around it, peering upward. Whatever they were, they were well hidden in the fronds, and they were celebrating. This scissoring sound was a jangle of angry joy. David listened for a while, until he was sure. Then he went on up the street, passing the café where he had his coffee in the morning, and there at the same sidewalk table was the same birdlike, behatted man who had told him about the mourning doves. And again the guy seemed to know what David was thinking.

"Oh, it's you," he said. "Have another bird you'd like identified?"

"I do, yes," said David. He explained that he was just on the corner and had heard what sounded like parrots in a palm tree.

"They *are* parrots," the man said. "Parakeets, actually, canary-winged parakeets. Escaped cage birds from Brazil. They come to my yard and try to crack the walnuts."

So this was the joy he had heard in the palm trees—the exultation of successful escapees. The cry of these cocky birds had been as different from "Polly-wanna-cracker" as possible. It had been more like "Fuck-you-we-got-out."

"Yeah, weird, huh?" said the guy. "They live off exotic fruits, you know, Japanese plums and the like."

"If you want to see real parrots, though," he went on, "there are real parrots living downtown. Around Telegraph Hill. A flock of about forty. Also escaped cage birds. They're all one species, just like the canary-wings. But bigger birds. Conures, actually. Somehow they manage to find each other."

10

Fern woke up in the dark, before her alarm clock went off. She had a knack for doing this, for waking up exactly when she wanted to. In spite of this she had set the clock, a fold-up brass item that she had rarely used on the trip, and had endured its ticking, impatiently. Sleep bored her. She had slept for days, while she'd been sick. So she'd lain in the stillness of the South American night, wishing it were morning already, so she could go up the ridge. And seemingly only a minute later the clock had gone off, ringing as annoyingly as it had run, a tinny clanging. Her hand was there to silence it before it squawked another second.

Outside, the jungle was as quiet as she'd ever heard it, even the insects done with their work. It had rained earlier, and the grasses and leaves were still soaked, but a few stars shone where the clouds had parted. Suddenly Fern felt anxious about this predawn hike. The trail into the forest, so familiar during the day, ended abruptly beyond the beam from her flashlight. She wondered for a minute if Leonin would fail to show up. The evening before they had pored over the map he'd brought her, trying to figure the best way up to the place called Las Manos. They'd found a branch from the main path that ran north along the ridge to the site. Leonin had been up the ridge on the reserva trail, but he had never noticed a second path and had been keen to see it.

Still, it was so early on a workday. And Leonin did not live on the reserva, but in his village down the road. He rode a bicycle to work. Leonin was young, ten years younger than she was, and he seemed like a kid to her in many ways. She assumed he still lived with his parents. Suddenly it seemed odd that she had not wondered more about his life. And even in the midst of beginning to wonder about it, she heard the rattle of the chain on his bicycle, as he rode up the bumpy path. How he could see to ride, she didn't know.

Leonin appeared out of the dark, a smile on his broad face. It was good to have a good guy around, especially at that moment. Leonin had asked nothing from her and had taken up her cause without her asking, because it had interested him. He leaned his bike against the wall of the cabin, then just gestured ahead and continued up the path, striding off into the dark. Fern put her light on him and followed.

The trail up the ridge took them some five hundred meters vertically, not to a huge height, but a steep one and a considerable climb under such conditions. After just fifteen minutes she felt slippery with sweat. Two summers before, Fern and Pepperbloom had walked for three days through the Chiricahuas, pine-topped peaks rising from the Arizona desert like islands in the sea. That walk had been hard and long, into country far from any house or road. This trail was as difficult, but otherwise utterly different, moist, hot, dark, and enclosing. Insects swirled in the beam of her light. Every few feet it illuminated a line that a spider had strung across the trail in the night. The forest around them pressed in, so dense it was solid in the dark.

They had allotted an hour for getting up the ridge. After that, nothing was certain. The map they were using was thirty years old. Perhaps the jungle had reclaimed any trail left unused since then. Leonin had made it clear that he had to be back at the reserva by eight, to do his job. Qualles was very strict—*riguroso*—about the time. They had just three hours to get up there and get back. Simply finding the secondary trailhead would be a great success for a first attempt.

They walked in silence, bending into the steepness of the trail and occasionally having to pull their boots from the muck. Fern still felt shaky from her days of illness. Her nausea rose when she pushed too hard. At least the darkness was easing. The trees around them began to show individual silhouettes, and in this twilight they came to the bridge where she and Leonin had seen the ocelot on her first day at the reserva. Here she rested a moment, putting her flashlight away in her pack. The path grew narrower after that. The bridge was as far as most people went, evidently, and few feet had worn the way beyond. The two of them pressed on through the damp undergrowth, pushing wet branches aside. Water dripped from the leaves, and looking down, Fern could suddenly see hundreds of tadpoles wriggling in a pool in the streambed.

The birdsong rose with the sun. Beyond the screen of the high branches, the sky brightened and the birds began the morning calls and cries that had so amazed her on her first day at the reserva. The chorus again bore dozens of voices, low notes as well as high, croaking and cawing, yoo-hooing and piping, yipping and whistling. It was funny, goofy, over-the-top, and it came from every direction. Through her discomfort, Fern began to recognize the dawn.

The light came up, the façade of the forest breaking into a million aspects. Looking at the climbers and creepers, the density of the undergrowth around the stream bank, the trees, ceiba and pigio and balsa, and hearing the birdsong resound through all of it, Fern felt lifted up, capable of thought. A passage from Darwin came to her.

Oddly, no one had ever assigned her the task of reading *On the Origin of Species.* For class, she'd read modern textbooks and articles on evolutionary theory, but she had decided to read Darwin on her own, in the summer after her first year of graduate school. To her surprise, she found that Darwin was not difficult. The voice in the book might have come from an old country uncle, with his examples from farm life, from the breeding of dogs and donkeys and pigeons. Uncle Charlie, she and Pepperbloom had called him. Darwin had gone to South America as a boy and had come home forever changed by the profusion and the strangeness of what he had seen there. He had borne the secret back to gray and staid England, where it lay dormant within him for years before blossoming in his great work, which though it was careful and thorough and clear-sighted and unassailable, even obvious in retrospect, was nonetheless ecstatic with the joy Darwin had felt in the tropics in his youth.

One passage in Darwin's book had moved her and stayed with her. At the end of the book, he imagined contemplating "an entangled bank, clothed with many plants of many kinds, with birds singing on the bushes, with various insects flitting about." This variety and diversity had a common source, Darwin wrote, a life "breathed originally by the Creator into a few forms or into one." Fern had memorized the passage that summer, and she especially loved its conclusion, which ended the book. "From so simple a beginning," he noted, "endless forms most beautiful and most wonderful have been, and are being, evolved."

As she followed Leonin up the trail at dawn in the Ecuadorian forest, she felt visited by the idea, not even as an intellectual thing but as a physical presence, a moment shared by all the creatures alive in it. She herself was part of it. As different, as foreign as she felt, having come thousands of miles to be in that place where there were dozens of kinds of trees, many of them unknown to her, still, they *were* her, and she was them.

The land gathered them in as it rose up around them. Rocks began to show in the trail, pale stone shelves erupting from the black soil, layers of the white limestone that underlay the whole region. The trail twisted into a creeper-draped ravine, up which she labored, filled with this sense of connection, of belonging. She could see herself, both of them, as from a higher perspective, and she knew she would remember the moment her whole life. She wanted to stop Leonin on the trail to tell him, but she couldn't formulate the Spanish—*¿Soy los arboles? ¿Soy los cantos de los pájaros?* He might think she was crazy. He was intent on his pace, pressing ahead up the trail, which grew narrower and steeper at every step.

Still, she called his name and when he looked back, could only mutely raise her open palms, like a symphony conductor presenting the players to the audience. And Leonin got it. He widened his eyes and nodded. He knew. At the top they had to climb. Here was sheer rock, and they found footholds in the little stream that ran down the cracks. The last four or five feet were nearly vertical. Leonin glided up, reached back, and put a big hand out for her. At last they emerged, on top of the outcrop and into the early sunshine.

They turned to look back over the tops of the trees. The view was clear all the way to the mangroves, which lay like a dense cushion across the eastern horizon, still dark beneath the new sun. Fern's heartbeat pounded in her ears. She was soaked with sweat and dew. Leonin let out a whoop of triumph.

They rested a minute, letting their breathing return to normal. Then they proceeded across the ridgetop, looking for the branching trail. It had taken them an hour to get up there. Soon they would have to turn back, or risk being late for work. The trail they followed wound around on top of broad stone ledges, eventually heading for a second ridge. At the base of that ridge, according to their map, the branch trail would appear.

They found nothing at first. The trail disappeared across the rock and reappeared again in the moist places where soil could gather. Then, when they had surely gone too far, they saw it, a distinct path heading north and running along the base of the second ridge. She and Leonin set up a pile of stones to mark the site. Then they hiked back to the brink, where they took in the vast view again and sat to rest a moment before heading down.

They had been there only a moment when she heard the sound, a sustained squalling from the treetops below. In another moment she could see them, a flock of parrots, their wings beating rapidly, making a straight course over the forest canopy, coming up from the direction of the mangroves and rising toward the ridge. Fern bit her lip and gazed intently. These could be her aratinga. She took off her pack and pulled out the camera.

She'd read many reports of the aratingas' behavior in flight. Mainly they'd been sighted on the wing, as they were so noisy and obvious in the air. They called out as they flew, to hold the flock together, some researchers had suggested. This flock, about thirty or forty birds, flew up the ridge just north of them, circled once, and dived into the canopy of the ceibas. Both Leonin and Fern watched them in silence until they disappeared.

"¿Son ésos?" Leonin asked her. Are those the ones?

"Creo que sí." I think so.

Leonin clapped her on the back in congratulations, but Fern hardly noticed. In a moment she was gathering her gear to go back up the trail. In explanation she could only think to say *"Más cerca"*—she needed to get closer.

Leonin objected, making it clear he had to go back. His work, he said.

"That's okay," she said, in English. She didn't care about her chores at the reserva at that moment, or about Qualles, or about anything else. She needed to see these birds. *"Ve,* you go. I'll be all right. *Estaré bien."*

"¿Y el director?" he asked.

"Dile que no puedo trabajar hoy," she said. Tell him I can't work today.

Leonin considered this a moment and gave a shrug, seeing the futility of trying to talk Fern into returning with him. He gave her the map and offered her his canteen. It was an old-fashioned canteen, a thick tin one with a strap and a cap, and it touched her that he would offer her his water. As much as Fern did not want to take it, she knew that his offer was sincere, that it would be rude to say no, and that he would insist and maybe be late for work, so she thanked him and put the strap over her shoulder.

"Y gracias por venir acá conmigo," she said. Thanks for coming up here with me.

"De nada," he said cheerfully, as he started down just below the lip of ridge. *"Daré de comer a los papagayos,"* he called, and she had to think about what he meant. For a second she thought he'd said something about eating the parrots. But he meant that he would feed the macaws for her. She'd forgotten that and called out again to thank him as he negotiated the first steep section. He waved and turned away, and she turned as well, heading across the ridge.

She found the cairn that marked the second trail and turned there. She had walked about a mile when above her rose delicate ridges of weathered limestone that looked like fingers. Perhaps this was Las Manos. The trail descended the ridge and continued under the trees again, and she approached the place where they'd seen the birds come to roost. The ceibas on that part of the ridge were truly enormous trees, their bald thorny trunks thick as redwoods, but bright green. The ceiba has no leaves most of the year, accomplishing its photosynthesis directly through the bark. Just then, though, there were new leaves on the branches, tiny ones. The sunlight, filtered through them, cast an even, almost glowing yellow-green light beneath the canopy. With her binoculars Fern saw that the limbs erupted with tiny scarlet flowers as well.

The trail wrapped around a jutting point on the ridge and came into a broad open space on the forest floor. Fern saw something moving in the air beneath the high branches, then realized it was something red, falling, twirling. Then there was another and another. When she trained her binoculars on the branches, she could see the birds there, roosting on the thick limbs, eating the ceiba blossoms and dropping stems and pieces of flowers as they did so. As she came directly underneath them, the red petals fell around her. She picked one up. It had been neatly trimmed off by a sharp bill. Then she lay down on the forest floor and trained her binoculars upward. She had to look for a long time before she was sure she could see the splashes of scarlet on the foreheads and shoulders of the green birds. She could hear nothing. The flock was, as the literature had said, quiet in the leaves.

She shot a roll of film, then got out her notebook and started writing down what she saw, with the date and time and the location. Las Manos? she wrote. She counted as many of the birds as she could—only fifteen—and she tried to be as objective as possible about identifying them. As much as she wanted them to be the birds she'd come to see, she needed to make room for her own doubt. And then she was given a sign. Something else dropped lightly from the branches. It was bright and twirled as it fell toward her in a wide spiral—a feather. It dropped to the ground some twenty feet from her.

When she got up to get it, they spotted her. She reached the feather and simultaneously heard a bird cry out overhead. Parrot flocks don't have a single lead individual, but vie constantly, which was, she supposed, safer for the flock in the long run. One of those birds had seen her. In an instant several birds had taken flight, also sounding the alarm. She peered up through the binocs and saw those lead birds circling as the others stared through the leaves at her. Then they, too, left the branches. The group circled once and flew off, moving eastward over the trees and down the ridge. The alarm squawk, the take-off squawk, shifted to the flight call. Fern stood there holding the feather—a green-and-yellow plume—and listening to this chatter grow fainter and fainter. She could hear it for a long time, until they were miles off.

She felt elated and lucky. She had seen them. She had pictures and notes. And the feather was physical evidence, something she could use to confirm an identification, which was the first and most important step in her work. All of her effort, all of her insistence with her parents and with Geoffrey and with Pepperbloom, had begun to pay off. It hadn't been a big flock, but it was a flock, and it might have been resident in this place for a long time—since 1963 anyway, the date she'd found in the file. Probably they had come to this place for generations when the ciebas were flowering.

She walked out, hungry suddenly, and wondering if she were really a scientist. Science took you down and down into detail, always seeming to promise to give you the whole thing. And maybe it finally did. But she wanted more. She was bringing back data, verifiable information, but she hoped she could also hold on to the feeling she'd had on the way up the ridge that she shared an origin and a larger existence with the life she was witnessing. Just then it was solid and real, as solid as the limestone shelves she was walking over. And though she was aware that she could not know it in a scientific way, she felt sure that the feeling had brought her to the flock.

So she had her notes and pictures. She was closer to completing this dissertation. But this feeling was the important thing. You could record details forever, you could be a scientist and still miss this. Could her work stay grounded in it? "From so simple a beginning," she thought. In ancient times, people had rituals when they sought an animal, rituals requiring a deep identification with the animal before the hunt might succeed. She had come to that identification through her studies, through ornithology and Darwin. Well, she was a Yankee and an academic, and that was her way. She pulled the feather from her shirt pocket and looked at it again. It was a flight feather, a remex, its asymmetrical vanes producing the lift that the bird needed to fly. One edge was narrower, to cut the wind.

11

On the morning after he discovered the parakeets in the palm tree on Dolores Street, David put his fingers to his right ear to remove his earplug and found no earplug there. The night before he had forgotten to put them in. Since the parrot's departure he hadn't felt so desperate about shielding himself from noises.

The apartment was a quiet place without a shrieking bird in it. The thought had even occurred to him a couple of times, on going to bed, that he might just skip plugging his ears, but each time he had perceived noises, the sound of a motorcycle, blocks away, speeding down Guerrero Street, climbing its gears, braking for a stoplight, then climbing its gears again, or the sound of the floorboards in the neighboring apartment, creaking as they were walked on, or just the sound of the wind, hooting in the gaps of the window frame. He had reminded himself that ordinary people slept through such noises. Then he'd put the earplugs in anyway.

This time he'd simply forgotten. He'd fallen asleep thinking about those parakeets, exotic birds that had found an exotic palm tree to roost in. Nor did he have much time that morning to remark on the fact. He was going downtown, to find the parrots if he could. He got up rehearsing the directions that Henry Peak had given him. Peak was the man in the funny Swiss hat in the café, an inveterate birder, it turned out. He worked nights as a security guard at a building downtown. He'd seen the downtown parrots often, at dawn, when he got off work.

David and Peak had sat for an hour the day before, talking about the bird called Little Wittgenstein. David told Peak everything, about getting the parrot from his father, about coming to like it, even about how he had tossed the bird out the window. "You're lucky," Peak had said, and David had thought for a second, Yes, I was lucky. The parrot coming into his life had been a lucky thing.

That turned out not to be what Peak meant. David had been lucky that Little Wittgenstein had been a cherry-headed conure, a species with amazing adaptability and a chance of surviving this far north. We're halfway to the pole, said Peak, cheerily. Did Peak think it was possible that Little Wittgenstein had survived and was living with the flock downtown? David had asked gingerly. It was definitely possible, Peak said. The place the parrots lived was on a sunny bluff on the lee side of Telegraph Hill, the warmest place in the city, protected from the constant northwest winds. "It's been called the Banana Belt of San Francisco," Peak said.

The falcons might have gotten him, though, Peak had added. He'd launched then into an account of the effort to reestablish peregrine falcons in nests on the eaves of skyscrapers downtown. The falcons had been threatened with extinction by poisoning with DDT, which reduced the tensile strength of their eggshells, said Peak. But now several nesting pairs were breeding on the high-rises and on the towers of the Bay Bridge. Wasn't that great? asked Peak. It was, David had agreed, though just then he didn't want to think of Little Wittgenstein hunted from above by steely-eyed birds of prey.

Peak said he went out with groups of birders to see the ducks in the Delta sometimes and to count the hawks in the Headlands. He'd taken David for a birder, or at least a potential birder, the first time he'd seen him, when he'd watched him staring at a mourning dove. And he'd asked if David would be interested in going out with a group sometime. David had said no, thanks. Something in him had recoiled at the idea of being a birder among other birders. A bird, yes, a birder, no.

David dressed hurriedly, preoccupied with the falcons and with Little Wittgenstein's fate. He was also worrying about getting to Telegraph Hill, a place in San Francisco he hadn't been in years. He would have to cross Market Street, the great divide in San Francisco, for a century separating respectable from disreputable, rich from poor. Many elderly ladies, living in the genteel neighborhoods of Cow Hollow and Russian Hill, had never in their lives crossed Market Street. South of Market was wilderness to them. For David, who lived far south of Market, it was the opposite. He didn't go to Cow Hollow or Russian Hill. When David ventured across Market, it was only to go to the public library, which was just a block north of it. Telegraph Hill was beyond North Beach, even, not part of his mental map. He'd had to ask Peak for directions. Peak, in the careful way of a birder describing habitat, had given him extensive instructions. David should take the cable car part of the way, then walk to a place called Greenwich Stairs. Once he got close, he might hear the birds. The flock ranges along the waterfront, he said, but they show up at the stairs a lot. Keep your ears open, he said, as if David had a choice about that.

Riding in a cable car was outlandish to David. Never in his whole life in San Francisco had he ridden in one. They were for the tourists, he thought. But he was not a man to improvise with directions. Emerging from the subway on Market Street, he lined up with the tourists at the roundabout. Many wore shirts emblazoned with the name San Francisco. Odd, he thought, that this proclamation of local identity should be the mark of outsiders. When his turn came, he climbed aboard the cable car. Among the others, with the bell ringing, he did feel foolish at first. But as the car began to climb Nob Hill, he got over it. It was a beautiful morning, and the bright bay rose at the end of the city streets, gradually framing more and more of the downtown buildings in blue. Good air poured through the open sides of the car. When at a stop some of the other passengers got off, David moved to one of the seats that faced outward, where he could see better. He still couldn't entirely relax, but he had moments of enjoying it, between which he clutched the pole by his seat and tried to enjoy it.

The city, his own city, impressed him. And the bay amazed him. Just as he had lately apprehended the obvious physical reality of the subway, here were the qualities of the water, its fluidity and brightness and largeness and continuity. It struck him with the force of a new idea that this water in the bay connected seamlessly with the waters of the oceans around the world. You might step aboard a ship here and step off anywhere, even in Ecuador.

At Greenwich Street, he got off the car and began walking uphill. It was steep. Gravity gripped him, made him lean in and breathe hard, and at the top he feared that Peak's directions were not right. Greenwich ended abruptly at the crown of the hill. He was blocked, and for a moment he felt his old fear rise in him. He stood there like Balboa, the bright water all around him, the exposure making him gasp. And what helped was nothing, just taking a moment and feeling afraid, until he calmed down. Nothing was good. If he'd had to come up with something, he might have been in trouble. But nothing he could manage, and after a few minutes, he was able to recall what Peak had said, that Greenwich would reappear below, where the slope wasn't so precipitous, and after another minute of imagining this, he made his way down the far side of the hill, taking Grant to Union and Union to Montgomery, which led him back toward the point at which the phantom Greenwich returned.

Still, by the time he arrived where he thought he was going, he wasn't sure anymore. Montgomery, a broad city street downtown, here seemed like a mountain trail. It grew narrower and more crooked, carved into the promontory crowned with Coit Tower. The land on his right dropped away, and he could see the wharves down there, small toothy projections into the blue bay. Then the street concluded in a cul-de-sac, where there was a railing, from which David looked down over the tops of trees. They looked like an odd collection of trees to him, palms and regular trees and the occasional red-leafed one, all in a sloping thicket.

And then, before he was ready for them, before he had stood at the top for even a minute, the parrots appeared. David heard a cry answered by a clamor that sounded like a troop of chimps in the trees, and at that moment a dozen or so of the birds flew out of the thicket toward him. They were bright green, and the flock banked together in formation in the sunlight. Their orangish underwings flashed in unison as they headed north toward Fisherman's Wharf. Even at that distance, with no special training as a birder, David recognized them. They were Little Wittgenstein birds, cherry-headed conures.

The sight made David so excited he shouted, "Wait!" at the retreating flock. A man standing nearby on a deck, talking on his cell phone, assumed that David was shouting at him. He put a hand over the receiver and shouted back, "The guy you want to see is down there." He pointed up the street, and following this indication, David found Greenwich Stairs, which dived sharply in several flights into the trees below.

He had not chosen this, David thought. Out of the blue his father had given him a parrot, and this chain of events had begun, which now included finding the birds in the palm tree on Dolores and meeting Henry Peak with his directions and now this stranger with a cell phone virtually ordering him down the stairs. But a sense of fate kept him going. Though more of the same was sure to follow if he went down there, he had to put aside any doubts he still had. He had come this far. Who was he to object, if it were fate? David descended the steps into the shade of the trees.

Once inside the park, he saw no other parrots, but kept going down anyway. When he had climbed down perhaps half a city block, he heard something and looked up to see not a bird, but a birdcage, on a fire escape. Inside the cage, a parrot was squawking, making a lot of noise. *Ska-walk, ska-walk, ska-walk,* he cried, this noise exactly Little Wittgenstein's iambic alarm.

As David watched, a man, long-haired and bearded, stepped out onto the fire escape where the caged bird was. David called out to him.

"Hel-*lo*," he yelled, his call an inadvertent parody of the bird's. "Do you know anything about those parrots?"

It took the man a minute to locate David, whose voice had risen out of the trees of the steep urban park. "Wait a minute," he called when he spotted David at last. "I'm coming down." He picked up the birdcage and went back inside the building. Then he emerged at the side of the house, carrying the cage and coming down the steps in a small alley that ran between the buildings. When he reached David, he put out his hand, said his name was Mike, and added—as a joke or not, David couldn't tell—"I see the flock has called you." Yes, was all David could say. He was looking at the bird in the cage, who looked very much Little Wittgenstein, only without his splash of red head feathers.

"This is Dean," said Mike, gesturing to the bird in the cage. "Well, come on in." David followed Mike into a small ground-floor apartment, a cell really, just off the stairs. The one-room place had been converted into a parrot aviary. It was sharp with bird smell inside. A small desk with a computer took up one corner, but the main item of furniture was a floor-to-ceiling roost, the trunk and larger branches of a small sturdy tree. Another parrot sat on one of the highest boughs. "That's Bob Seger," Mike said.

Mike proceeded without explaining much. He had an intensity David recognized. Like David himself, Mike was a man in the middle of a long concentrated train of thought, and either he had no patience with bringing others up to speed, or more likely, he simply didn't stop to consider whether they were up to speed or not. For this reason alone, David liked the man immediately.

These two birds were cherry-heads from the flock, Mike

explained. He opened the door of the cage he had been carrying, and the fire-escape bird called Dean flew immediately to the perch. "Dean's just a baby," said Mike. "Bob Seger could be thirty-five years old." Bob Seger's head was entirely scarlet, David noticed. By this measure, Little Wittgenstein could have been as old as David's teenaged son, if he'd had one. His red feathers had extended halfway down his neck.

Mike said that one day Bob Seger had fallen at his feet on the fire escape. The flock knew that Mike would take care of them if they got sick, he said, and Bob Seger had been deathly ill. The vet—Mike took these birds to a vet—had said that it looked like the parrot had eaten some poisoned bait set out for pigeons. The younger bird, the one called Dean, had failed its first flight, Mike went on. Somebody found him on the street and brought him in. Dean had fledged too early, said Mike, meaning he had tried to leave the nest too soon. Usually the baby conures fledged or took their first flight in one two- or three-day period in September, he added.

Mike was housing these two birds together, letting them recuperate. He hoped that Bob Seger might teach Dean some flock skills. "Like not eating pigeon poison," he said pointedly to the birds, as an aside.

"Parrot flocks have culture," he said. "That means that their behavior has to be taught, one generation to the next, as it is in human culture. They have big brains, mostly empty at first. They need a flock. Like we do."

As if on cue, the two birds in the room began squawking. This was the call that David had lived with for months, though the reason for their cries was as mysterious as the meaning of Little Wittgenstein's had always been. But Mike divined something by it.

"The flock's back," said Mike. "Come upstairs—I'll introduce you."

The two of them left the little bird hospital and climbed the narrow steps of the alley beside the building, emerging at the front door of the house. Inside, the place was airy and open. Shells and driftwood were piled on the table. Across the broad living room, the wall was all window, filled with the trees in the park and the blue bay, above which stood a panorama of the coastline, the northeast corner of the rocky peninsula where the city had started. The water framed two islands, Alcatraz and Angel Island. David felt transported, a world away from his apartment, which was, after all, just a few miles behind him, across the city.

As Mike had predicted, the rest of the flock was arriving. Three dozen green birds wheeled in over the trees and settled on the railing and the steel rungs of the fire escape, which stood outside the windows and glass door of the kitchen. Mike picked up a big wooden bowl filled with sunflower seeds and went out to greet them as they came in. Latecomers landed on the rim of the bowl and on Mike himself. David stayed back, watching through the glass door.

"You make them nervous," Mike called back. They made David nervous. They were very alert and feisty, crowding the food bowl and flapping and vying with one another. It was a flock of Little Wittgensteins, with the same expressive eyes, black pupils surrounded by that white wrinkled membrane. The more excited birds dilated their pupils, as he had seen Little Witt do.

Mike stood among the birds and talked to them as they ate, and David looked at each bird, searching for one he knew, a mature conure with a crook in his beak, but he didn't see Little Wittgenstein in the hopping, eye-popping bunch. Then, gradually feeling more comfortable with the birds, David decided he might step out onto the fire escape with them. His first movement startled them and in an instant they shrieked as one. With a collective whacking of wings against the air, they were gone. It was an explosive exit.

Mike came back into the kitchen with his bowl of sunflower seeds. "I told you that you made them nervous," he said. "But they'll be back." The two men waited there in the kitchen, but the flock's cries diminished. They flew south, toward downtown.

"Just now the flock has thirty-five birds," Mike said. He had named each bird, those names a catalog of popular references, many from the '60s. He listed a few: Cassius, Hubert, Tricky Dick, Twiggy. Mike had also pieced together a history of the Telegraph Hill flock. He'd found people who'd been watching the birds for years, and they had told him the story.

In 1983, a single escaped conure had appeared on the waterfront. By 1985, another had joined it, presumably of the opposite sex, because in two or three years this couple had five young parrots flying around with them. Then around 1990—the same time, Mike said, that parrot habitats around the world were coming under extreme demands from human populations—maybe a dozen new birds arrived, overnight. All of them were wearing quarantine bands. Mike explained that ever since the parrot fever scare in the 1930s (the birds were wrongly thought to spread the disease), all imported parrots were required to spend thirty days in quarantine before they could be sold. If they lived through the quarantine, he said, they were banded and shipped to wholesalers. So all of these new birds had been sent through the system. But somehow they had escaped, en masse. Maybe a crate of birds, destined for sale, had broken open on a dock down there. Mike gestured out the window. Or maybe some caged birds sensed the presence of this family of conures on the hill and managed to join them.

"Whatever," said Mike. "Suddenly there was a real flock here."

"They stay here?" asked David.

"Parrots everywhere have limited ranges," said Mike. "A few miles. They don't migrate. These guys stay on the waterfront. At night they roost in the poplars of a small park downtown." Mike sometimes followed the flock on his bicycle, riding from the financial district to the Golden Gate Bridge.

"You know what keeps them here?" said Mike. "Hawks, raptors. That's their main enemy. The Golden Gate Bridge is a major migration route for red-tailed hawks. Like parrots, hawks don't like flying over open water. So they fly over the bridge. And even the speck of a hawk, way up overhead, scares the hell out of parrots. So they don't go past the bridge. And on the other side, downtown—"

"Peregrine falcons," said David.

"Exactly. You know about this," said Mike. "Carefully and expensively reestablished. On window ledges and bridge towers. Peregrine falcons can strike from above at 150 miles an hour. You'd never know what hit you."

Only then did Mike think to explain his own connection to the flock. Mike himself had noticed the parrots several years before, he said, when he had first moved to Telegraph Hill. But he wasn't much of a bird-watcher then, he said. One day he thought it might be interesting to put out some seed for them. Gradually the birds discovered the seed, and then had begun showing up, expecting it. Mike, meanwhile, found himself becoming more interested in the flock, and he had patiently accustomed the birds to his presence. "I stood where you were standing for months," he said to David, "before they would let me sit out there with them. And it took a year before I could feed them by hand."

Mike looked at David seriously, then. "What I think now," he went on, "is that they were training me. They were recruiting me to the flock, as the human member who supplies the seeds and gets them to the vet. They chose me, not vice versa. In fact, I tried to quit once or twice, and each time they came to the window and insisted. They've chosen you, too."

David didn't know about that. "I never gave birds a thought until my dad gave me one of those last spring," he said, pointing to the empty fire escape where the birds had been.

"Your dad gave you a cherry-headed conure?" said Mike. "What happened to it?"

"A friend of mine, a friend of mine and I, threw it out the window. In the Mission." David then told Mike the whole story of Little Wittgenstein: his arrival, his life in the apartment, his departure.

"You think he joined this flock?" asked Mike. "Is that why you're here?"

"I was kind of hoping to find him down here," said David. "But I didn't see him."

"Do you want him back?" Mike asked. It was a question David hadn't thought of. He'd wanted to find out what happened to the parrot, but it had never occurred to him to try to bring him home, to restore him to his former life.

"I don't think so," said David. "Not if he could live in a flock like this."

"It's not easy for them, you know," said Mike. "They get real scaggy in the winter. There's pigeon poison around. A lot of times they rely on handouts."

"What do you think?" asked David.

"Like I said," said Mike, "I think they chose me and I think they've chosen you."

Sure, David thought, any number of odd things had happened to bring him to this place in this moment. But he resisted the idea that he had been chosen. It seemed mystical, and David wasn't comfortable with anything mystical. Never mind that the work of his life had been to dismantle the structures of rationalism; he had always tried to be rational, even about such dismantling. And now he found that he couldn't answer. In the resulting pause, Mike seemed to understand. He tried to explain.

"Look," he said. "Here's how I think it happened. Like I said, all over the world, parrot species are threatened. Many are already extinct. And this is not occurring in isolation—the parrot is literally the canary in the coal mine. They let us know how sensitive and critical habitats all over the world are doing, how the whole planet is doing. That's why biologists are working hard to maintain parrot flocks in the wild."

He put the bowl on the counter and scooped up a bunch of sunflower seeds. "It's just like human beings," he said, "to try to control everything." This David understood. Abandoning that kind of control had also been the main effort of his poetry.

Mike stood with his back to the sink, pouring the seeds from hand to cupped hand. "But right here in San Francisco," he said, "these birds are doing it for themselves. They're carving out a niche. They're finding a way to survive among human beings on a planet dominated by human beings. And, like I said, this is bigger than just parrots. It's about whether nature itself can continue."

He had stopped the pouring and now held some of the seeds in each fist. He lowered his voice, as if to avoid appearing extreme. "And again, here's the thing," he said, confidentially. "These birds—I don't know how else to say this—have enlisted certain human beings in the effort. I keep meeting people just like you, people who never had anything to do with birds, who now find themselves connected to this flock. This happened to me, too. Really, I was minding my own business one minute, and now all I want to do is hang out with them and keep them going."

This seemed extreme to David. "That would mean," he said gently, "that this flock was communicating with me in some way. I certainly didn't feel that."

"You didn't feel it?" said Mike. "You are sitting here, aren't you? How do you know they haven't been trying to reach you?"

Right, thought David. He couldn't know that they weren't. But that didn't make it true. But again he said nothing. Years of arguing with the X poets had given him a clear sense of when not to talk.

Mike wouldn't let him get away with it. "Look," he said, "you remember those two birds downstairs? You remember how they called out before the flock arrived? They called out, I told you the flock was coming, we came up here, it was maybe five minutes later, and the flock arrived. Did you hear the flock coming?"

David had to admit he hadn't.

"I never hear them," said Mike, "but this happens every day. The birds know when the flock is coming. Doesn't it seem strange to you that these birds—all the same species—can find each other in the first place, in a big city? Individual birds like Little What's-his-name get loose, and right away they find the flock. There must be some signal. Maybe you're getting that signal, too. You don't know it's from them, but you act on it anyway. And here you are."

David was still dubious. "One example," Mike said. "Down in Arizona, these researchers released a flock of thick-billed parrots, who used to live there, before the cowboys shot them all in 1906. So they released these captive birds with transmitters, and they tracked them for a while, but after a couple of years, the transmitters stopped working, and they lost the flock. So they took an old thick-bill out of the San Diego Zoo—and this parrot had been in the zoo since 1956—and they put a transmitter on him and set him loose. Within a week he had found the other thick-bills. Somehow he knew. After all, parrots have been around a lot longer than human beings, millions of years longer. They come from a much more ancient line."

"Really?" said David, interested.

"Oh yeah," said Mike. "There's a parrot fossil forty million years old. Found in Europe, of all places. The oldest human bone is about six million. The line of parrots is older than most other living birds. Hawks inherited their bills, woodpeckers their feet, cuckoos their tongues."

I am talking to a man about cuckoos' tongues, David thought.

Mike was on a roll now. "Some researchers think that the original race of parrots lived on the vast continent that broke up, eons ago, to become South America, Africa, and Australia. Gondwanaland, it was called. And maybe very old equals very smart," he said. "We know they can learn our language.

There's an African gray parrot called Alex who seems to grasp the concept of zero. Show him a tray of different things and ask him which are the same and guess what he says?"

"I don't know," said David. "'Get outta here?'"

"'None.' He says 'none,' in English. This is the concept of zero, the null set. This is the Mayan Calendar." Mike was racing ahead, making the connections only he could make.

"Come on." David gave him an outright skeptical look.

"Well, whatever," said Mike, conceding the point and still passing the seeds from hand to hand. "But I think they're far smarter than we think they are. They've had millions of years to perfect their communication. So I think we can start by giving them credit for knowing the world, for grasping its predicament at the moment and their place in it. And for communicating to us. I'm telling you, they've picked us out. Me and now you."

This was enough for David. He had done a lot that day already. He had ventured all the way across town, had found this flock of birds, had met this strange guy, and now, well, the whole thing was just over the top.

"Listen to me, going on," said Mike amiably. He put the sunflower seeds back in the bowl. "Anyway, look. You probably have to be somewhere. Don't worry about the grand theory. Just"—and he gave David a knowing look, an ironic gaze—"just welcome to the flock."

Mike showed him to the front door. How had he gotten there, Mike wanted to know. David hesitated, thinking that Mike was going global again, and then Mike laughed and said no, had he walked or what? David explained that he had taken the subway and the cable car. If he went down the steps, and south along the waterfront, Mike said, he could get BART at the Embarcadero. That would be easier.

"By the way," Mike added, as they reached the door, "there was a new arrival in the flock this spring."

A new cherry-head had shown up. The flock didn't seem to like him. He screeched a lot and fought with the others for food. So he was still pretty much a loner, though he came around, once in a while, to get seeds. Mike called him Brando.

12

When Fern returned to the reserva from her hike up the ridge, it was nearly noon and her elation was fading. She had missed the morning feeding, and she felt a rising sense of guilt. It wasn't like her. She was reliable. But she'd had no choice. And she couldn't feel bad about it, she told herself, though she did. Halfway down the ridge, this sense of her own irresponsibility shifted into a feeling of anger at Qualles. He had put her in this bind. In spite of the glowing acceptance letter he'd sent her, in spite of what he had said about supporting her research, he had tried to block her at every turn.

When she reached the base of the ridge, she didn't stop at her cabin but went straight to the macaw cage. At first, everything looked normal. The aluminum food tray was there and empty. The birds had been fed. Leonin had covered for her, as he said he would. But as she was turning to go back, something struck her as odd. And indeed something was not right. There were only three birds in the cage. The two scarlets perched in the lower branches, but only one of the Buffon's sat above, Truman, the smaller of the pair. Eisenhower was gone.

The sight made her frantic. Somehow, in her absence, the macaw had gotten out. She couldn't think how this had happened—had Leonin left the cage door open? Had she left the cage door open? She walked quickly past the other cages, looking for Leonin. But the place was deserted. All was still, immobilized by the heat of the day and the whining of the insects. Then it occurred to her that she had missed the lunch truck. She headed back to the main building. The truck was not in its space. All of them had gone to the cement factory. Except for the gate guard, she was alone on the place.

So she spent a miserable hour hunting for Eisenhower. She'd read somewhere that escaped birds tended to stay nearby, and so she returned to the macaw cage to look. She called him, yelling his silly name—"Eisenhower!"—into the high branches of the ciebas. She walked wider and wider circles into the forest beyond the compound. But no response came from the trees.

She heard the grinding of the truck's engine for a long time before it came into view, then she walked over to the roadside near the main building with a sick feeling in the pit of her stomach. The half dozen workers in the back all looked at her as they pulled up, Leonin among them, with a worried expression on his face. Qualles was driving. He avoided her gaze, and she knew then that he would take every advantage of the situation. Still, she went over to meet him, as he got out of the truck.

"There's a problem," she said. "One of the macaws got out. One of the Buffon's. He's gone."

Qualles looked at her a moment and then simply said, "Yes, I know." He needed to see her in his office, he added. He ushered Fern ahead of him and followed down the walkway, like her jailer. They went into the main building and into the shaded inner office, where he closed the door behind them. He told her to sit down and then he let her sit in front of his desk for a long time while he busied himself, pulling out the file containing her résumé, finding paper and pen, and setting in order his already spare and neat desk.

"You failed to do your job this morning," he said, taking notes on his own words as he said them. "You neglected the birds. These are rare and valuable animals and you might have done them serious harm."

"Eisenhower's okay, then?" said Fern. "You know where he is?"

"Never mind that," said Qualles. "That's not what we're here to discuss. What we're here to discuss is your performance. Since your arrival here you have been insubordinate and rude to me, you have faked an illness to avoid your work"—here Fern protested, but Qualles put up his hand and without looking up from his notes spoke more loudly—"and as I said, this morning you were absent without leave. I make it a rule," Qualles said, "to give interns three chances, and that's three for you."

Qualles then told her that he was canceling her assignment at the reserva.

"I'll do whatever job you want," said Fern.

"I'm not talking about that," said Qualles impatiently. "I'm letting you go."

"Listen," Fern said. "I'm sorry. I never thought that one of them might get loose."

"You're still not getting it," said Qualles. "You're fired."

Fern could not believe what she was hearing. "You're firing me?" she said. She had never been fired from anything.

"We can't have someone working here who endangers the animals."

Fern tried to explain that she never would have endangered the macaws. She'd had a chance to see the aratinga that she'd come here to study. Her first opportunity.

Qualles simply asked her to have her things packed by the end of the day. Leonin would drive her to Guayaquil in the morning. "But I can't leave now," she said. "I've only just started my work here. I don't have a plane ticket."

"You should have thought about that before," said Qualles coldly. He told her she could use the phone to make her arrangements. The phone in the outer office, he said pointedly. With that, he returned to his notes, made a final punctuation point, put the page in the folder and closed it. "That's all," he said. There followed a minute of uncomfortable silence, during which Fern groped for something to say. She thought of nothing at first, but then her anger rose and she surprised herself with her outburst.

"Fine," she said, "because I can't wait to get out of here. Because this is a miserable little zoo, with no real relationship to nature or zoology or anything else. It is, as you call it, just your *collection*."

"That's correct," said Qualles.

"And that's just the attitude," Fern continued, "that has brought everything to this point where our own survival is in question because of collectors and exploiters like you. Well, all I can say is good luck, because you'll need it. Because nature will have the last word and it won't be one that you will want to hear."

Qualles laughed. "There's no *nature,*" he said condescendingly. "Nothing left, at any rate. That's what little would-be Ph.D. types like you can't understand. Nature's gone. We have these bits and pieces to show us what it was. And to do with as we please."

This flabbergasted her, and she got up and walked out, saying nothing further. She didn't stop in the outer office, where Sonia looked at her with wicked pleasure. Outside, Leonin was waiting, but she could not think to speak to him in Spanish. He just slowly shook his head, and this was enough to start her tears. They turned and walked together away from the main building.

Suddenly she remembered the macaw, though, and asked Leonin. *"¿Dónde está Eisenhower?"* Where is he?

"No puedo decirlo ahora," he said in a hushed voice. *"Te diré más tarde."* He couldn't tell her that now. He'd tell her later.

"No puedes?" You *can't*? She was astonished at this, too.

"No, no puedo," said Leonin, and he pointed his thumb surreptitiously over his shoulder to indicate something about Qualles.

Fern suddenly felt desperate in the face of this turn of events. She started crying again and began speaking to Leonin in English, not caring it he couldn't understand.

"I don't get any of this," she was saying. "What did I do that was so wrong? I was really sick. Didn't you tell him I was really sick?"

Leonin didn't understand her, and she dismissed the thought. Of course, Leonin had told him.

"I missed one feeding," she went on. "And I came down here to do my research. That was clear from my first letter. But he stood in my way the whole time. And I can't go to Guayaquil tomorrow. I don't have any place to stay, and I can't get my work done there. I'm supposed to be in the mangroves. I was supposed to be in the mangroves weeks ago. What the hell am I supposed to do now?"

Leonin listened and nodded. Then he said, as if helpfully, in his slow English, "We go to Guayaquil tomorrow. *En el coche,* in the car."

"I can't go to Guayaquil," she said. She felt as if no one had been listening to her for weeks, for months. "I need to go to the mangroves!"

"¿Los manglares?" he said.

"Sí," she said. *"Los manglares. Para mi trabajo. Para los papagayos."* For her work. For the parrots. It was hopeless to try to convey anything in this other language. It made things feel worse, to be there in the presence of her shock and grief without saying something about it. She felt alone and helpless.

But now Leonin got it, or at least he did not need to speak about it any further. They walked up the path together, quietly, and she wished he would put his arm around her or just pat her on her shoulder. Still, she was grateful for his presence.

He left her at the door to the cabin. Once she was inside, her anger returned and she began to pack furiously. She threw her clothes and books on the bed, starting to stuff things into her bags. She just wanted to get out of there. But then she saw that her things wouldn't fit in her three bags if she did not pack them carefully—as she had when she'd left Tucson. She wept and held her head in frustration, then started over, folding things properly. She thought ruefully of the way the cabin had looked when she arrived. It looked then as it would when she was gone, as if someone had simply thrown the essential items in a bag and got out as quickly as possible. This was a bad place.

The work took her a couple of hours, during which she decided that she would simply go to Guayaquil, find some cheap place to stay and decide from there what to do next. Then she heard a knock, and for a moment she thought it was Qualles, come to apologize and relent. But it was Leonin.

He'd ridden up on his bicycle. It was the end of his workday and he was on his way home. He didn't come in, but stood outside her door.

"Okay," he said. "It's okay. It's okay. *Vamos a los manglares en la mañana. Pero no le digas nada al director."* They would go to the mangroves. But she was to say nothing to the director about it.

"No comprendo," she said, truly not understanding. He repeated himself and added, *"No te preocupes."* Don't worry. And again he told her not to say anything to Señor Qualles.

"No te preocupes," she said in return. Don't you worry. She hoped never to say anything to that bastard, ever again.

He rode off down the road on his bicycle, leaving her to wonder what he meant. She was hungry, having missed lunch, and she peeled the banana she had left. The kinkajou—the dog of the mountain—came to her window as usual, and since it was her last day she broke her rule and put a bit of banana on the porch. He left the screen to get it but returned to eat it there, as he hung from the screen with one humanoid little hand and she ate her own banana inside.

She was ready to leave by the time the sun set. The cabin looked clean and barren, all of her things packed in her bags. When it grew dark she couldn't take just sitting there any more and went out. The moon had risen and was just past full. The trees cast inky shadows. She made her way down the cages and stopped to see the macaws. To her shock she found Eisenhower asleep on his usual perch. He hadn't been lost, she thought. Qualles had taken him out of the cage deliberately, she thought, just to make her absence that morning seem worse. Still, she was glad to see the bird back safely. Hoover, the big scarlet, woke up with a squawk as she stood there, and muttered his usual "Don't give me any crap."

"Don't give *me* any crap," she said.

She walked past the other cages to where the cats were kept and on an impulse continued to the last cage, the big one where the Bengal tiger was. She didn't see him at first, but she could feel him back there, amid the rocks that had been stacked up to give him shelter. And then he came out, having scented her, crouching in his walk, his dark eyes glinting in the moonlight, just his white stripes visible. He stalked her for a few steps as her heart leaped, then he went back out of sight.

Something in this last encounter summed up her whole experience at the reserva: a thrilling meeting with the wild world, followed too quickly by the recognition, in her and in the wild creature itself, that they both were captive, that the situation was contained and limited, that the wildness was no longer. She walked back to her cabin, no longer angry at Qualles or upset at herself, but feeling empty and shocked that even here she would find the human world containing all the rest.

Yet the gleam in the tiger's eyes stayed with her. In that look there was no resignation, no acceptance of the bars, just a recognition that this, once again, was not his opportunity. In those eyes, immense patience, ever-present readiness, wildness, stood, undiminished. This thought calmed her. She, too, would await her opportunity. When she lay down in the bed, she was able to sleep for the last time in that place.

In the morning there was nothing from Qualles. Fern didn't want to go to the main office even to use the phone, and so she stayed in her cabin until after eight, when Leonin pulled up in the same green station wagon he'd driven when he had picked her up in Guayaquil. Without pausing for ceremony, they loaded her bags. She wondered for a moment if there might be some sort of formality closing her time at the reserva. Maybe someone would come out of the main building to bid her good-bye. But when they drove past, there was nothing, and even the gate guard avoided her gaze. He looked down, feigning boredom, as if he had seen others like her come and go.

When they got to the main road, Leonin turned left instead of right—the direction of the cement plant and Guayaquil—but Fern said nothing. Her dismissal, even by the guard at the gate, had affected her. She'd felt this kind of official rejection only once before, when she'd been turned down for her fellowship at school, and then, too, for a while she had not known what to do. This was all she could come up with to console herself.

There was something too neat about it, she thought, a rehearsed quality to Qualles's words when he fired her, the way the cabin had been abandoned by the previous occupant, even the gate guard's practiced boredom. She wanted to ask Leonin about it, but again her Spanish failed her, and she could only think to say *"¿Soy la primera?*—Am I the first?—and to draw a finger across her throat.

"No," said Leonin.

How many? she asked. *"¿Cuántos? ¿Dos? ¿Tres?"*

"Más," he said. More.

"Más?" she said, incredulous.

"Veinte," he said, *"más o menos. Sí, todos."*

"Twenty!" she said, lapsing into English. "That son-of-a-bitch bastard! Twenty!" He fired them all, Leonin was telling her. This was part of his regular routine. She was one of a line. After a moment she had to laugh.

Leonin dared to smile then, too. *"Sí, veinte,"* he said.

"Todos." And then he began to laugh, and the two of them cracked up. And suddenly she felt present again. How seriously she'd been taking everything at the reserva. Any little world could capture you completely, if you let it. It was embarrassing and it hurt, but the pain lessened then. Especially if there had been twenty before her, if this creep just liked to bring people all the way down here, to use them as he could, and then to fire them. For his own ego, she supposed. Just to give him a sense of power and importance, out there in the true boondocks. She asked again, Twenty? And again he said yes, and they laughed some more.

"Wait a minute!" she said. "*¿Adónde va,* anyway?" Where was he going?

"A los manglares," he said. *"Pero primero a mi pueblo, Puerto Alegre."* He was, evidently, taking her sightseeing, to his village and then to the mangroves.

"Está bien," she said. Fine. Anywhere out of the reserva was fine.

The road ran along the foothills. The sun rose higher, and the steamy breeze that poured through the open car began to smell of water, of swamp. On her right, off the shoulder of the road, the ground dissolved into marsh, and she saw again, for the first time in weeks, the mangroves standing on their tall red interwoven roots. The first rank of trees blurred with the motion of the car. Beyond them was more open water, and beyond that more mangroves and even farther back the flash of more water. Fern felt enormous relief and gratitude to Leonin for showing them to her, this last time. Of course, the sight reminded her of old plans for her work in Ecuador, work she had failed to do, but she couldn't think about that just then.

After a while orchards appeared on the dry side of the road, citrus orchards, and then they turned right, onto a gravel side road that ran into the mangroves. The car rode along on a kind of levee, the swamp on both sides. After a mile or so the levee widened to accommodate a village, Puerto Alegre, Leonin announced, which consisted of a dozen small houses.

It was a plain but pretty place, thought Fern. The houses had corrugated tin roofs and stood beneath palms, and most were swathed in tropical foliage, bougainvillea and other creepers and vines. This was Leonin's village, and he showed it to her with pride, pointing out one house and saying, *"Es mi casa."* The road concluded in a roundabout, at the dock-side, where a few larger buildings stood. One was a school. Kids ran and played or just sat in the courtyard. The sound of the children—that happy chirping shriek of kids in a school yard—was immensely welcome. Fern felt returned to life.

Leonin stopped the car near the school yard and they got out. He called to a man standing with the kids. He was tall and blond, skinny, with a big Adam's apple and a face weathered by the tropical sun. When he walked over to them, Leonin introduced him to Fern in a touchingly formal way, as Frank. Frank was also from the United States, he said. From California.

"Hi," said Frank. "They call me Frank El Surfiste. There used to be another gringo here called Frank, but he didn't surf."

Frank was in Ecuador with the Peace Corps, it turned out. He taught the kids geography, among other things, and he pointed out a big mural on the schoolhouse wall, which was a map of the world that the kids had painted, with Ecuador at its center. When he wasn't in the classroom,

Frank said, he spent every free moment on the water. Just half an hour south on the main road, there were great waves, with nobody on them.

Frank and Leonin spoke familiarly in fast Spanish for a moment. Fern couldn't get what they were saying, and she was surprised to see how Leonin changed, talking this way. She had never seen him speak so fluently. In his element, in his own language, he had grown up in an instant. At the reserva, he'd held back this aspect of himself, speaking in slow English and Spanish with her and saying little to anyone else. There he'd been like a younger brother, a teenager. But talking with Frank, he suddenly became the man he was, and Fern was chagrined to have seen him in any other way. In that moment she caught a glimpse of how he might have seen her, as halting, not quite articulate. Had she appeared childish, too?

When the two finished talking, Frank turned to her. "Want to get a snow cone?" The three of them walked to the dock, a concrete pier extending into a wide place in the stream. On both sides of the dock, the shore had been built up with stones, and several boats lay tilting on this rocky slope. Out on the pier was the ice seller with his cart. They each got flavored ice in a paper cone, hers mango. Then they returned to the plaza and sat at a table there.

"Leonin has been telling me about your work," said Frank. "I think we can arrange to get you into the mangroves, if you want."

"Today?" said Fern, thinking that she still had to get to Guayaquil that night.

"Not today," said Frank. "We have to make some arrangements. But tomorrow."

"I don't know how I can get back here tomorrow."

"Back here?" said Frank. Then he said something quickly in Spanish to Leonin who answered, *"No no no no, aquí aquí."*

"He says you can stay here," said Frank. "He didn't tell you that yet? We talked about it last night."

"Sí, aquí," said Leonin.

"Here where?" said Fern.

"Well, at the moment there are only two of us bunking at the Peace Corps house," said Frank. "It's funky and we'll have to charge you a little rent."

"The what?" said Fern. And then she understood and shrieked, yipping with happiness. Leonin was beaming at her and all she could say was *gracias.*

Frank had to go back to his work, then, and he told her that he'd show her the place after school was out. He called to the children as he walked onto the playground, and they lined up to go back into the building. Fern and Leonin walked back through the village. At the house he'd pointed out, a young woman carrying a baby stepped onto the shaded porch. This was his wife, Yolanda, said Leonin, and his son, Pablito. Fern couldn't believe it. She shook hands with Yolanda, and said *"¿Su niño?"* Your son? to Leonin, who, grinning even more broadly, said, *"Mis hijos,"* for here behind her mother came another child, a beautiful little girl of about two, called Rebeca. Then Leonin's mother also came out of the house onto the porch, and Fern had a further shock—this woman, Concepción, seemed only a bit older than Fern herself. Fern had to laugh. She had been seeing things the way they were up north, where this man Leonin would still be a kid.

All of them welcomed her. They invited her into their house and sat in the parlor to drink tea, the adults in chairs, Leonin's mother taking the baby, and the little girl peering at this stranger shyly from behind her grandmother. Both Yolanda and Concepción spoke to Fern in a kindly way, asking about her home in Arizona, and Fern gave them the sentences that she had memorized back in Cuenca.

"¿Eres casada?" Concepción wanted to know, and Fern misunderstood her and answered, *Un poco,* meaning that yes, she was a little tired, and then in the quizzical silence that followed, Fern realized what Concepción had said—*casada,* not *cansada*—and quickly said no, she wasn't married. Everyone laughed, including Fern, as obviously one could not be a little married, but in the moments that followed she felt a wave of sadness. She'd put aside her breakup with Geoffrey, not even writing him back, so that she could get on with her work. But among this family it suddenly felt real. Yolanda reached and put her hand on Fern's and by the look in her eye, Fern could tell that Leonin had told her about the letter. For a moment Fern felt embarrassed. Then she asked how old the children were, and the focus shifted to them. The little girl came forth to be introduced and suddenly was not at all shy, hugging Fern's knees and chattering in the language of two-year-olds, which Fern understood both not at all and completely.

Leonin and Yolanda left the children with his mother and showed Fern around the village. They walked back to the dock and watched as a boat motored up out of the swamp. It was a slender craft, like a canoe, though it had a small outboard motor on its squared-off back. Two men sat in it, between them a piled net and two white plastic buckets full of fish. The men called out to Leonin. *"Es mi tío,"* he said to Fern. One of the men was his uncle. When the boat reached the rocky landing, the man in the front hopped expertly out and pulled the boat up. The men brought their catch ashore and the three of them inspected it, dozens of small silver fish that still wriggled and gaped in the buckets and three big orange fish that looked like carp, which flopped on the wooden planks of the dock. Leonin's uncle was Señor Enrique Something and the other fisherman Señor Jorge Something Something.

Behind them, school suddenly let out and the children poured through the gate. There were maybe fifty of them. Many dispersed to the houses of the village, their mothers appearing at the doorways. Some walked down the road carrying books. Two boys came to the dock and stood waiting. They were Enrique's sons, and after a moment he got back into the boat with them and, saying his good-byes, shoved off, heading into the mangroves.

When Frank appeared, strolling out of the school with his gangly surfer's gait, Yolanda and Leonin went back to the children, and Frank took Fern to the Peace Corps house, which was a concrete bungalow near the inland end of the village. Three surfboards stood on the porch. Inside, it was extremely simple, like a camping hut. There were just three rooms, the two at each end sleeping quarters with bunk beds, the one in the middle a kitchen and pantry. One of the rooms, apparently Frank's, was cluttered with schoolbooks and wetsuits.

The other room was neat. Someone had lined up bottles of lotions and skin cleansers, a woman's things, on top of a dresser. On the wall was a Sierra Club calendar, many of the days marked with notes in a clear hand in blue ink. The top bunk was empty—that was to be hers, Frank said—and there was another dresser for her things. Fern would share the room with Donna, another Peace Corps volunteer, who worked with the local citrus cooperative. Frank and Donna had talked it over the night before, and she was happy to have a roommate.

The living room was outside, said Frank, meaning the porch. And the bathroom was way outside. He pointed to an outhouse across the narrow backyard, where the mangroves began. There was no running water in the house. They retrieved their water with everyone else, from the pump in the plaza, and then they boiled it. Frank had rigged a cold-water shower over a wooden platform in a stall next to the house. The kitchen stove used a small propane tank that they filled in the market. Frank apologized that things weren't more lavish, but things were wonderful to Fern. In fact, they were perfect.

13

Within a week of discovering the downtown flock, David got an eviction notice. It came in the mail, a letter addressed "Dear Mr. Huntington," alerting him with regrets that he would have to vacate the apartment. At first he'd thought that Bozuki had simply made a mistake, not telling someone in his office that they had already worked out an arrangement. But it was no mistake. On the phone, Bozuki confirmed it. Yes, David was being evicted.

"But we agreed on the new rent," said David.

"My son wants the place," said Bozuki. "What can I say?" He was adamant this time. There was no negotiating him out of it. David would have to be out of the apartment by the first of October. That was only six weeks away, David said, and Bozuki just said, that's right. He didn't even say he was sorry. David called the city rent board, where the machine put him on hold, while Beatles music played until he hung up. Then he looked around at his jammed apartment, at the moldering heap of paper on his desk, at the heavy new furniture placed there a few months before. The whole thing was impossible. And yet, he could see the place in his mind, the blank floors running up to the blank walls, as if it had to be empty.

For a moment he considered calling his father, who had been in the business for years and knew, from the landlord's angle, every aspect of tenant law. But this would be a mistake, he knew. He would simply be giving his father a reason to gloat over his son's misfortune. Then he called Peter, who was his most practical friend, and without even saying hello first, told him he was getting evicted.

"Yeah, you and everybody else," said Peter. "It's the dot-com thing. Goony nerds from the 'burbs buying up the place like there's no tomorrow."

"There is no tomorrow," said David gloomily. "What am I supposed to do now?"

"What do you want to do?" said Peter. "And what have you been doing, anyway?" It was a good question.

"I don't know," said David. He'd have to think about it. And when he got off the phone, he could do nothing else but think about it. What had he been doing? He was spending a huge amount of time and energy on his new pursuit, parrots and parrot lore, giving it days of intense activity, perhaps unequalled since his time at college, days of reading and thought. In just the past week, he had gone back to see the flock twice. He was already grooving a new passageway for himself through the city, taking the subway to the Embarcadero and then walking past the wharves to the base of the steps. The first time he had stood up in a train full of morning commuters. When he had climbed the steps he found no flock, just Mike sitting on the steps with an unsurprised look on his face. Together they sat quietly until the birds arrived in a squawking bunch from the direction of downtown.

Mike told David the birds' names, pointing out which were mates and which were young birds. Mike had honored his heroes by naming the parrots after them. Among them were Bashō and Jane Austen, Thelonious and Dizzy, Cal and Ted and Mickey and Willie, also Leonard and Pee Wee Herman. Many names came from the movies: Bogart and Bacall and Hepburn and Redgrave and Brando, of course. Mike said he'd been thinking of the Brando in *The Wild Ones,* not the Brando from *The Godfather,* as this bird had arrived noisy and cocky, like a biker. David was, of course, particularly interested in seeing this bird. But Pepito–Little Wittgenstein–Brando did not show up that day. Mike said not to worry. The flock was not complete. Many of the birds were tending nests. When the young ones fledged in September, David could expect to see the whole population.

The next time David came to the steps, he found himself alone with the birds. Before he'd seen them he'd heard them clucking and cooing above him as he climbed. They were roosting and playing on the phone wires and the branches around the stairs. The birds seemed to know him, or at least not to fear him. They'd hung around for an hour, playing on the wires like kids, whacking and squawking at each other, even hanging upside down. It calmed David to sit there watching them.

David thought about this and called Peter back. "I still don't know what I want to do, but I can tell you what I have been doing."

"What?" said Peter.

"Actually I've been bird-watching in your neighborhood." David would not have admitted this to anyone but Peter.

"You're kidding," said Peter, and David told him the story.

"You're telling me that the bird you had in your apartment is part of this flock?" said Peter. David said he didn't know. He was the same kind of parrot, though.

"I went back there to try to find him," said David. "He might be called Marlon Brando now. He might be doing fine, even though the other birds don't like him much."

"O-kay," said Peter, both humoring him and letting him know he was humoring him. Peter told David not to worry about being evicted, in any case. He had money. He could move somewhere else. "You could move to Telegraph Hill," he added facetiously. David dismissed the idea, but it appealed to him more than he let on.

"Whatever," said David. "But I have to do something soon. I've got less than six weeks before they throw me out of here." Peter said he'd think about it and that he would keep an eye out for For Rent signs. He was sorry he couldn't be more help, he added. It was a horrible town for housing.

David got off the phone after that, feeling better. Peter was right. David could do something about this. He had the Wadsworth. He could do what he wanted. All he had to do was figure out what that was.

Even as the deadline for his eviction bore down on him, he studiously put aside the question, dodging his anxiety by plunging into books. His reading took on a sense of urgency, as if it held the answer to the question of his future. In the library, the clerks who gave him the bird books now recognized him and took him seriously, though they never asked about his reasons for studying these matters so intently. Mike's insistence that the flock was trying to communicate with David in some way, that he was getting a signal from them, worked on him. He raced ahead in his reading, from the *Anodorhynchus purpurascens* and the Carolina parakeet to the natural history of parrots in the Western Hemisphere in general.

He found that America had been identified with parrots since it was first called America. Parrots had arrived in the Caribbean long ago, perhaps during some Ice Age, when so much seawater had been locked in the poles that the islands had been connected by land. Then parrots could have migrated from the mainland of Central America without flying over open water. However they arrived, they found no natural enemies on the islands and flourished in flocks of tens of thousands. Such numbers of parrots flew above the islands that on some later European maps the whole continent would be labeled *Terra Psittacorum,* Land of Parrots.

Then sea levels rose again, flooding the land bridges and separating the islands. As the eons passed, distinct parrot species arose on each separate island. The types remained the same—the *Ara,* the biggest parrots, among them macaws; the next largest the *Amazona;* and the smallest the *Aratinga*—though in each particular place, parrots evolved in a particular way. Even just reading about these ancient flocks, David felt that he stood in their presence, before the time of human beings, watching huge flocks spiral over the mountains and trees and beaches, on each island their calls and their hues slightly different, like living flags. This was the pure and full array, the life-force of the New World, dense, brilliant, vital beyond anything one might see now.

The descriptions surged through him. He'd never thought about nature in this way. In his dim cubby in the library, he got a lump in his throat as he read. It startled him. He'd lived so enclosed and urban a life, consuming himself for so long with human meaning only. Why him? Why should *he* come to this passion? But then perhaps he'd made a vacuum, a void, into which a vision like this might flow. He toyed with the notion. In truth, David Huntington, né Hirsch, the X poet and city man, was hoping he had been called, as Mike had suggested, called to incorporate within himself the deeper history of the flock, called to help them survive.

In a volume about early European explorations of the New World, David found the log Columbus had written on his first voyage. In his current state of mind, David saw that the journal was all about birds. He was no naturalist, Columbus, though he had kept an eye out for birds from the first. As his little fleet plunged ahead into the unknown sea, Columbus held an abstracted and steady course at twenty degrees of latitude and looked for birds as signs of land and as indications that his theories about the globe were true.

But Columbus's theoretical globe was far too small, so his search for birds became more and more desperate. Becalmed in the empty environment of midocean, having already traveled some four hundred miles beyond his estimate of the distance to Japan, Columbus needed the birds. "Toward night two or three land birds came to the ship, singing," he wrote. "They disappeared before sunrise." Columbus seemed quite nutty to David, quite crazed. He could have been Coleridge's Ancient Mariner.

In the end the birds did bring Columbus to land. One morning the crew of the *Niña* sighted what seemed to be a coastline. After sailing all the following day, they found that this phantom shore consisted only of huge flocks of birds. By then it was October, and the ships were passing beneath the great migration routes of the birds of the Americas. These were the flocks David had been imagining. Columbus, who had marked the birds one by one for weeks, now looked up from the deck to see millions of them: ducks, geese, passenger pigeons, vast, trumpeting, avian multitudes, all heading southwest.

Still he would not abandon his course at twenty degrees of latitude, until the captains of the other two ships convinced him, with some effort, to follow the birds. The Portuguese had found land following birds, they said. So they changed their course and fell in beneath the flocks. "All night heard birds passing," Columbus wrote in his journal, and David shuddered reading it. For four days and nights the ships followed the flocks. On the fifth night, they came to land.

Nor was this the last of birds in the journal. Ashore, the Europeans now found parrots, to them exotic eastern birds. The Arawak people who lived on the island swam out to meet the ships, bearing gifts of parrots. For some forty of these birds, Columbus traded "beads, red caps, hawks bells, indeed whatever we chose to give." And Columbus found parrots wherever he went in the Caribbean, on island after island. "Groves of lofty and flourishing trees were abundant," he noted as he went, "as also large lakes, surrounded and overhung by foliage in a most enchanting manner. Flocks of parrots obscured the heavens."

On his return to Spain in 1493, Columbus displayed the parrots he had acquired on his voyage to the king, the queen, and "an immense multitude" at court. David imagined their cries ringing in the chambers of the palace, as Little Wittgenstein's had in his apartment. This account of a European man insistent on his own abstract and diminished calculation of the world, delivered by birds, at first by ones and two, then by millions, into a dazzling parrot-crowded paradise, this struck David as his own story, and he read it with a sense of shock and recognition, even embarrassment.

David couldn't go home when he left the library that day. He felt drunk, high on what he had read, and he did something he had never done, simply turning his steps toward the bay and letting himself find the way to the stairs at Greenwich. He felt drawn there, solid in his aim as he walked through the Tenderloin and Chinatown, past golden ducks hanging dead and naked in the windows of restaurants, past the hawkers outside the strip clubs on Columbus Avenue. Soon a vista of water opened, and suddenly he recognized the street.

It was the narrowing way he had taken when he had first found the stairs. And then, as if they knew he was there and had come to salute him, the flock appeared overhead, plunging momentarily over the space of the street, their wild flight calls cast down on the pavement like strafing fire. His heart leaped to hear them. The individual birds plunged past him, maintaining the gesture of the flock in flight. When they disappeared behind the buildings, David could still hear them sustaining their calls as they flew into the broad open space where the city dropped away. He hurried to the top of the stairs and from there saw them again, turning and rising and falling like a single joyous protoplasmic thing above the city in the low glowing sunlight at the end of the day.

David stood and listened and looked. The cry he heard echoing over the streets and wharves was the cry of those extraordinary flocks of old over the islands of the Caribbean, the flocks that Columbus had said obscured the sky. Then it was not just the same cry repeated but a continuous cry, sustained over the centuries. And not just the cries were continuous—so was the flock itself. Wheeling in the golden light, this flock was that flock, that collective life ongoing despite the deaths of generation upon generation of the individual birds in it, like a body continuing to live despite the deaths of its every individual cell. That age-old voice of the birds called from the depths of life's origins, before parrots came to the Caribbean or to Ecuador, before human beings lived on the planet, before the vast southern continents split apart. He could hear it, the call of every parrot who had ever lived, the cry of the earth itself.

He heard it and a rush of gratitude ran through him. Somehow, though he had worked to avoid the larger world for his entire life, he had been favored with this. One parrot had brought him the message of its species, of its kindred, and of the life of the whole planet. Reaching the railing of the steps above the steep urban forest, he put his warm hands on the cold steel, knowing that he had received it, sure now that he had somehow been chosen to receive it, and that he would never be the same.

14

That afternoon Fern was left alone to move into her new home. In the mangroves at last, she was happier than she'd been in months. She put her things away in drawers that had been emptied for her, and then she walked back to the dock, where she sat contemplating the water and the vast swamp that began on the other side of the stream. She had a feeling that she was being looked out for, a feeling she could not explain. It made her hopeful about doing her research there.

When she returned to the house, music was pouring out the door, the same Ecuadorian music that she'd danced to in Cuenca and had heard on the bus. Her roommate Donna had come home from work and was in the kitchen, making dinner. Donna was an African American woman, from Mobile, Alabama, tall and strong, and she welcomed Fern with a firm handshake. She was cooking, in one big skillet, a dish of rice and beans and fish with greens. Whatever it was, it smelled wonderful. "I tend to eat rather simply down here," said Donna. "You know, toward the bottom of the food chain. But if you'd like some of this, you're welcome to it." Fern, who was hungry, just said yes and thank you.

"I've been eating bananas and mangoes for dinner for weeks," she said.

"This will do you some good, then," said Donna, handing Fern a plate.

Donna knew all about the reserva and about Qualles, it turned out. Leonin had been telling them stories about her since she had gotten there.

"It's not a good place, up there," she said, meaning the reserva. "Leonin has seen them come and seen them go." She laughed. "It's good you're out of there. We were wondering how long you'd last."

Fern laughed, too. It was such a relief for her to have her sense of the reserva confirmed by someone on the outside. Still, she didn't want to talk about it, and so she asked Donna why she was in Ecuador.

Donna had been to college at William and Mary and had majored in economics. When she'd graduated, she'd gotten various job offers, one from the Federal Reserve Bank in D.C. But she had turned to the Peace Corps, to apply her economics training on a small scale, where it might make a difference. "I'm learning a lot about oranges," she said.

The farmers she worked with had never been able to take their fruit directly to the international market. They'd sold to the big companies—actually, to one big company, Donna said—at whatever price they were offered. She was working to find them markets in the United States where they could compete on their own. She spent a lot of time online, she said, e-mailing wholesalers and checking commodity prices.

Fern said that she'd found the reserva on the Internet, and Donna just laughed. "Yeah, well, it's all there," she said, "the good, the bad, and the phony."

Frank the Surfer came in, carrying a bundle of student papers. "That smells good," he said. "What is it?"

"It's the thing," said Donna. "You know, the thing."

"Love that thing," said Frank.

"Tomorrow make something besides the thing, would you?" said Donna to Frank. To Fern she said, "We eat this a lot."

"Hey, let me cook tomorrow," said Fern, and both of the others instantly agreed. Though they traded off on the cooking and the chores, they clearly welcomed a new cook in the house. They'd take the truck down to the market, Frank said.

When they had pushed the plates aside, Frank asked Fern about her work, and Fern tried to explain that she hadn't done much of it yet in Ecuador. She told him about the aratinga. Frank was interested and asked for a description. They were small green parrots with orange underwings, said Fern. They moved in a flock and made a lot of noise in the air. Frank said he had seen something like that. They buzzed the boat sometimes, he said, when he went out fishing in the morning.

Fern said she had had only one sighting so far, and she tried to describe what she had seen on the ridge above the reserva. The flock had appeared to come up from the mangroves. But it wasn't clear whether they roosted there. And there was nothing in the literature to that effect.

"Honey, there's nothing in the literature about a lot that goes on down here," said Donna. She added that she was surprised that Fern had gotten any research done on the reserva.

Fern said sheepishly that she hadn't thought it would turn out to be a zoo.

"A zoo isn't all that it is," said Donna. "I guess you noticed that that man Qualles deals in wildlife."

"Deals?" said Fern. "You mean he *sells* them?" Though

Fern had been suspicious of Qualles, she was still shocked at what they told her then. Leonard Qualles ran a lively business in endangered species, they said. The zoo was a kind of front, a holding facility for animals for sale. They'd heard about it from Leonin and also from the fishermen in the village, who had been given a standing offer of cash for certain animals they brought in.

Fern said, "I didn't see anything like that going on there."

"He didn't want you to see it," Frank said. "He can't afford to have anyone around long. They might get wind of the operation."

How could he get away with it? she asked them. There was CITES, the treaty that prohibited trade in endangered animals. There were agents at the airports.

"We hear he works with them," said Frank. "The guys at the airport get a piece of the action, even when they bust somebody trying to get a parrot or a jaguar out of the country. In fact, from what we hear, some of the animals get sold over and over. They catch the buyers at the airport and send them home with a serious warning. And the animals go back to the reserva to get sold again."

"Eisenhower," said Fern, to the general puzzlement of the people at the table. She explained that a rare parrot had been missing the day she had been dismissed, and then had turned up again mysteriously.

"Sounds like it," said Frank. "Also sounds like the reason you had to go. But you'll have to ask Leonin to be sure."

"Leonin *knows*?" Fern said.

"Sure he knows," said Donna. "That's why he helped you. He'd like to get Qualles out of there. The reserva wasn't always like this. It's been around for years, and it used to be legitimate. Even now, Qualles has got to act like it's for real.

I'm sure the fact that you came down there to do research will turn up in all his official reports, as a sign of official support from the U.S."

"Ugh," said Fern, putting her hand to her forehead. "Still, I don't know what I can do about it."

"Just let people know, when you get back," said Frank. "Anyway, you can do your real work."

Fern was grateful for what they had told her but also embarrassed to have been so naïve. How could she have lived there and not known? She and Frank cleaned the kitchen after dinner, and she was quiet as she went about it.

"Look, don't feel bad," said Frank. "All of us Yankees who come down here get an education we don't expect. Life in the States doesn't quite prepare you."

No, she had not been prepared. She had come out of her life of amenities and reassurances, grad school and boyfriend, the wide paved spaces of the United States. And she had brought that life on her trip. Though she'd meant well, she hadn't been in Ecuador. At least now she had really arrived.

Fern took another walk around the village after dinner, looking at it as if for the first time. People were shutting down their houses for the night, doing their last chores. In the sky above the trees, wisps of high cloud shone as if with their own pink and violet radiance. When she got back to the house, she found Frank grading papers on the porch. "I give them homework and they give me more," he said. She asked how she might get into the mangroves in the morning.

"I'll take you for a look before school," said Frank. "We have to get on the water at low tide, though, and that's really early."

"Why low tide?" she said.

"If you go at low tide," Frank said, "you're sure to have

water, coming back." Fern thanked him for his offer, feeling inadequate as she said it. He and the others had already done so much for her. Still, she was in no position to decline.

The next morning, Frank put his head in the door of their room and said "Rise and shine!" Below her in the bottom bunk, Donna groaned. "You guys rise and shine," she said. "It's the middle of the night." Fern climbed down from the top bunk, pulled on shorts and a T-shirt, over which she wore a loose field vest with lots of pockets. The night before she had stuffed them with things she thought she'd need in the mangroves, her notepads and extra pens, two kinds of bug repellent, sunscreen, her binocs, a light mosquito net that she could fit on her hat. The hat was billed like a baseball cap and had a flap that draped her neck. Most of these things had remained packed for months. She'd packed a light backpack, too, with a plastic water jug, a dry shirt and socks, her bird book, her camera, and other things.

She came into the light of the kitchen fully equipped. Frank, who was dressed in flip-flops, flowered baggie trunks, and a U.C. Santa Cruz Banana Slugs T-shirt, looked at her, but mercifully said nothing. She sat heavily in a chair and laced up her boots, saying again that it was so nice of him to do this.

"I'm glad to have the company, this early," he said, explaining that he usually rose before dawn to drive to the beach and surf a few waves, before school.

He'd made coffee and offered her a piece of mango bread. Just five minutes later, as if they were rushing to catch a train instead of the tide, they got up, shut off the kitchen light—leaving the house as dark as the middle of the night could be—and went outside.

Using a flashlight Frank gathered some gear on the porch, his wetsuit booties and a broad, battered straw hat. *"Superfino,"* he said, putting it on. *"El producto del Ecuador."* He gave Fern a couple of life jackets and shouldered a pair of oars. As Fern stepped off the porch, a rooster screamed in a nearby yard and was immediately answered by two or three others, farther away in the village.

They walked in silence to the dock, the *malecón,* Frank called it. Many of the houses had lights on already, and the smell of woodsmoke hung in the air. At the shore the rocks were slick, the surface of the water far lower than the day before.

"There's a three-meter tide here, this time of year," said Frank. "That's miles and miles of mud, when it goes out."

Standing there, Fern felt the sea, distant but potent, drawing its water out of the estuary, as if it were inhaling in its sleep. The salt water drained through millions of mangrove roots, thousands of miles of twisting stream channels. On the far bank, a low mist wafted through the trees. *"La garúa,"* said Frank, "That's what the people here call the night fog."

The exposed roots of the mangroves glowed palely, a riot of crossed and looping fibers, some of them knobbed like knees. Above them, the trunks of the trees rose straight and tall, some of them to fifty or sixty feet. Frank readied one of the boats, untying it, putting in the oars. As the light came up, the inner depths of the forest began to reveal themselves as a single texture, a world of mangroves.

Mangrove seedlings, slender beanlike hypocotyls, could float with the tides and currents for a year or more. They might take root at the foot of the mother tree or in a mudflat halfway around the globe. So mangroves had come to ring the world in a belt of tropical lowlands. These mangroves were all mangroves, Fern thought. The dark thicket suddenly felt deep in time as well. Fossil mangroves had been found that were seventy-five million years old. The trees may have originated even longer ago than that, three hundred million years before, even before there were flowering plants on land, when human beings were still unimaginably far in the future.

Frank got into the middle of the boat and asked her to sit in the stern. Using one of the oars, he poled them off the rocks, and the hull slid silently out into the channel. Frank put the loose oar into its lock and began to row. He drew the oars easily, without straining. They made hardly a sound as they passed through the water.

"You need to navigate," he said. "I know this channel, but you never know when a mudflat will build up. So let me know if I'm headed for something besides open water." She looked ahead, over his shoulder, as they proceeded. The stream channel immediately took a full turn around a bend and headed in the opposite direction. Frank explained that they were going downstream, heading out with the tide into larger channels, tidal creeks as wide as rivers that eventually opened into the bay itself. Frank rowed on comfortably.

"You don't use a motor?" said Fern. Frank replied that he hated the noise. "Everybody hears you coming," he added.

Fern tried to make some observations, to push through her sense of bewilderment at the swamp around her, and began identifying the mangroves on the nearest bank. They were red mangroves with slender trunks, the most salt-tolerant of the eight New World mangrove species. They exuded a film of salt through their waxy leaves, she knew, and looking at the closest branches, she could indeed see the white lines the salt made there. This was satisfying, like finding the proof of a theory. She could hypothesize, too, that farther inland, where fresh water was more abundant, would be the others, in zones, the gray mangrove, the black mangrove, and at the line of the highest spring tides, the buttonwoods.

But which direction inland might be was lost to her at the moment. The shoreline opened with dozens of watercourses, some of them as broad as the stream they followed, and soon she was sure that if she were out there alone in the serpentine maze of channels, she would not be able to get back. They had been rowing for only a few minutes and already she knew she'd be lost.

Just then, everything was undergoing dawn. That was how it felt. Rosy light suddenly brightened the sky to the east. All around them the islanded groves began to radiate with birdsong. Frank looked at her with mock alarm, acknowledging the cacophony. It was a great sound, equal parts joy and shock, as if the coming of the day were something that had never happened before. "It's happening!" the birds called, not, "It's happening again," as she might have, as her mental species, having seen the days come and the days go, might have. She had to smile, hearing it and feeling herself new with the day.

Frank rowed down the winding channel for nearly an hour. The tide turned. Water began to fill the meandering troughs like stems climbing a trellis. They passed many birds, herons and egrets standing still in the shallows and small ducks that moved silently into the shelter of the roots as they passed. On a thick branch above the stream a long-necked black-and-white bird, strange to Fern, stood sentinel-like, its large wings spread as if to warm them in the new light. On another bare branch a pair of sharp-beaked kingfishers surveyed the water. And constantly from the thicket around them came the purrs and clucks and tweets of tiny birds, invisible to the eye.

They passed a pair of fishermen pulling nets out of the mud, many fish flashing silver in them. They'd come at high tide, said Frank, and had strung their net across one of the side streams so that all the animals in that channel were literally up the creek. When the tide went out, the net took them all. The fishermen waved to Frank, seeming to know him.

After a while, Frank rowed up one of the smaller channels, which narrowed until the leaves of the mangroves brushed them on either side. Here a still silence hung heavily over them, the breath of the warm wet atmosphere. As they sat there, motionless, Fern began to notice that the whole scene—the bottom of the channel, the roots, the bank, the trees—was covered with living things. On the leggy, interwoven roots near the boat, periwinkles and barnacles and clams hung in clusters. A crab with its eyes on two slender stalks raised a single blue claw. Many things, fish and shrimp, flashed in the clear shallow water and wriggled and burrowed into the mud. A small cayman or alligator blinked and disappeared, rippling the water. The branches were strung with dozens of webs. The lines of gossamer gleamed everywhere. Every few feet, there was a huge web, a spider at its center.

Fern contemplated one of them some three feet from her face: a black spider big enough to look furry. It was spotted with red and lifted its grotesque jaws in her direction. Fern began to feel stings and itches and realized that many smaller insects, midges and mosquitoes, had begun to harass them as they sat there. Suddenly, the whole swamp seemed too close and too alive. The miles-wide, steaming, green watery place had become a single, vital, many-mouthed organism with an appetite for her own flesh. For a moment she fought off a feeling of claustrophobia and rising panic. Then Frank, slapping his forearms, suggested they get out of there.

"That was intense," she said, when they had pulled into the broader channel.

"Uh-huh," said Frank. "That's the mangle, up close and personal."

They moved steadily up the waterways, the tide running with them now. The place was immense, and so was the project she had taken on. At home in Tucson, reading about life in the mangroves, the dropping of their leaves sustaining shrimp, fish, mussels, clams, all the beginnings of life, she'd been moved. Now she felt starkly the inadequacy of mere reading. Until that morning her conception of mangroves had been theoretical. Now she'd seen them, had felt their living presence, and it stunned her. How was she going to get around in them by herself? How would she find her way, let alone locate a single species of parrot? With one glance at the real mangroves, she could see that the task she had set for herself could easily be a life's work.

She thought about it, as the boat glided along the water, which was perfectly still, reflecting precisely the trees that overhung the channel. The sky had been brightening as they'd gone in beneath the trees, and by this time—not even seven—it was a cool blue, deepened in its reflection in the water. Now it looked tranquil, beautiful.

The Delta of the Ganges, in India, bore the largest mangrove concentration in the world. She remembered the stories she'd read about the place, home of a particularly fierce red species of Bengal tiger. These animals pulled people out of boats and ate them. Here in Ecuador were jaguars, somewhere nearby, perhaps watching their boat between the roots of the mangroves. She remembered the tiger at the reserva, its glance acknowledging but not accepting its life in a world dominated by human beings. That made him dangerous. This was as it should be, she thought. The life of the mangroves also insisted, resisted. It remained, to the last mangrove, an unconquered and unconquerable presence. This was dangerous, too, and would eat her if it could, just as the tiger would.

"How'd you find your way here?" she asked.

"Water's the common denominator, I guess," said Frank. "Started surfing when I was eleven."

"No," she said, " I mean how do you find your way *here,* in the mangroves?"

"Oh," he said. "I went out with Enrique at first. Enrique lives in the swamp. He took me when he went fishing."

"You think he would take me into the mangroves?" she asked.

"He might. We'd have to talk to people about it. They've seen a lot of outsiders come and go down here, and usually things just get worse for them when they leave. He'd need to know your reasons."

"Of course," she said, wondering about her reasons herself.

"One thing will help," said Frank. "Getting thrown off the reserva. That's a plus."

"I did, didn't I?" she said, having to grin.

15

More than four hundred feet long from bow to stern, the ship chugged along in the open ocean, seeming to surge ahead with every explosion in the barn-sized engine that pounded away below. The main deck stood four stories above the engine, and the cabin superstructure rose another four stories above the deck. On the third floor was the bridge, where white-uniformed Chilean sailors steered the ship amid a hundred blinking lights, the radar, and the depth finders and the radio and the other instruments. And on the fourth floor was David, making his new home in a little seagoing room where the furniture was bolted to the floor. He unpacked. He put out his books. He would be at sea for three weeks, and he had much reading to do before the ship reached Guayaquil.

Early that morning, they had passed beneath the Golden Gate Bridge, and David had stood out on the deck, watching with a pounding heart as this enormous soaring orange ironwork, representing his whole life up to that point, swung by overhead. David was amazed at himself and amazed at the capacity of life in general. Things had proved so much roomier than he had imagined.

The date was October 1, a day he had worried about for weeks, thinking that for all he knew that he would be homeless by then. But here he was, heading out to sea, his old apartment empty and ready for new people, and all his stuff placed in storage in a single red corrugated container, stacked neatly with hundreds like it on the Oakland docks.

In the end, it was Peter who had helped him, first by convincing him that he had no reason to remain in San Francisco. Why not travel for a while? Peter had said. Why not live in Italy, for instance? Peter had suggested this when the two had met at Babar. The place was nearly empty, on a Wednesday night, and David was as full of anxiety as Peter was expansive.

"Everything changes," Peter said. "You just have to go with it and see what happens next. If you have to move, why not embrace it?"

Even the bar in which they sat, in which they had gathered for years, was closing. Lenny, the bar's owner, a guy from Ann Arbor, had gotten a huge offer for the place. Lenny was buying some land in Costa Rica, said Peter. This appealed to David.

"I'd rather live in South America than in Italy," he remarked impulsively.

This was all Peter needed. "Where would you go?" he asked David, and when David said he was only kidding, just being hypothetical, Peter said, "Fine, let's be hypothetical. Where would you go?"

"Maybe Ecuador," said David. Peter was surprised at this. Not Bahia or Buenos Aires or Patagonia? "No," said David. "Ecuador."

How would he get there, hypothetically? Peter wanted to know. That would be a problem, David admitted. He wouldn't want to fly. He still had his dread of aircraft. Fine, said Peter, no airplanes. How about a boat? Peter knew about boats from his work on the docks.

This boat idea struck a chord in David, because he had been watching the ships lately, as he had walked along the wharves on his way to see the flock. To Peter, he said only, "Well, that might be all right." Peter had said, "I'll tell you what. I'll figure this out for you." They dropped the matter for the rest of the evening and for a couple of days, until Peter called him and simply said, "Well, I found you a ship."

It was a Chilean freighter, called the *Lircay.* It booked a few passengers and traveled the Pacific Coast from Seattle down to Valparaíso. It left Oakland in mid-September, and made port in Long Beach, San Diego, Mexico, then Ecuador.

"It stops at a place called Esmeraldas and then in Guayaquil. Or you can stay on it and go all the way to Peru and Chile."

"No," said David. "I couldn't do that. What about all my stuff?"

Peter said he'd thought of that already. A dockworker friend of his ran a self-storage business in West Oakland, near the docks. "They put the stuff in ship containers and stack them off the ground," said Peter. " It's safe and it's cheap."

Still, David persisted in refusing. It was an outlandish idea. And all Peter could do was to ask that he consider the matter. "Listen, Dave," he said. "Nobody I know needs a change of scenery as much as you do. Not only that, but like I said, you have to move. You have no choice. And you can move. You have the money. Just think about it."

So David had considered the matter, obsessively, day and night, all weekend. He stayed home and thought about it. Friday night passed and Saturday night, nights he might have gone out on a date with a woman, if he'd known any.

When Monday morning arrived, the other residents went off to their jobs and the silence of the empty apartment building greeted him once again, and he felt idle and yet could not look at the pile of paper he had once thought of as his book. So he decided to go see the flock. Maybe he'd find the bird called Brando this time.

He got off the subway at the foot of the Embarcadero and walked along the waterfront. Now the sight of the water truly tugged at him. A ship went by, a blue-and-yellow tourist-line boat, but still a ship, cutting a foamy wake into the blue of the bay, and David watched it with a sense of wistfulness that grew into an actual pain in his chest. It represented everything in life that was going somewhere—if only out to Alcatraz and back. When he reached the stairs and climbed up into trees and shrubbery, he found not the whole flock but only a few birds, twittering on the wires. David had turned to climb back down when a commotion above made him look back. A new parrot had joined them. It flapped its wings on the swinging wire where it had landed, and it screeched loudly and familiarly.

David climbed the stairs and stared at the new arrival. The bird was an adult, with a spattering of red feathers on his head and neck. It peered down at David with one white-rimmed eyeball and then the other, as David peered up at him, thinking he could see a crook at the point of the bird's bill. Then the parrot stared outright at David, both eyes bulging around the crown of its beak, and gave forth its familiar screech, and it was clear. Here was Little Wittgenstein, alive and apparently well, in fact, looking better than ever.

"Hey!" exclaimed David. "How've you been!" The bird squawked back. "Long time no see," said David. Squawk. "How's life been treating you?" Another squawk. Little

Wittgenstein's squawks were pretty much the same as ever. Maybe there was some anger in the squawk—a little "How-dare-you-imprison-me-and-then-throw-me-out-the-window"—but it sounded more to David like the announcement of a free creature, on his own in the world and not caring who knew it. Maybe this had always been the bird's declaration. If David had heard ridicule in the bird's cries, maybe it had been his own ridicule, he thought, the expression of his own rising disdain for his narrow life, projected onto the squawking bird.

"You're Brando now, I hear," said David, and Little Wittgenstein squawked his squawk again. The new name, like the old ones, did not reach him. David watched the bird for a while, as it clung to the wire and preened itself. Then another bird flew up and landed on the wire quite close by. And as David watched, the bird he knew as Little Wittgenstein began to preen the newcomer, nibbling into its feathers with his beak. A mate, thought David. He's found a mate.

When the two parrots flew off together, David climbed down the stairs and headed back toward the subway. Across the bay stood the docks in Oakland, where Peter worked. Gazing over the water, David suddenly knew he was going to do it. Back in his old apartment—it was his *old* apartment, like a shell he had already cast off—he called Peter. "Tell me the rest of it," he said, when Peter answered. "Because I want to go. I've got to store this stuff. I've got to get a ticket."

In the following weeks there was much to do. David got shots and a passport, and these involved finding places in the city he had never been. But the fact that he was going to South America put his navigations around San Francisco into an adventurous context, and he found not only that could he manage it, but also that if he let himself, he could actually enjoy finding his way. So he found the passport office. And he found the clinic they sent him to for shots, where he sat in the waiting room with others about to travel, three men in suits and a couple in hiking clothes. After the nurse injected him with vaccines against yellow fever and hepatitis, he sought out a store where he bought himself hiking clothes, roomy shorts, a khaki shirt and a vest, and luxurious Spanish hiking boots. At that point he still had no idea what he would do when he got to Ecuador, and so he found a travel agency, where he was shown brochures for tours of the Galápagos and the rain forest. But organized tours did not appeal to him, and he left without booking anything. At night he read and reread his now-worn Ecuador book, which in a twinkling had turned from a theoretical text to an actual guide.

It occurred to him that Mike, the caretaker of the flock, might be of help. The next time David went to Telegraph Hill, he knocked on Mike's door. Mike opened it and ushered David into the kitchen, where they waited for the flock to arrive on the fire escape. David told Mike that he was going to Ecuador, and Mike received David's plans with his usual unsurprised air.

"You're going to find the flock down there," he said, and David nodded, though it was the first time he had thought of his trip in such explicit terms. That was a good idea, said Mike. Whatever information David could find out about the flock's home environment might help them survive up here. Mike got out a map and showed David the area where the flock came from, a region around the Gulf of Guayaquil, near the border between Ecuador and Peru. David had not seen a map of the place on such a scale. Most of it was a maze of streams and tributaries. It made him dizzy to look at it.

Mike was taking down David's phone number when the flock arrived, swirling in around a big cypress that rose above the others in the park, then settling on the metal rungs of the fire escape.

"I think I met Brando," said David, "and I think he's Little Wittgenstein." The two of them searched the incoming flock until they found him. He was perching apart from the others, in the limbs of a tulip tree nearby. "That's him," said David. "I really think that's him." Near Little Wittgenstein perched the other bird that David had seen.

"Yep," said Mike. "And it looks like Brando and Kim Novak are an item."

Mike called the following day and said he was sending David something in the mail. A thick envelope arrived, and in it David found a short note—"From the archives. Actually, I'd been hoping to make this trip myself. M."—and scientific articles about the *Aratinga erythrogenys* in its native habitat, a copy of the map, and a page of bird references in Guayaquil, including a phone number and address for INEVS, an Ecuadorian organization working to save local endangered species.

David's last month in San Francisco passed quickly, every day filled with errands and hard work. David had underestimated all that had to be done, and he was relieved to hear from Peter that the ship had been delayed. They were doing some engine work in Portland and would be two weeks late. This was fortunate, as it turned out that David needed every minute of that time. Peter and Lyle came over to help him pack. Lyle was quiet and acted concerned, as if David had lost his mind. Without a qualm, David loaded the papers of his would-be book into cardboard boxes, marking them simply Old Poetry. David reserved a few books—a Spanish grammar, the works of Samuel Taylor Coleridge, his own copy of *Parrots of the World,* purchased the week before, and his Ecuador guide, among others—and packed up the rest, surprising himself with his relief.

Then the movers arrived, and they bore everything out of the building and up a ramp into their truck, which they double-parked all day in front of David's building. Peter and David followed the truck across the Bay Bridge in Peter's vintage VW bug, then took the lead when they reached the Oakland docks, directing the driver to the storage yard.

On the docks everything was larger than life, out of scale. Huge white cranes stood like gigantic horses at the water's edge, their booms raised as if they were looking far out to sea. At the storage yard, they helped the movers put David's things into a single boxcar-sized steel container. They packed it carefully, filling every space. The new pale velvet couch slid into the opening like a lozenge. David was shocked then to see how easily the yard operator lifted the red corrugated container, up, up, everything he owned assuming a lesser and lesser scale, until, when the crane placed it neatly into a stack with dozens of others, it looked like a shoe box, a minor item. David signed some papers, gave the operator a check for the first six months' storage, and then went home to his empty apartment, sleeping that night and for two nights following on an air mattress Lyle had lent him. Lyle had become a believer, in the end. He was, he said, totally impressed at what David was doing.

David had to stay in the apartment until the very last

day, September 30, before the ship had docked in Oakland and was ready to take him aboard. That morning he packed up the last few things and swept the place out, finding in the sweepings a green-and-yellow feather, which he slipped into a book that he had put with his travel things.

The new tenants showed up as David was finishing. They were a young couple from Palo Alto, and they were irritated with the place. The kitchen was so small, said the woman, and the whole thing would have to be painted.

"You wouldn't be Mr. Bozuki's son, would you?" David asked the guy.

"Oh god no," he answered, genuinely horrified.

That afternoon David went to the bank and got a bunch of hundred-dollar bills. He didn't trust traveler's checks. He put the money in a sock among his other socks. That evening Peter drove David to the docks, and Lyle came along to see him off. Peter gave David a couple of books—the works of Pablo Neruda and *Lord Jim.* Lyle was awestruck by the docks, silent for once in the presence of the cranes, the stacked containers, the piles of raw steel, and the ships themselves, their steel sides rising high overhead, all of it monumental under brilliant golden floodlights.

David was thrilled and terrified and glad to have his friends there. Peter found his way to the right dock, and there was the *Lircay,* with its own orange cranes and its gangplank, a rugged, battered steel affair. Some of the crew lined the railing and watched with interest as the three of them came aboard. They carried David's stuff up four flights of stairs inside the superstructure of the freighter, to the Officers' Deck, so-called. The cabin was small and neat, with two rounded rectangular portholes gleaming with the lights of the docks.

They dropped David's luggage—two seagoing duffel bags, a backpack, a suitcase, and a plastic trunk, actually a cooler, holding his books. Then they went back down the gangplank and drove into Oakland, where they had dinner at a Vietnamese place called Le Cheval. David was by then in a state of shock, the ship having made it all quite real.

Over dinner, Peter tried to be encouraging and Lyle tried not to appear worried about his friend. David had a second drink and then a couple more, until the streets swam by as Peter drove them back to the dock. At the foot of the gangplank they hugged, all three of them suddenly emotional.

"I don't even know when I will see you again," said Lyle. On Lyle's insistence—"You have to have a way to get home, if you need to"—David had purchased an open-ended airline ticket from Quito to San Francisco, though he hated the thought of having to fly. Now Lyle's fear seemed prudent. At last David clambered up the gangplank, looked back once to wave at his friends. Then, stumbling over the high steel thresholds, he made his way to his cabin, where he locked the door and fumbled in the dark onto one of the single beds. Drunk and exhausted from the sheer hard work of the past few days, he fell deeply asleep in his clothes, not stirring until dawn, when a definitive nudge against the hull jolted him awake, and he jumped up to the porthole to see one of the big white cranes moving past. They were under way.

Still groggy, David left his cabin and walked to the door at the end of the hallway. It opened to the outside, and he found himself on a steel staircase. He came out on an upper deck, then walked to the railing. A tugboat was pushing the ship away from the dock. Whirlpools and eddies opened in the water below like mouths gaping in surprise. Then the throb of the ship's own engines began, and the ship entered the channel. The steely Bay Bridge passed overhead. In a few minutes they had traversed Treasure Island and then the whole skyline of San Francisco came into view.

This was his city, his only city, yet he had never seen it from the water. In the clear early light it looked toylike and perfect on its hills. The buildings downtown revolved as one as the ship went by. Telegraph Hill rose up and he could see the green swath that was the park by the Greenwich Stairs. He strained his eyes to see any sign of the flock. For a moment he thought he could hear their cackling flight above the thrum of the engines, or he may have supplied it himself. In any case, that jangle rang in his ears, a piercing salute for his departure.

Next came the wharves of Fort Mason and then the rocky beach leading to Fort Point, and then the soaring orange bridge, passing gracefully over the ship. David felt scared, having done it, having left, but the huge ship had its own schedule and momentum and the step he had taken was at that moment irrevocable. The strait slid away behind them, their broad white wake leaving a trail all the way back under the bridge to the dock. As the coast disappeared and the wide horizon encircled the ship, he was going, he was going, and then he was gone.

Suddenly he felt exhausted again and went back into his cabin and fell on the bunk. He was awakened by a knock at the door. It was the captain, a courtly German, who welcomed him aboard and informed him that he was the only passenger on the ship. He also suggested that David might be lonely eating by himself and invited him to eat with the ship's officers. David accepted, and that night ate the first of three weeks' dinners in the Officers' Mess, where he had an assigned seat between two Indian officers—the first mate,

Roy, from Bombay, and the radio officer, Surojit, from Goa—both of whom talked a lot and were glad for the new company. The two were impressively familiar with American literature—as well as English and Indian; Surojit recited a long passage from "The Rime of the Ancient Mariner," which David couldn't help having mentioned.

After dinner the captain invited David to tour the bridge, where the officers looked at the charts and at the revolving green radius on the radar screen, which illuminated the glowing shape of the coast. Beyond the wide windows, the ship's cranes and stacked containers rocked together as the ship split the swells, and beyond the decks in a sky like black silk the stars were brilliant. One constellation stood directly ahead of them in the south, and David asked which one it was. "That's Scorpius," said the captain, a mild tone of surprise and exasperation in his voice, as if he couldn't quite believe that someone would not know Scorpius when he saw it.

When he left the bridge, David climbed the steel stairs to the top of the ship, reaching a small railed deck out of which one of the two enormous funnels rose. The damp wind blew in his face, smelling strongly of the sea, the air drenched not just with the odor of salt, but with the smell of some vast organic matter, like miles of underwater kelp forest. David looked up at millions of stars. Under the lights of the city, he realized, he'd only ever seen one star or two at a time. But every tiny patch of the night sky held clusters of stars. The constellation that David now knew as Scorpius still stood ahead of the ship. David, deciding it didn't look much like a scorpion, suddenly saw it in minute detail as a lily on its stem, every fold and vein of its petals outlined in stars, dozens of them.

Lying in his bunk that night, David did not believe he would be able to sleep. For a moment he wished he had brought his earplugs. The engine throbbed below the decks and sent its pulsing shudder throughout the ship, setting off all sorts of small vibrations and squeaks in his cabin. But David did fall asleep, though he had a dream in which machines were out of control, and he woke up in the dark, not knowing where he was, shouting, "Stop!"

The next morning dawned bright and blue. David walked around the ship. Beyond the railing of the steel staircase, the side of the ship dropped away starkly, some fifty feet. On the horizon a single oil platform stood like a lone castle. The water near the ship was dark and blue and so clear that the air beaten into it by the bow floated beneath the surface in cloud banks. It seemed as if the ocean alone were moving, bearing bunches of brown grapelike seaweed into the waves breaking on the bow.

Then he noticed strange winged creatures, flying fish, he realized after a moment, leaping out of the waves and gliding away from the ship over the blue surface. One big fish glided forever, over swell after swell, looking so right yet so odd with its widespread wing-fins. And David, no longer anywhere, though certainly somewhere else, he, too, was odd but oddly right.

16

Leonin's uncle, Enrique, a small man with a deeply lined face, listened gravely as Fern explained that she was a scientist. Frank translated this for her, but the old fisherman said nothing in reply. Next she said she was hoping to show everyone the beauty and richness of this place and to save it for the future. That had slightly more meaning. Anyway, Enrique nodded. But what finally convinced him to take her into the mangroves was the picture she showed him of the aratinga in her book of South American birds. In the photograph the little parrot stood on one leg on its perch and gazed side-faced at the camera with its white-rimmed eye.

"*¿Es éste el loro?*" said Enrique. Is this the bird? The picture charmed him, and he showed it to his son, who stood at his side on the dock as they conducted the interview. Yes, he would help her find this bird, he said at last.

So almost at dawn every day for two weeks, Enrique had taken her out in his boat, saying nothing as he steered the outboard motor. She took pictures and notes and drew maps in her notebooks of the layout of the waterways and the few landmarks she noticed. By the end of the first week, she knew her way through the first series of twisting bends in the channel. Twice they heard parrots, the first time the screech of a solitary bird, and the next time, just after sunrise, the raucous group chatter of a flock in flight, somewhere beyond the screen of the trees. Then for many days there was nothing.

Slowly the fierce heat of the summer—the sky most days like hot silver—was giving way. And with so little accomplished, Fern had to reconsider her objectives. No longer did she feel that she would be able to make any long-term observations of the aratingas. Back in Tucson, she had imagined herself like Diane Fosse among the gorillas, sitting close to the flock and observing their habits for hours. But there was a good reason that the birds roosted in the mangroves—they were deeply hidden and safe there. Her goal became simply to sight a flock and get pictures that would confirm its existence, then perhaps to learn something of its movements.

After two weeks, Enrique apologized and told her he could not take her out any more. He needed to fish for his family, he said. Fern might have protested, pointing out that Enrique fished much of the time while she took her notes, but Frank had already told her that Enrique's wife objected to her husband spending so much time with *la mujer de los loros,* the parrot woman. So there was no option but to go into the mangroves alone. Frank argued with her about it. It wasn't about her being a woman, he said. It was dangerous for anyone to go out without someone to back them up in case there was some kind of accident. He had gone out alone many times, though, so he could not persist against her decision to get this research done. And in the end he let her use his boat.

After just a few days of going out by herself, she felt her boat skills come back, though she'd had to push the boat off the mud several times, occasionally having to get out into waist-deep muck to do so, before she learned to read the channels by the color of the water, the ripples, the flotsam on the current. Her arms and shoulders began to grow sinuous from the work of rowing every day. The bugs never let up. She covered all of her exposed skin with insect repellent each morning and kept it handy in the boat, and even then she came home with a dozen welts. She took notes on what she could, but it was frustrating using Frank's boat. She could go only so far into the swamp by rowing, and it was not far enough to find the flock.

In the house she did her part, driving their truck to the nearby town of San Lorenzo to shop on market day and cooking for her roommates when her turn came. Fern spoke to the younger class of the two at the school about her aratingas, with Frank's help for translating. "How many of you have seen a bird like this?" she said, holding up the picture, and almost every hand in the room had gone up, a hopeful sign, she thought. But one boy said that his uncle had such a bird as a pet, and others chimed in, and then, when she asked how many had seen this parrot outside, the children hesitated.

She and Donna had become close friends, often talking and laughing in a slow easy way in their bunks after the lights were out. At dinner, they listened to Frank's narration of the day's waves, sometimes rolling their eyes at his unending enthusiasm for surf. One night as Fern and Donna sat on the porch after dinner, she'd told Donna about Geoffrey and had gotten the letter out to show her, and Donna had been righteous and indignant on her behalf. Fern had told no one about it up until then, and she tried to tell the story in a casual and funny way, but her voice caught and betrayed her. Donna said, "This guy doesn't deserve you," and then cooed, "Oh come here, honey," and had given her a hug as she cried about him one last time.

"Same thing happened to me," Donna confessed. The man she had been seeing at home had found someone else when she'd gone to South America. "Professional hazard, I guess," said Donna.

Fern had gone to Donna's office, a cluttered shack on the edge of the orange groves, to send e-mail. It seemed forever since she had used a keyboard, and once she sat down, she wasn't sure whom to write. Not to Geoffrey certainly. Her parents weren't on e-mail. So she wrote to her old teacher, Pepperbloom, to report on the trip so far. Things hadn't worked out as planned, she wrote. She loved Puerto Alegre, she said, though the mangroves were hard and she was on her own and didn't know how much data she was going to be able to get.

The next day Donna brought home Pepperbloom's response. "Leave it to Ron to get you down there without help," she wrote. "Still, I'm proud of you for hanging in there, and I'm sure that no matter what you get out of it for a dissertation, this will prove to be a great experience. Remember, this project is the first step of your work in the field, not the last. Just keep your eyes open and be careful out there in the swamp." Fern felt a surge of love for Pepperbloom when she read the note. This was the way Pepperbloom had always been, so full of pure enthusiasm for the work. The note renewed Fern's faith in her project. She didn't have to know what she would find there. She just had to keep looking.

After a couple of weeks of letting her use his boat, Frank had helped her get one of her own, taking her to a boatbuilder in San Lorenzo. She'd expected to choose among several boats on a lot, as at a car dealership back home. Instead, the place was a workshop, the floor covered with sawdust, hand-tools lining the dim walls. She described what she wanted and paid the man half. It was a big expense, but when they returned the following Friday it was ready, a beautiful blue flat-bottomed boat with a graceful prow and a red motor and gas tank, and she loved it instantly. It came with broad paddles and an anchor and line, and was built for the mangroves. With the motor tilted up to take the prop out of the water, it could ride in just two inches of water.

The boatbuilder and his brother helped them load the boat and the other equipment into the pickup. As they finished, a small, handsome man and a redheaded woman approached them, saying hello to Frank. The woman was carrying a briefcase, Fern noticed. It wasn't something she'd seen often recently. Frank introduced them as Renato and Raquel, and Fern remembered that she had met Raquel before at the INEVS office in Guayaquil. The two were charged with preventing the sale and exportation of native species. Some days they worked out of their field office in San Lorenzo, where they might observe the animals that the fishermen brought in. Raquel explained this and asked if Fern and Frank would like to have lunch.

They left the truck and the new boat in the care of the boatmaking brothers and walked a few blocks to the main market square, where there was a café with two tables outside. They sat under the umbrella at one of them. Renato, who spoke excellent English, said that they had heard about Fern's work, about her search for the aratinga, and about her difficulty at the reserva. Had Fern not already spent a month in the village, she might have been shocked to have her business so publicly known. But in the village everyone knew everything, by osmosis as it were.

Lunch, *almuerzo,* was usually the big meal of the day in Ecuador, and they all ordered *sopa* and *segundo,* a bowl of soup and a main course of fish. Frank and Renato and Raquel spoke in Spanish then, and though Fern could still not speak with them, she realized she could understand what they were saying. Renato asked about the kids Frank taught. He, too, had come to Frank's classroom to speak about endangered species and to try to impress upon these children—and through them their parents—that Ecuador's wildlife was their heritage, that capturing and selling native birds was wrong, that it betrayed the country's future. Frank had organized an ecology club at the school, and he told Renato that several more students had joined the club since his visit to the school.

Seeing that Fern was following the conversation, Frank told her that he had once called Qualles, to ask if he might bring the students to the reserva. "He wouldn't permit it," he said. "He told me that the animals would be stressed by the presence of children."

"Funny, Qualles loved giving tours to visitors," Fern said. "But not to kids."

Renato and Raquel were interested in her remark. Had she known any of these visitors? Renato asked her. Had she ever witnessed any animal being sold at the reserva? She hadn't. She hadn't known about any of that until she'd heard it from Frank and Donna. And only one animal had gone missing while she was there, though it had turned up again.

"Which animal?" asked Raquel.

Fern said, "A Buffon's macaw called Eisenhower." Raquel

pressed her on the matter, asking her for other details of the bird's disappearance. But beyond giving her the date, Fern couldn't really help. She'd been there to do her own work, she told them.

Lunch was served, and they ate and talked about her work and other matters. They asked her about Arizona, and she told them about the attempt to return the thick-billed parrots there, birds that had disappeared in the early 1900s. "It was a difficult project," she told them, "and not really successful."

"Esperamos que no tengamos que hacer eso aquí," said Renato, *"después de que se vayan estos pájaros."* Let's hope we don't have to do that here, after these birds are gone.

They lingered over coffee and dessert, and then the two wildlife officers walked with them back to the boatyard. Raquel asked if Fern would take her into the mangroves sometime to see these birds. "Sure, but I'll have to find them myself first," said Fern.

That afternoon she and Frank put the boat in the water. Frank helped her install the motor and the tank, and several men from the village came over to the dock to watch. She and Frank put the paddles and life jacket cushions aboard and slid the boat down the stony beach into the water. It was her boat, and she was going to start the engine, though she let Frank instruct her on setting the choke. "Now pull," he said, and with the village men watching, she pulled the rope that spun the motor. To her amazement, it started, and the crowd on the dock whistled and applauded, to which she made a bow, as much of a bow as she could make, seated in the boat. Then she clicked it into gear and opened the throttle, and down the channel they went, Frank shouting "Excellent!" as she banked around the first turn.

She loved the boat from the first, and she took it out every day. The ways of its motor she'd come to know intimately; how to mix the gas and oil she put into it; how much gas flooded it; how long to wait when that happened. The boat was nimble and fast when she opened the throttle all the way. And she learned the trick of tilting the motor forward and gliding over the shallows.

The mangroves began to reveal themselves to her. Each day she saw something she hadn't noticed before and each day she felt the presence of the place more deeply. Its uniformity, which had been so bewildering at first—each part so much like the others, each new tidal creek so like the last—slowly gave way as she learned to see it, to tell one particular bank by its mix of mangrove species, to recall how a certain stream angled into the main channel, to note a certain ancient tree reaching above the others on higher ground in the middle of an island. She became familiar with the fishermen she saw on the water. She began to learn some of the subtleties of tides and the weather, and she pushed on, extending her trip into the groves by five minutes each time.

When she neared the place she had chosen for the day, she cut the engine and paddled in, slipping silently beneath the trees. Putting out the anchor, she stayed as long as she could while the tide came in, filling the creeks and covering the mud. When the tide crested, she pulled up the anchor, started the engine, and headed back.

She compiled a list of species that she had sighted—it grew to several dozen. She'd seen perhaps a thousand egrets, wading and hunting in the mudflats, and she had identified three species among them: the great egret with its long yellow bill and the superb S-curve of its throat, the snowy egret with its crest, the smaller cattle egret. She had listed six species of herons: the black-crowned night heron, the chestnut-bellied heron, the boat-billed heron, the rufescent tiger-heron (she had seen just one, a young male, striped like its namesake), the capped heron, and the little blue. White and green ibises, also, with their curving bills.

Some of the birds were familiar, like the grebes and coots and ducks she had seen in lakes and ponds back in Minnesota. The kingfishers and woodpeckers and hummingbirds were just slightly different from their cousins up north. But many were strange to her. Using her book, she identified birds she had never heard of, their names like odd stones, willet and gallinule, jacana and starthroat and jacamar, tyrannulet and potoo. Potoos, which were like nightjars, liked to perch stiffly, mimicking a bare branch. One day she sat close to a potoo for half an hour, not seeing it until it startled and took flight. Always there were dozens of unseen birds near her, calling and peeping from the mangrove thicket. She recorded a white-necked puffbird and an olivaceous woodcreeper and a black-tailed leaftosser.

She heard, almost daily, cries and screeches from the thicket that might have been parrot calls, and twice sighted a pair of yellow-headed Amazons heading in the same direction at the same hour of the morning. But no aratinga. She felt that the birds she and Enrique had heard, just after dawn, were the same group she had seen from the ridge, but she'd had no sign of them for weeks. Still, the hope of seeing them got her out of bed in the darkness every morning with an increasing sense of urgency. In November, the rains would begin, making her work in the swamp difficult, if not impossible. Then there was the date on her plane ticket home: December 12. These two events loomed, closing off the time for her research.

Enrique had taken them swiftly out to a place he thought the bird in the picture lived, but she hadn't known the swamp well enough that day to mark the place in memory, and there was no asking Enrique where it was; at least it wasn't something he could tell her. He'd have to show her again, and she didn't want to have to ask him. So each day she took her boat deeper into the mangroves, almost always setting out in darkness.

Learning the tides in that place was the work of years, she realized. You had to be wary. The tidal flow in the Guayas estuary was immense. A place in the mangroves where she had drifted over blue water in the morning might be mudflat by evening. But tides and parrots weren't on the same schedules. The best times—the only times, really—to find a flock of parrots were the early morning and the evening, when they set out for feeding sites and when they roosted for the night. At these times they were noisy, calling out to keep the flock together. Fern knew it was futile for her to try to navigate the mangroves after dark, so that left her just the early morning hours.

When Frank had first taken her out on the water the day after her arrival in Puerto Alegre, the tide had been perfect—the low tide of the day occurring at almost exactly sunrise. But the tide advanced a little every day, and soon she found herself setting out at higher tides at dawn. That meant that every afternoon the danger grew that she'd find herself deep in the mangroves on a lowering tide.

One morning Frank had warned her, as the two of them sat in the kitchen in the predawn dark. If she kept pushing it, he told her, she'd get stuck. She should at least take some extra supplies, food, water, a light, some mosquito netting.

She knew he was right, but did nothing. That very morning, she heard again, above the sound of the motor, that continuous peal of parrots in flight. She cut the engine immediately, and as the boat coasted silently, she closed her eyes to listen harder. Yes. There they were, the calls receding into the trees as the birds headed westward. She spent that day searching for a big tree that might be their roosting site. She was so involved in the work that the tide surprised her, turning before she noticed it. The boat worked against the current as she came back to the dock.

Before first light the following morning, she took Frank's advice and loaded some extra gear into the boat. She headed toward the place where she'd heard the parrots the day before. But when dawn came, she heard nothing. Just the usual bird chorus, no parrots. So she pushed on, deeper into the mangroves than she had ever gone. In the midst of her note-taking she felt the tide shift, but she'd made it back all right the day before, so she decided to look awhile longer.

The spot where she had anchored lulled her. The broad bright water seemed yards deep. But when she started the boat and turned upstream, the tide was running strongly, and she recalled Frank's warning that certain places drained more slowly than others so that she couldn't always depend on her immediate surroundings to judge the tide. Just as she had that thought, she felt the hull strike bottom, throwing her forward as the boat ground to a halt, its propeller slowing dramatically as it dug into the mud. She tried to push the hull free using an oar, but by then the tide had stranded her. She was going no farther until the tide came back in.

Actually, she was going no farther until it came back in twice. The whole afternoon passed, and her boat didn't lift off the mud. The sun dropped behind the mangroves on the western bank, shadowing the water, and finally the boat spun on the last point of its grounded hull and drifted free.

By then, it was too late for Fern to return to the dock. The light had already drained from the sky in the west, and the channels upstream would still be impassable for another hour or more. So rather than risk getting lost in the dark in the mangroves, she turned back downstream and tied up for the night in the deeper water of the place she had reached earlier that day.

The mosquitoes arrived in clouds at dusk, biting her a dozen times on her wrists and ankles and on the back of her neck before she had doused herself with Jungle Juice, a strong repellent that smelled like kerosene. She'd brought a dozen plastic bottles of the stuff from Tucson but had gone through most of it, and so during the day she had begun to use it sparingly. But now she just slopped it on. Thanking Frank mentally, she unfolded the mosquito netting and lay under it, veiled in the bottom of the boat, watching the last rays of the sun reach higher and higher, touching a few wisps of cloud with scarlet then indigo then violet in a sky that had darkened to cobalt blue.

A clatter of flapping made her sit up. At the far end of the open water, a dozen roseate spoonbills were landing, the last still flying in low over the water, braking to land, lifting themselves upright and spreading their huge pink wings. The big birds came in with such delicacy that the water around the roots hardly rippled. They preened themselves, folding their necks over their backs and digging in their feathers with their paddle-shaped bills. Then, each on one leg, they settled in for the night.

Fern settled in also. The darkness came quickly. She'd packed a small battery-powered lantern, and she switched it on to find her food and water. The lantern made the darkness seem more intense, almost solid beyond the lighted interior of the hull, and she became aware of the vast symphony of insect sounds rising in the night. She ate cold chicken and rice, left over from the previous night's dinner, which she'd packed in a plastic container. The lantern drew dozens of moths and other flying insects. She shut it off and lay in the boat watching the stars appear. They were the stars of the south, many of them unfamiliar to her. She found the Southern Cross, but the rest made strange patterns in the sky. The moon rose, a sliver, casting little light. Over the black mass of the mangroves, the separate stars gathered, until they appeared as a radiant cloud bank or a reef shining in the dark.

As the night deepened, the mosquitoes thinned a bit. She hoped that Frank and Donna weren't freaking out too badly at the house. Frank would probably know what had happened—he had predicted it, after all—and there was nothing anyone could do until morning. She herself wasn't worried. The tide was still high and the boat rode comfortably in midchannel. Whatever might walk or crawl into the boat if it sat on the mudflats couldn't reach her.

In the night she awoke suddenly, startled and bewildered. The moon was gone, and the dark was thick about her. So was the silence. The insects had stopped. The quiet pressed heavily on the air. Yet something had woken her, a scream, she thought. Then it came again, a shriek, extended and hysterical, for all the world the wail of a little girl screaming bloody murder. It sounded unearthly and could have come from a cat or a bird. For a third time it rose and fell in the thick silence. Now she was entirely awake. She lay curled on her side on the bottom of the boat, which was tilted at a funny angle. Her shoulder ached and she lay with her head downhill. She pulled herself to a sitting position and realized what the trouble was. The boat no longer rode in the water, but lay on the mud, rolled slightly to one side. The tide had left her grounded.

She found the lantern and switched it on, finding that she had misjudged the channel. The water glinted nearby. She wondered what, if anything, to do. The cat, or whatever it was, had been close, not more than fifty feet away, a jaguar maybe. She sat quietly, lifting the lantern and peering into trees on the embankment. The small illumination failed at the water's edge. She felt observed, watched on all sides.

It seemed like a good idea to try to get the boat back into open water. She lumbered to the bow with the lantern, dragged up the anchor—a ball of mire—and put a foot over the side. Her boot disappeared into the muck and continued to sink until the mud reached her knee. The bottom felt solid enough there and she stepped out of the boat. Then holding the bowline in one hand and the lantern in the other, she tried to drag the boat to the water's edge.

It was real work. The boat budged inch by inch out of the impression it had made in the mud. When it finally pulled free, she fell forward, plunging her hand, with the lantern in it, into the muck. With great effort, she got herself back upright and dragged the hull another ten or fifteen feet, finally feeling, rather than seeing, the water. She scrambled back into the boat and pushed with an oar in the mud, groaning and then falling as the boat slipped free. She dropped the anchor and fell back down, panting.

She was exhausted, feeling foolish and no safer for having made the huge effort. The stinking mud was heavy on her clothes and made her itch. The lantern was useless now, and the darkness was still intense. For a long time, hours, she lay in the boat, trying to wipe the mud off her clothes and hands. She'd never been more uncomfortable in her life, she thought. Finally, the sky began to brighten.

And then she heard them. First one squalling cry and then others, as the flock roused itself. Their cries rose from the trees to the southeast. They were still at a distance, perhaps a hundred yards, but there was no mistaking them. The sound of their cries grew as more of the birds joined in. Then all at once there was a collective screech, and as if they had sensed her, they flew toward Fern, calling out. Suddenly the lead birds appeared, tumbling over the trees and into the clearing that the water made. They squalled and beat the air as behind them the rest of the birds poured over the trees.

Her heart pounding, Fern fumbled for her camera and tried to count the birds as she clicked the shutter: six, ten, twenty, thirty, then a bulk of dozens of birds, still dark against the predawn sky. They dipped into the air over the water and flew right for the boat. There could have been a hundred birds, small parrots she could not identify for sure until she saw the orange underwings of the last few stragglers. It was the aratinga, her aratinga. She sat in the blue boat, mud covered and openmouthed, firing the camera, so startled that she could not even exult at having seen them until the flock had already passed, their cries receding as they drove inland.

17

The ship had been perfect for David, like taking his apartment building to sea. He awoke in his cabin and climbed to the open deck as if to the roof. Instead of the hills and avenues of San Francisco, there stretched the broad sea, huge and different every day, sometimes so blue it was almost black, sometimes sheened with cresting waves like foil.

There were many little things he loved about the ship: the rubber corduroy flooring in the halls, the heavy-duty toggle switches on the solidly affixed bed lamps, the hinged porthole that locked down with a heavy threaded ring. He loved the ship's routine, its regularity and steady slowness. Bells and horns went off all day, sounding the hours. The ship sailed at about fifteen miles per hour, Roy told him, and David decided this was the perfect speed for a journey. There was none of the instantaneous change of scene that made flying so disorienting. At fifteen miles per hour you might watch what floated by, and each day's segment of the trip felt actual and sensible, every foot of the distance between San Francisco and Ecuador apparent.

So they proceeded. When they came to port, a pilot came aboard to guide them in. The pilot arrived in a boat that was small and fast, and neither boat nor ship stopped for the transfer. The pilot simply stepped over a gap, the rushing ocean below, onto the freighter, which had a door in the lower hull for the purpose.

When the ship was in open ocean, David was allowed to visit the bridge. Blackboards, on which the course bearing and other data were written, hung beneath the large windows. David took an interest in the charts and the gauges and liked especially to note the GPS units—position indicators with digital readouts that took their data from a network of satellites around the earth. David got into the habit of checking every day as the GPS units clicked down from 40 degrees in latitude, which they'd read when he'd first seen them. Each day, the minutes diminished as the ship neared the equator. With these assurances of direction and consistency, with the ship's indicators revealing its progress, its alignment with an abstract yet constant matrix of longitude and latitude, broadcast from outer space, David loved the bridge. The bridge made the ship different and even better than his apartment building, he had to admit.

He ate with the crew. On the ship there was always something to talk about—the ship. If he felt ill at ease, he'd ask the officers some technical question, and the chat would continue. How far off is the horizon? he asked Roy at dinner one night. That day in particular the question had arisen because the sea had been flecked with whitecaps. Near the ship these showed themselves as large breaking waves, thousands and thousands of which appeared on the ocean, marking the distance. How vast it was, and how huge the earth by inference. Yet David wondered how much, exactly, he was seeing.

Roy had been precise in his answer. Maximum horizon radius from the bridge on a good day was fifteen miles (an hour's sail, thought David, happily). Once in a while when cool air undercut a hot patch of air, the refraction formed a kind of lens that let you see beyond the curve of the earth, but that was rare. Then the other officers chimed in, describing the clearest days they had ever seen, off the Seychelles or in the Arctic.

The talk at the mess was a single round of conversation on one theme: How long do we sail? When will we reach port? How long will we stay? When do we sail? They'd made port first at Long Beach. They arrived in the night, and David awoke to find the view from his porthole crammed with the vast machinery of the industrial port, the cranes and parked barges and fuel tanks and pipelines, fields of pavement crossed by tiny yellow forklifts, the water itself hemmed in tightly and speckled with litter. Roy and Surojit pounded on the door of his cabin and told him he was going to Rodeo Drive with them. So they became his guides in a strange new city—David had never been to L.A.—and they spent a long day in traffic going slower than the freighter did, at the end of which they had real Indian food, with fiery curries and thick yogurty sauces, in a restaurant at the Marina. With one of his hundred-dollar bills, David bought new sneakers, orange-and-black ones, which Roy and Surojit thought quite loud. They had bought loads of gifts for their families back in India. David climbed back up the gangplank at midnight, carrying among his own bundles the Barbie doll set Surojit had bought for his daughter.

It was their only big outing ashore during the voyage. None of them left the ship when it reached San Diego—as this was a short layover and they had just been ashore—and in the dark of the next morning they began the longest leg of their ocean voyage, three days at sea before reaching the small port of Manzanillo in Mexico. On these warm days,

David left the porthole open. He loved hearing the wash of the wake below, a rushing sound that rose and fell as the ship rocked in the swell of deep waters. By then the vibrations from the ship's engine were quite lulling. He felt the ship's constant pulse—as if it made its way a foot at a time across the ocean on millions of tiny treads—and then lost his sense of it. At night now he slept more soundly than he had in years, wrapped in the low throbbing and rocked by the ocean itself.

Every day, every moment, they dropped southward. The GPS read thirties and then twenties and then teens. Each day the sun burned hotter over the decks, and in the afternoons, thunderheads rose from the sea, vast uplifted clouds like the ancient gods, David thought, titanic, regal, burgeoning, white jellyfish dragging blue curtains of rain.

Living in San Francisco, David had rarely known hot weather. All his life he'd worn a sweater or a jacket in the evening, and now he expanded in the warmth, his muscles unfurling, until he felt longer limbed, taller even, loose and large. After dinner when he climbed the steel staircase to the top of the bridge, he was amazed by the sensuous, unthreatening tide of warm tropical wind washing over him.

One night he climbed to the upper deck in the light of a full moon that had risen behind the ship. The towers and capstans and funnels cast black shadows forward, and the sea was illuminated broadly with pale light. Ahead of the ship rose one of the thunderheads he had seen in the daytime. He watched as the freighter made its slow progress toward it. Lightning fired within it, the bolt dramatically backlighting tendrils and banks inside the cloud, these visible just for an instant, a sight never to be glimpsed again. As the ship drove forward beneath the cloud, it passed into a warm shower, and the moonlight thrown into this mist cast a ghostly rainbow, without hue but still graduated like its daytime version. It hung directly in front of the ship in a pale, shimmering arc, falling to the sea on either side. It was so subtle a thing that David shook his head to see if he was not simply seeing some image on his own retinas. But there it was. It stood for some time, a gate of light, the stars visible through it. It broadened as the ship neared, and then in an instant, vanished. They had passed through.

When he returned to his cabin, he studied his Spanish, which he hadn't thought about since high school, and made a list of irregular first-person verbs—*doy, hago, pongo, salgo*—which he posted on the back of the door and which he came to consider his best poem in years. He was awake to language in a way he hadn't been for a long time. In the ship's lounge he found *Madame Bovary,* which he couldn't stop once he picked it up. "She had nothing round her neck, and little drops of perspiration stood on her bare shoulders." He read this sentence and had to read on. It resonated with the new sensuality that had risen in him, and the words were palpable, stinging him with sweet desire.

The port at Manzanillo was little more than a slot in the beach, lined with concrete and sprouting towers and maritime cranes. A tug pushed the big ship in, as David stood at the rail. As they came to the dock, one of the crewmen threw out a rope, with a ball of a knot at the end—a monkey's paw, an age-old sailor's knot. Someone below caught the light line and hauled over a huge yellow-and-black plastic hawser, thick as a thigh, that secured the freighter. The gulls flew over the decks, making their cry that was like a trill concluded with a sigh: *brr-eh.* Above them hung frigatebirds, large graceful creatures that could soar far out to sea, their slender silhouettes like the m-curves schoolgirls use to draw birds.

When the ship left the port, a group of porpoises chased the pilot's boat into the open sea. As the smaller boat pulled alongside, David could see a pair of porpoises shadowing it, their gray forms appearing and disappearing beneath the surface. The freighter's wake spread wide as it slowed, and the porpoises burst in tandem from the face of a wave just below him, including him in their astonishing animal joy.

The next day, after breakfast, he made his way to the bow of the ship. They were amidst the El Niño current, Roy had told him, and David wanted to see if he could see it. He walked forward through a tunnel beneath the containers, stepping over hoses and wires and passing four huge tractors, chained to the foredeck. At the point of the ship was a steel platform with a railing, and here he stood in the sweet warm wind, his view of the sea unobstructed. Far from the engine, he heard no sound except the onrushing waves. A flock of large brown seabirds (albatrosses?) hovered in the air off the ship, hunting the flying fish that leaped from the water. The birds waited for a telltale trace—the streak the fish's tail left as it emerged—then dived and snapped up their prey. Often the birds let out a cry when they saw a fish, seeming overcome in their excitement.

From the bow David watched the birds for an hour, feeling solemn. By accident, a parrot had come into his life, and because of it this whole world had opened to him. The change had come because, after years of his labor and denial, he was poised to change, ready to crack open. Any small shift might have triggered it. Now each bird he saw, each cry he heard, confirmed that there was a larger life on earth, directing his own. Just where it was taking him he didn't know, but he wasn't worried. This force, expressing itself in these creatures, was big but benign; he could trust it. He watched the birds hunt until a larger swell began to come up, favoring the fish by giving them more cover.

That night the ship crossed the equator. David had hoped to observe the event from the bridge, watching the GPS latitude units click through zero and start to climb again. But he'd been asleep when it happened, in the predawn darkness, and had awoken in the Southern Hemisphere. The next day they reached Esmeraldas, a tiny port in Ecuador. David stood in the bow and saw South America rise from the southern horizon, a coast steep and, true to the name, emerald green. Skinny nearly naked workers climbed on the containers and hung from the cables on the cranes, doing the work huge machines had done in the north. The sight made David shudder and wonder what was coming next. The ship was one thing—it felt safe and familiar—but in two days he had to get off. He had the list of contacts that Mike had given him, people who worked with wildlife in Ecuador. But really, what was he going to do? He didn't even have a hotel reservation.

That night at dinner he asked the officers' advice and got plenty. They had all been to Guayaquil and knew about places to stay. The chief engineer suggested one hotel above a casino downtown. David listened politely but knew he wasn't going to that place. Then the Russian engineer, Mikhail, who spoke only a little English, said that he was going on shore leave in Guayaquil. If David would like, he would show him a place, he said.

The next two days went quickly, and the serenity David had known on the ship disappeared. He packed his things and hoped that Mikhail was as good as his word. In the late afternoon of the second day, a day as gray as those in San Francisco but steaming hot, the ship entered the Gulf of Guayaquil. The pilot's boat came racing toward them, made a broad turn, and pulled alongside. The pilot stepped over the flashing gulf between the two decks.

The ship proceeded slowly up the narrowing bay. Low banks appeared to the north and south, green and unmarked. These gradually closed upon the ship, until it was chugging slowly up a river, pale and muddy, though still miles wide. The sun dropped into view for the last few moments of daylight, burnishing the cloud banks behind the ship. Then tiny lights came up here and there on the shore, a tangle of streams and low ground covered with small trees whose bare roots stood exposed on the bank. The air held a thick sweet swampy smell. A tug gave a high-pitched whistle, which was answered by bird cries on the far bank. Then a few houses came into view. It was Friday evening, and David could see a gathering of people at one of the houses, an outdoor party. He heard the thump of bass and the trill of some reedy piping and someone, a man, singing in Spanish through a microphone.

It was somebody's home, but not his. David turned to go down to his cabin. Then he heard something in the air behind him, and he turned to see a pair of large birds flying toward the ship from the other bank. The cackling thick-necked yellow-headed birds flew over the deck and across the river, where they spiraled swiftly into the trees. They had to be parrots, Amazons, he thought, going to their nests to roost. The sight lifted his spirits. It was a good sign, a welcome even.

When he awoke the next morning, David checked the porthole and thought for a moment that they had run aground on some sandbar in the Guayas. The ship was stopped, and he saw only the brown river and the wild far bank. But when he dressed and went out on deck, he found that the near shore was the dock, the industrial maritime world, with its hoists and tanks and stacks of iron and acres of concrete. At breakfast Mikhail told him that he had called them a taxi. They had to be off the ship in an hour. And so, with the help of the Indian officers, he got his bags—all five of them—down the stairs and the gangplank. The taxi was waiting.

Surojit told David that if he wished to go back to San Francisco on the ship, he should meet them in December when they returned north. David said he didn't know if that would be possible, but thanked him. Roy wished him luck finding his bird—they knew all about his quest by this time, of course. The taxi took him and Mikhail across the wharves and out of the port. At the customs checkpoint, they were simply waved through. David felt a stab of fear as the taxi raced on, into the crowded streets of this strange city of millions, where he knew no one, except this Russian, Mikhail, who, once he had given the driver an address, said nothing and did not smile.

The taxi stopped on a busy avenue at a house behind a gated arch and a tiny plaza with a fountain. It was a boardinghouse, an *hospedaje* run by a squat Russian woman, whom Mikhail introduced as Madame Cherchenko. She, too, knew very little English, but Mikhail arranged lodging for David. The woman showed David his upstairs room, which was cool and dim and had a high ceiling with a skylight and two plain single beds over which stood ornate Russian crosses. A curtained window looked out into the hall. Left alone, David put his things into a wooden wardrobe and repressed a desire to get inside it himself. He concentrated on putting his clothes and his shoes away and then putting his books on the desk. He opened the parrot book and turned to the page for the cherry-headed conures. There was the tiny map of South America with the shaded circle around the region in which he now found himself. The coast encircling the gulf looked like lips on the west coast of the continent. He could not believe he was there.

At one, he ate lunch with Mikhail and his new landlady. It was a big meal, as was the custom there, and was a mix of Russian and South American food: cabbage and a stew of beef and vegetables, with pieces of corn-on-the-cob floating in it. The Russians talked in Russian. At one point Madame Cherchenko looked up at David and said, "You are looking for birds?" and David said that yes, he was looking for birds. "Many birds here," she said pleasantly.

That afternoon and over the next few days, David slowly expanded the area in which he felt comfortable. He explored the house and sat in the small plaza, which had a circular fountain surrounded by blue tile work. Then he ventured out onto the avenue. After another day, he went to the corner, where there were rows of tables at which vendors sold all sorts of odd things, like rubber stamps and panpipes. The next day he found a bank, where he cashed two of his hundred-dollar bills for many hundreds of thousands of colorful Ecuadorian sucres. He rolled the wad up and stuffed it into his pocket, feeling as if he had crossed one more boundary toward truly being in the place.

At the end of the week, Mikhail checked out, wishing him good luck and leaving him alone, the only guest in the place, as he had been the only passenger on the ship. He was still not enjoying himself, still had a slight anxious pressure in his chest sometimes, though it had lessened. Madame Cherchenko served him a midday meal every day, as it came with the room, and sat at the far end of the long table. After her first attempts at English, Madame Cherchenko apparently forgot that he could not understand a word of her language and talked to him in Russian. He answered her in English. And weirdly, considering this arrangement, he came to know what she was talking about. Perhaps it was her hand gestures. Da-veed, she called him. She was a widow, he gathered, and her husband had been a violinist with a symphony orchestra in what had been Leningrad. She made those bowing gestures, in any case. And it was during one of these lunches, some ten days after his arrival in Guayaquil, that David, without realizing it at first, finally relaxed.

One day he brought down his parrot book to lunch and showed Madame Cherchenko the picture of the cherry-headed conures and talked to her in English about them. She was as patient with his language as he had been with hers. He had owned one of these birds, he said, and had thrown it out the window—he made gestures of throwing it out the window, as she nodded—and then it had joined a flock of others and he had found that flock. Now he wanted to find the big flock, the parent flock, of which these birds in San Francisco had been a part. *"Da,"* said Madame Cherchenko, *"da."*

After lunch he got out his list of contacts. Rather laboriously, he translated a few sentences of introduction into Spanish. He was an American, looking for a certain kind of bird. This one. Could they recommend a bird-watching tour? He went down to the sitting room, which was furnished with heavy Russian furniture covered with lace. Madame Cherchenko sat in the stuffed chair that she occupied on most days. David gestured to her that he wished to use the phone.

All of it was unfamiliar. Even the ringing of the phone on the other end was indicated by a beep, a sound that in the United States would have meant the line was busy. And when, in the midst of this sound, someone did answer, David was startled and launched into his memorized speech, getting in return a torrent of Spanish he did not understand. So the first three calls resulted in nothing but confusion. Madame Cherchenko smiled beneficently at his efforts.

David was at the point of giving up, when on his next call a woman's voice interrupted his speech to say in a clear and steady voice in English, "Why don't you stop by the office and we'll see if we can help you?" David was so relieved he almost hung up without getting the address, and the woman had to remind him. They were on the avenue called the Tenth of August, she said, near the parque Bolívar. David wrote down the number.

The next morning, David showed Madame Cherchenko the address and asked about a taxi, but she insisted he could walk, producing a worn map of the city to show him. The downtown was an even grid for the most part, and the parque Bolívar was several blocks north and a few blocks west of the house. So, remembering the day that he had found his way from the subway to the waterfront in San Francisco, he set out with a hand-drawn version of the map.

Guayaquil's sidewalks were much more crowded than San Francisco's; it seemed as if the whole city were on foot, and he was washed forward in a tide of pedestrians. So many people, beautiful women and neat businessmen, workers and salespeople, white-eyed blind beggars and peasant girls selling a few items laid out on blankets, their babies in slings on their backs or lying whimpering on the sidewalk.

David found the only intersection at which he had to turn and walked down the avenue called the Tenth of August, feeling less nervous and seeing more. The crowds increased as he approached the heart of downtown. He found the address he sought and rested in the lobby a moment, trying to calm his overwhelmed mind. Then he took an elevator to the eighth floor and found a frosted glass door bearing the name he sought in neat black letters.

18

Fern was beginning to appreciate the subtleties of swamp stink. The mud, which was the color of chocolate, had a pungent odor of rot, of course, and at first this was all she smelled in it, not really wanting to smell it at all. But after she was around it and in it, after she had worn it for days, she began to distinguish in the smell a complexity of odors, like notes in a chord, some of which were at certain times more dominant. Amid the rank stink arose a grainy thick smell like beer or summer grass and a sharper scent like vinegar, even a sweetness of wine. When her nights in the mangroves began, she started catching a more elusive, more exquisite smell, a quintessence of muck, an ambergris of rot. It was so subtle she wondered if she might be making it up. Eau de merde, she called it.

This parsing of the mud stink was one dimension of her experience of the swamp, which had continued to intensify. She remembered her panic, that first time Frank took her into the mangroves, when she could only feel assaulted by the vastness and vitality of the place. Then she had worked to break down the experience into bulky but intelligible parts, until she could at least see, if not grasp what she was seeing. Now at last she had arrived and could take pure pleasure in the details, as the place divulged itself. More and more she took in the minuteness and strangeness of its parts, the chaotic yet perfect knitting of branch and creeping vine, the exact accommodation of creature and habitat. Now she read in each pool the workings of a world unto itself. And the sum of these worlds upon worlds was the whole of the mangroves. Infinity whispered to her there, beyond knowing.

But this sense of the whole was momentary, a hint, a delicate implication. Reaching it was such hard work that she came to it at the edge of her energies. Still, she pressed on, unwilling to let it go. After that first night in the mangroves, she was finally with the flock, and the place was opening and opening, and she couldn't hold back. Though she was taking a chance and she knew it, she made a further decision. She would defy the tide by leaving the dock in the afternoon and tieing up for the night at the place she called the cove. She'd let the tide trap her, as it had that first night, and stay out, if need be, every night until the rains arrived.

On the second afternoon she passed Frank on her way out.

"What's up?" he called from the school yard. Fern just shouted that she'd be back in the morning. Then she started down the channel, pleased at the way the outgoing current drew her into the swamp. The maze of the mangroves itself, she imagined, wanted her there.

The next morning, the flock again rewarded her with an appearance, and the danger she faced seemed justified. There was some plain logic in it. The birds relied on the tides to protect them. When the tide ran favorably for the approach of human beings, they'd naturally be warier and hide themselves deeper in the mangroves. And when low tide cleared the channels of boats, they'd come out. So she just had to challenge the tide, to be there when they were. Even as she reasoned it out, she felt less rationally that her willingness to be trapped by the lowering tide, to take on this risk, had somehow earned her the right to observe the flock. She had to show her courage, her worthiness, as if this were her own private vision quest.

The birds themselves confirmed it. That second morning they lingered over the boat, interested. They came in lower, flying a little less frantically, and swept over the water in one wide turn, observing her, even, she thought, congratulating her. They weren't obvious about this. Fern felt their interest the way she sometimes felt the sly observance some men made of her in public places, dignified men in business suits, polite men, who didn't want to show themselves obviously, who looked at her sideways and briefly, making a pretense of doing something else, readjusting their newspapers or dusting their lapels as they glanced at her from beneath their eyebrows.

But the flock's interest, this shared observance, this congratulatory pleasure was surely there. They welcomed her. There was some knowledge between them. While she was learning Spanish, a moment occasionally occurred in which the fact of Spanish disappeared into the reality of communicating with other people. And here, too, in the mangroves, she came to know without noticing that she knew. She shared that mind, as if, when she slept in the boat deep in the mangroves, she had dreamed the flock's dream. Of course, she would not have included this in her field notes, which she knew had to have a hard, verifiable edge. Heading back to port that morning, just to wash and change and set out again, she argued with herself about it. It was surely superstition, some part of her insisted. Unscientific, anthropomorphic, egotistical, reckless. But she could not dismiss it.

That afternoon she avoided Frank entirely, purposely casting off before school let out. He'd say she was taking too many chances. That night she slept uneasily in the boat, though quite exhausted, and her inner alarm clock failed her as she awoke several times in the dark, each time groping for the flashlight and finding that it was too early. The last time she sat up and waited for dawn. She intended to time the passage of the flock overhead, using the second hand on her watch. She didn't doubt that they would appear. That certainty was part of the knowing.

They did appear, calling out at first in the dim thicket, then rising as they had before. Their appearance and disappearance was now a distinct and predictable set of events, which she saw with utter clarity, even through the camera's viewfinder. She noticed distinctions between individual birds. She could tell the stronger, bigger birds, the leaders, from the younger ones that followed. She watched little interactions among them as they flew. Their flight intertwined, as each darted into and out of the group. Some pairs played tag. Some young birds followed their parents. She heard some of them cease crying out and others taking up the call, which remained unbroken, a single syncopated ongoing rhythm.

She saw them see her. She saw *it* see her, rather. That was how it felt. The flock, one entity, alert and reacting, took her in with its many eyes and, further, *included* her, made her part of it. When they were gone, when the last bird disappeared and the call faded, she seemed to awaken to herself, shaken from the effort of being with them. Then she was shocked to see that the whole experience, their entire passage, had taken just eleven seconds.

She'd seen them, now, three times, for probably about that same brief interval each time, and she'd been with them, as briefly, when she'd watched them feed in the ciebas on the ridge. When she added it up, she realized that she had observed them in total, in a scientific way, for just a few minutes, at most, over several weeks. Looked at objectively, this amounted to a tiny bit of data, not anything that might support any certainties. But totaling up the seconds still did not make her doubt—it only made her wonder at the power of this feeling, at what they had communicated in the short time they had actually been together.

Now she was elated, no longer afraid of the mangroves. The place, too, embraced her, protected her, and this sense of belonging wasn't even displaced when, after the birds had passed, she saw in the mud beside the grounded boat the undulating track that a large snake had made in the night, as it had explored the hull and then moved on. This might have bothered her, she managed to think; actually it should have bothered her. But at that moment even this mark made her feel welcome, encircled and safe.

Her roommates, by contrast, were convinced that Fern was whacking out, as Frank called it, and putting herself in danger. When she got home after that day, exhausted but still high from having seen the flock, a state in which everything was very clear and very particular, Donna was waiting for her. Fern had grown accustomed to coming home to the quiet of the empty house, while the other two were at work, and the sudden presence of her roommate sitting silently, rather sternly, in the little kitchen scared her off her feet. All Donna had to do was say "Hey," before she'd seen her, and Fern sprang in alarm like a surprised animal.

"Sheesh, you scared me," she said, leaning on the table. "Why aren't you at work?"

"I'm *supposed* to be working," said Donna, "but I'm sitting here thinking about getting up a rescue party."

At that moment, Frank walked in. "I heard the boat," he said. "You all right?" He was serious now, for once not goofing around.

"I'm fine," said Fern. "I'm back."

"You're looking fine," said Donna.

Fern was a mess. Her arms and shirt were coated with mud, the result of a struggle with the anchor, and her feet and legs crusty with swamp goo and plastered with weeds and grasses. Her hair, which had grown wild since she'd had it cut off back in Tucson, was flared and bleached. Her nose was freckled and peeling, and she had a couple of welts on her forehead, from insect bites. She bore that multifaceted mud smell, too, that stink she had come to know so well.

"Oh," she said. "Yeah. I guess I should shower."

"Listen," said Frank. "We don't want to be telling you your business. But you've only been here a couple of months, and you don't know the place as well as you think you do. It's too risky for you to stay out there at night alone."

"I have to," she said. "You know how the tide's running. I can't get out there any other time. I've got maybe three weeks until the rains start." She raised her voice as she said this, until at the end she was practically shouting, something she'd never done there before.

Donna said, in a low and serious voice, "You're pushing your luck, girl. You want to hear a few of the things we've been thinking about? Just a few of the things that can happen? Ordinary things that can happen easily out there in that swamp? I mean, we don't even have to talk about poisonous snakes." Fern flashed on the track she had seen that morning in the mud around the boat, but didn't say anything about it.

"We don't have to mention big cats or creeps with guns," said Frank, taking it up. "We could just concentrate on the stuff that's easy to imagine—like falling out of the boat and watching it drift out of reach on the tide."

"Yeah, like that," said Donna. "Or even just getting dehydrated and lost."

"There's plenty of water," said Fern.

"There's plenty of water that will make you sick," said Frank. "Water that will make you want to die a long time before you do."

"Easy," said Donna. And in that one word, Fern felt the real fear that they'd felt for her as they'd waited. All teasing aside, they had really thought that there was a chance that she would go into the mangroves and not come out.

"Oh, you guys," she said, suddenly feeling love for them. The wave of exhaustion she'd been resisting—from three nights in the boat and three days of work—washed over her. "I just had to be out there. I've seen them. They're out there. And listen—I have to tell you this. I know I'm okay. It's like they want me there. It's like I know their thoughts."

She regretted saying this as soon as it was out of her mouth. The two at the table were not reassured by these words. She had to seem a little crazy. She'd been out in the swamp without enough sleep for too long. And maybe they were right, she thought. She was past her limit, she who had never pulled an all-nighter for an exam at school.

"All right," she said. "I'll get some sleep. And I won't go back out there until we talk some more. And thanks, you guys, for thinking about me."

And they left it at that. It was all Fern could do to drag herself to the outdoor stall, pull off her encrusted clothes and stand under the cold downpour. When she returned to the house in her robe, she found that they'd left tea and bread and had gone back to work. But Fern didn't have the strength to eat. She could only fall into her bunk. Even the noise of their return, the sounds of making dinner and their talk about her at the table didn't wake her up.

Not so far away, in Guayaquil, David was making his own explorations. He had traversed the downtown—for him a major accomplishment. The Ecuadorian Wildlife Institute proved smaller than he expected and rather makeshift, just two rooms jammed with file cases and overstuffed shelves. David stood waiting, as the woman at the front desk completed her phone call. Out the window stood the columns of the office buildings in this strange city, and beyond them green hills rose in the distance. The walls inside bore perhaps a dozen posters, some of them faded and partially blocked by files, showing the wildlife of Ecuador: penguins and blue-footed boobies and jaguars and other animals. One depicted yellow-headed Amazons, and one, which David would have liked to get a closer look at, showed macaws in flight. It was an aerial shot of a fleet of gold-and-green parrots, their wings spread and long tails straight out, flying over a river somewhere in the jungle. Where was that? he wondered. Was that anywhere near Guayaquil? He made a mental note to look these birds up when he got back to the *hospedaje.*

Then the young red-haired woman hung up the phone and said, *"¿Sí?"* in a pleasant way. This was Spanish, of course, but it took David by surprise, and the sentences he'd studied in his room flew out of his head. All he could do was hope that she was the same person who had spoken to him on the phone and begin speaking in his own language. He was an American writer, he announced, in Ecuador to do research on a certain species of parrot. This sounded odd even to him. Until that moment he had not thought of writing about these birds, but he felt he had to say something quasi-businesslike to justify his peculiar interest—not to say obsession. Then, trying to diminish the oddness, he added apologetically that he was interested in bird-watching tours. His sense of getting anywhere ebbed as he went on.

She paused before she spoke, and he was sure that he had simply been blurting out foreign nonsense to her, when to his delight, she answered him in English. There were a number of tours, she said. Which species was he interested in seeing?

"I've come to Ecuador to find the cherry-headed conure," David said, feeling more foolish and sounding, he thought, like some kind of dorky nineteenth-century explorer. The woman said she was not familiar with that particular bird. She asked him where it lived. Around here, said David, thinking of the lips on the map that were the Gulf of Guayaquil. The woman turned to the bookshelf behind her desk and pulled out a well-thumbed bird guide. Could he show her? she asked.

David paged through the book, found the section on parrots, and leafed through it until he found the smaller species. There were several pictures, but none of the Little Wittgenstein birds. Amid an unillustrated entry in Spanish, though, he found the Latin name, *Aratinga erythrogenys,* in parenthesis. When he pointed this out to her, a glimmer of recognition passed over the woman's face, and she asked if he would wait a moment. Then she got up from her desk and went into the other office. In a moment she returned with a man of slender build, who introduced himself, in a formal way, as Renato Diaz-Huerta. This is my colleague, Raquel Molina, he said, and David shook hands with her as well. He told them his name, still feeling like the dorky explorer. He was even dressed for the part, in his boots and outdoor costume.

The particular bird he was asking about was in some difficulty, said the man, adding, in a casual way that gave David a shock, that its habitat had been destroyed. So it would be hard to find. Most of the bird-watching tours in Ecuador went to the Galápagos or to the Amazon, and this species did not live in those areas.

David was wondering how to proceed when the man asked him if there were some particular interest in this bird in the United States? David said that he didn't think so.

"How did you yourself become interested?" the man said. "If you don't mind being asked." Leaving out the part about throwing Little Wittgenstein out the window, David told them about the parrots in San Francisco, a wild flock of these particular Ecuadorian birds flourishing in that city in the north. This was news to the two wildlife officers. Raquel said, her English faltering for the first time, that the habitat once occupied by these birds was very big, very broad, with mountains and oceans, and so these birds might be very—she checked the word with the man before she said it—very adaptable. Able to live in other places.

"Yes," David said, wanting to say something more but not knowing what.

"We don't really know how best to locate this bird," said Renato. "But we will look into the matter." He asked for the phone number where David was staying, but David didn't have it. He'd have to call Renato back, he said. And then, shaking hands with the two of them again and saying a formal South American good-bye, David left the office. In the lobby he headed for the light beyond the glass doors and was out on the street before he could breathe again.

There he stood still, letting his nervousness about talking to the INEVS people diminish. It was replaced, in spite of the crowd on the sidewalk and the unknown city that confronted him, by a growing sense of triumph. True, he hadn't exactly learned anything, visiting the office, but he had traversed the strange city—*traversed,* he used this word to himself. It was a mountain-climbing term that properly described his sense of overcoming great difficulty. He'd found the place he sought, he'd spoken to these people, he'd come away with a further plan. This was real exploration, for him.

And now what? He took his time, figuring out which was the right way to go to get back to Madame Cherchenko's and then, with a positive thrill, starting off in the opposite direction. He was a big, tall, hapless American guy in hiking clothes with a funny transported look on his face, striding down the avenue among strangers and going he knew not where. And it was great. He felt so confident that he let himself wander the downtown streets, keeping, it must be said, the general direction of Madame Cherchenko's in the back of his mind, but feeling sure he could find the avenue no matter what.

It was the noon hour, and the streets were pale in the heat, the shadows dark in the city's doorways. He went with the crowd as it poured along down the sidewalks and flowed across the intersections. He looked at the sky, the Ecuadorian sky; he scouted the side streets and peered through the archways. He looked in shop windows. Walking past the open doors of a small church, he could feel cool air scented with incense wafting out of the ancient tall pointed nave. He remembered flying over Ecuador in his sleep and knowing every peak and spire and tree, and felt that he had actually come to live his dream.

A shady plaza opened amid the avenues and he crossed the street and walked through iron gates into the green square inside. Before him, enormous on a horse in midstride, towered a hatless Bolívar, the hero framed in the ornate rose window of the city's cathedral and flanked by its two white gothic spires. Bolívar! I'm in South America! David proclaimed to himself. He let himself loiter, actually loiter, in the shade of the trees in the square. Amid the ornamental gardens, giant iguanas waddled and snoozed, providing him with further evidence that he was in a strange and distant land. Still undaunted, he went on, leaving the park, walking westward on a whim.

He walked toward the *malecón,* the waterfront, passing the doorway of the Hotel Rizzo and strolling past more shops and office buildings and across the broad boulevard that ran along the water. Along the river was a promenade, and he proceeded across it to the iron railing. The wide water sparkled like a lake. The tide was high. The water lapped the wall beneath his feet.

Far off, wavering in the sunlight stood another shore, low and green. He'd always remember this moment, he thought. In truth, he would, though not only because of traversing the city and being in South America and making his way alone and not feeling any fear—in fact, feeling happy about it. Afterward, there would be something else, even more important, connected to the memory of that bright water and the far green bank.

David returned to Madame Cherchenko's *hospedaje* without incident, though he got home in a roundabout way, taking unfamiliar streets until he had completed the circuit he'd begun that morning. He had only a little anxiety, when his path reintersected the avenue of the rooming house and he was for the moment unsure which way to turn, deciding finally to turn toward downtown, so that if he were mistaken he would find himself in familiar territory, at least, rather than farther out in the vast city. But within a block, there was the arch opening on the little plaza with its fountain, and he was safely back.

All this was quite enough for him, for one day, but he still had one small task to accomplish. After Madame welcomed him, he asked her if he might use the phone, and he called Renato at the INEVS office to give him the phone number there. Renato, as pleasant and formal on the phone as he had been in person, thanked David for calling, and then added that he already had some information about the parrot that might interest him. Another researcher, Fern Melartin, from Sonora State University, was in the country studying this bird. Did he know her? David did not.

Renato suggested that perhaps David's best opportunity lay in contacting this person. This seemed like a long shot to David. Could he call her? he asked. That was a difficulty, said Renato. Professor Melartin was at the moment living in a remote village in the Guayas Estuary, where there was apparently no phone.

At this point the effort that David had made that day weighed heavily on him, and he could only say, "Oh." He could not venture further, and his "oh" allowed not much of a rejoinder. Renato added that he hoped to see David again before he left the country, then said good-bye and hung up. David put the phone back in its cradle, which sat on a lace doily as if on a lily pad on the little black table in Madame Cherchenko's parlor. And despite what he had accomplished earlier, despite his traversing and his elation, he had a vague feeling that the prize of the day had escaped him, as indeed it had.

In her dream, they were circling, shining in new light above a landscape still dark. They followed one another, spiraling up, beating the air with dozens of bright wings, and calling out, that familiar cry seeming also to shine. They were pausing in their flight, the call rolling from bird to bird, suddenly focused on one object—on her, she realized. They were searching her out again, chiding her. Where was she? Why hadn't she returned? I'm here, she called back, opening her eyes. And in her room it *was* just dawn, the day's first light still pale behind the blinds, that cry still seeming to roil the air. Off in the mangroves, above the place she called the cove, the flock was indeed circling, looking for her. She knew this, certainly, for a waking moment. And then the sense of its reality abruptly ended, like an electric current switched off, and Fern fell back into a dreamless sleep.

She woke again some hours later, in the heat of the day, and jumped up almost frantically, as if she were late for work. She rushed to dress, to get back into the mangroves, and she didn't remember that she had told Frank and Donna that she wouldn't do so until she had spoken with them again. Loading the dinner leftovers into a plastic bowl, she did remember it, though, and then she only said "Shoot," out loud to no one and kept working. But when she left the house carrying her food and gear, she felt bound by what she'd said. She couldn't go out again without a word.

Even so, she went to the *malecón* first, to load the boat and check the tide. The water was high, but had already turned and was ebbing fast. The movement of the tides was like a train schedule for her by then, and she could tell immediately that it was already doubtful that she would make it back to the cove that night. If she left any later, she'd probably find open mud blocking her way. Fuming with frustration, Fern turned away from the water and went to find Frank.

The school had only two classrooms, one for the younger children and one for the older ones. From the small lobby, Fern peered through an open door and saw Frank at the front of the older class. He was reading to them from a book in English, and she had to wait for him to look up. He translated the story into his own Spanish and made comments. Fern recognized what he was reading, a book she had loved in her own childhood, *The Wind in the Willows,* about Rat and Mole and Toad. *"En el invierno, El ratón durmió mucho,"* Frank translated, admonishing the kids, *"Pero no duerman ahora."* Pausing then, Frank noticed Fern standing outside the door, and the children did also. *"Un momento,"* he said to them, and they responded by oohing and laughing as if they'd caught him at something.

Frank was not happy to be interrupted. "I'm in the middle of this," he said.

"I know," said Fern. "I just wanted to let you know that I'm heading out."

"Heading out where?"

"Into the mangroves. To see the aratinga."

"You can't wait?" he said.

"Tide's running."

"You can't take a day off? You've been out there for a week."

"Three days," said Fern. She squirmed impatiently. "I'm running out of time here. I'm just letting you know."

Frank sighed. "Just come outside and talk to me for one minute," he said in his teacher's voice. He turned to bid the class *cállense* and told them to read, and then, as the class made another, longer, ooh, the two of them stepped out the door into the sunshine of the playground.

"Look, this isn't my business," said Frank. "You can do what you want, of course. But one thing—these people in the village are good on the water, better than anybody I ever saw in the States, some of them. And every year, in one of these towns, we lose somebody in the mangroves. Somebody gets killed, somebody drowns. It happens, and it happens to people who know what they're doing and who know the water. Anyway, it's your life, it's your work. But I'm telling you, if I were you, I'd take a day off."

Fern told him that she appreciated what he was saying, but that she just couldn't. "It's my only chance to see them," she said quietly. Frank just looked at her seriously, a little sadly.

"We want you to take one day off," he said. "Just one day. But I guess you'll do what you have to do." He turned away and went into the classroom, leaving her there.

Fern went back to the boat. The tide was rushing out now, and she read it with a sense of futility, knowing that even at that moment, the water was draining at three particular broad flats in the channel. Still, she untied the line and got the boat going. But her resolve failed as she negotiated the first curving banks. What Frank said worked on her. Better boat people than she had been killed out here. And she was already tired. Maybe she could stay home and write up her notes. Take a day off. Why not? So she argued with herself until she turned around. Still, she groaned as she unloaded the boat and was in a foul mood by the time she returned to the house.

19

David felt contained, frustrated. Suddenly, the rooming house with its little plaza and fountain was too small. He had been there for ten days. At first the place had seemed like quite enough for all of South America. But after his venture across the city he couldn't stay there all day again without feeling that he was hiding from something, that he was missing the real trip. The sense of successful adventure that had filled him the day before had evaporated.

He felt restless, a novelty for him. He'd made it to the INEVS office, but in fact he hadn't come away with any further plan. His only lead was this American parrot researcher whose name he hadn't even written down and couldn't quite recall. He'd have to call them back and ask again. Fern Something, who couldn't be reached, down in the Guayas Estuary. The map in his guidebook showed this to be a huge area, a tangle of rivers and islands, with no bridges marked anywhere. Many of the towns marked on the map were utterly isolated, not even connected by a road.

Madame Cherchenko was surprised to see David up so early, but she gave him strong tea and chattered to him in Russian, letting him understand in her mysterious way that she was off to do her shopping. David called the INEVS office at eight, hoping they started work at that hour, but there was no answer and no answering machine. He waited impatiently until nine, but still no one answered. At that point he got his guidebook and went out into the city.

He walked, naturally, by the route he had taken the previous day, heading downtown, and soon came to the building housing the INEVS office and went in and took the elevator, hoping to speak to someone in person. But on the office door was a sign that read (oddly, since it was a Wednesday, the middle of the working week) CERRADO—closed. This was bad. He had not seized his opportunity, and now it was gone. There was no one to help him.

He descended and returned to the sunny pavement and then simply stopped. He was holding back the sense that he had come all the way to this foreign city in South America in vain. Yesterday he had been full of daring and purpose, but now the place appeared as a single high wall, a blocking façade, with signs in a strange language. Not knowing what else to do, he proceeded as he had the day before and walked to the river. He sat on a bench by the water, thumbing through his worn Ecuador guidebook, hoping that the book, which once had seemed like a fantasy novel, might now give him some practical help.

Thinking he'd find a pay phone and call the INEVS office again, he looked in his book under "Post and Communications." Wistfully he read the paragraph about international calls, imagining whom he might call back in San Francisco. Peter would be able to help. For a moment he thought he would even welcome talking to Lyle—though in the next moment he came to his senses. This gave him an idea, anyway.

The map of Guayaquil noted the location of the EMETEL office—the place to make international calls—and it wasn't far. He began walking, racking his brain to recall the name that the INEVS guy had said, but still only remembering part of it: Fern, that unusual first name. He also tried to compose an utterance in Spanish, "I want to make a call to the United States," but his Spanish deserted him and he could only think to say, *"a los Estados Unidos."*

Still, when he found the place on the ground floor of an office building and waited in line for his chance to talk to a woman behind a window, this proved to be sufficient. He was given a piece of paper with a phone number on it and told *"Diez y siete,"* which was for booth seventeen of the twenty in the office. When he had dialed the number he'd been given, the operator first answered in Spanish, but then when he asked to make a call to the United States, spoke to him in clear English, another small triumph.

The victory, though, was momentary. With some difficulty, he reached the university operator in Tucson, but then could only say that he was looking for a professor named Fern. Could he be any more specific? the operator asked. She couldn't search for a first name. Did he know her department? Ornithology, he guessed, but was told there was no ornithology department. Zoology, maybe, he said, and could hear her huff as she connected him. But there he was stymied completely, when the guy answering the phone just dismissed his question—"Did they have a professor in the department named Fern Something? —and hung up. David swore in the little booth, and began the intricate process again.

The Biology Department had no professor named Fern, either, though when the receptionist checked the directory, she did find a Fern Melartin. That was the name, he said. Ms. Melartin was a graduate student, but unfortunately she did not teach in the department, and the receptionist had only her home phone, which she couldn't give out. Still, she rang the graduate office, where he might find more information. "Oh, Fern," said that receptionist. "She's not here. She's working in South America this term."

David knew that, he said. He was in Ecuador studying the same kind of bird that Ms. Melartin was studying. Did she have any idea how he might contact her? She didn't, she said, and for a moment David thought that this call, too, would end fruitlessly. But then the voice informed him that Fern was doing her dissertation under a Professor Ronald Hudson and put him through to that office. At Hudson's office, though, he reached a machine on which, above the international static, guitar music strummed while a male voice informed him that Ron was best reached at home late in the evening. When the beep came, David hung up.

The gleam of communications in this moment of history seemed like a mirage to David. More people were connected by more means than ever before, which meant that he had more means than ever before for leaving unanswered messages. More ways of not finding out anything. If he were that dorky nineteenth-century explorer, he could not have been more cut off in South America, he thought. That he could hear distant recorded voices just made the isolation worse.

Still, David decided to make one more intercontinental electronic foray, and he called the graduate office back. To his relief, he heard the same voice on the line. He explained what had happened. "Oh, I forgot," she said. "Ron's never here. He keeps odd hours."

David was at a loss at this point and just asked if she knew any other way of finding out where Ms. Melartin was in Ecuador. She didn't, but she asked him to hold, and he did, for so long he began to wonder if he were still connected over all the miles. When she returned to the line, she said she'd asked one of the grad students, who had told her that Fern was close with Professor Francine Pepperbloom. This sounded hopeful, until she added that Professor Pepperbloom was no longer with the department. She taught somewhere in Boston. That was all she knew.

David thanked her and hung up the phone again, left with just this last tiny lead, and not much hope that it would turn into anything. But he called the international operator again and asked for information for the Boston area. There, to his delight, they did indeed have a number for a Francine Pepperbloom and when he was connected a real person actually answered, a woman who was, it turned out, the same Francine Pepperbloom who knew Fern Melartin from Sonora State University.

"Really, that aratinga," she said, when David told her why he had come to Ecuador. At this mention of the bird's Latin name David felt almost as elated as he had the day before after negotiating the streets of Guayaquil. Pepperbloom said she'd had an e-mail from Fern just a few weeks before. But she couldn't remember where in Ecuador Fern had said she was. Maybe she could find it, though. She was at her desk, and he could hear, over all those miles, the clacking of the keys as she looked up the note on her computer.

"Here it is," she said. "She's in a place called Puerto Alegre, down in the mangrove swamps. I don't have any idea where, exactly, that is." This time David wrote down the name. Pepperbloom offered to send Fern another e-mail, telling her about David.

"She doesn't know me," said David.

"No matter," said Pepperbloom. "I'm sure she'd want to know that you are doing fieldwork on the same parrot."

David agreed, feeling slightly fraudulent. That *was* what he was doing, though, when he thought about it. He thanked her and hung up, finally emerging from the booth and paying at the counter hundreds of thousands of sucres for the calls. Seventy or eighty dollars, he thought, for this one bit of information, the name of a town somewhere in the mangrove swamps of Ecuador.

Back in his room at Madame Cherchenko's, he studied his map of Ecuador and found Puerto Alegre in the midst of a region shaded with green dots, which he expected indicated a watery condition. It was near the gulf, forty or fifty miles south of the city, a tiny place, its name in tiny type on the map. Unlike some of the other towns, though, it was connected by a slender red line to the main highway running south from Guayaquil. He made a decision, momentous for him, and put a change of clothes in his smallest duffel bag, the green one.

At dinner, he made Madame Cherchenko understand that he was taking a trip in the morning and didn't know how long he would be, but that he wanted to keep most of his things there and to continue renting his room. Then, after a restless night, in which all his old fears clamored and threatened, he went out beneath the little arch, bag in hand, and hailed a cab, making his destination clear by showing the uncomprehending, then dubious, then delighted driver the map.

"Puerto Alegre!" said the driver. *"Ese lugar está muy lejos."* It was far out of the city, in the mangrove swamps. David said, *"Sí,"* and got in.

Having been forced to abandon her trip into the swamp, Fern was not in the best mood. Donna brought her the message, a short e-mail note from Pepperbloom. "I got a call today from a David Huntington (know him?)," she wrote. "He is apparently in Ec to do work on your aratinga. Told him you were in Puerto Alegre. Hope that was all right. Do take care. Francine."

Fern was annoyed at the note. She hadn't heard of Huntington, though she felt she should have. She didn't want any other field biologist coming down here to the mangroves. This was her turf. She'd worked hard to get here. She feared being scooped on the presence of these birds, something that hadn't been definitively reported, as far as she knew. Pepperbloom, of course, couldn't have withheld the information, but Fern hoped she hadn't given him enough to enable this Huntington character to find her.

After dinner, she sat quietly on the porch with Frank, as the corrugated roofs of the houses in the village vibrated with the glow of the sunset. She was worrying about the contents of Pepperbloom's note. Frank, unfazed by her silence, removed and replaced a layer of wax on one of his surfboards. Fern had begun washing some of her work clothes in a bucket, wringing mangrove mud out of a shirt, when she saw a car come through the village. Its driver stopped at the plaza near the dock and made an inquiry of the children playing there in the last light of day. The kids, as Fern watched, pointed up the road at her, and the car swung around and pulled up to the house.

It took Fern a moment to recognize the two people who got out, and she did so only after noticing the briefcase that the redheaded woman carried. It was Raquel, the INEVS worker she'd met in Guayaquil and her partner—she couldn't recall his name—who had been with her in San Lorenzo, when she'd bought the boat. Frank called out, *"Buenas tardes."*

Frank pulled up two more chairs and got the visitors Fanta—they had declined his offer of *cerveza.* Fern had assumed the two had come to see Frank, as he'd known them previously. But they had come to see her. The man, Renato, pulled his chair around to face her obliquely and started formally and politely praising Fern's work in the mangroves. They were quite aware, he was saying, how important her work with the birds was. "So we hesitate even to ask," he said, "but we wonder if we might ask for your assistance with another matter?"

Fern was reluctant to hear about it. She had so little time left in Ecuador to do what she had come there to do. All she wanted to do was get back to the flock. Why couldn't everyone just leave her alone? Still, she responded politely, in her best Minnesota manner.

"Ask away," she said.

"Yes," said Renato. "We remembered your experience at the reserva and thought we might work together on the matter," he said. Raquel put her briefcase on her lap and unlatched it. She pulled out a thick file.

"This is information on illegal wildlife sales at the reserva," she said. "We have been looking into this for more than one year. We believe that the director at the reserva, Leonard Qualles, is engaging in selling prohibited animals. But so far we have not been able to do anything about it."

Renato added that their biggest problem had been that no one who had purchased an animal or bird from Qualles had been willing to give them any information about the transaction. "These people have not been prosecuted. They live in other countries," he said. "They're not professionals in the animal trade, just embarrassed visitors who have lost their money. They don't know anyone in Ecuador. And they just don't want to . . . ," he said, reaching for the word.

"To deal with it," said Fern.

"That's right, they don't want to deal with it. There's no reason they should say anything, especially if they would implicate themselves."

Renato leaned forward in his chair. "If we could bring those people back here to Ecuador to testify, then maybe we could do something," he said. "But our office is not a big agency with a budget. As it is, we must ask for help."

"What do you want me to do?" she said

"We are looking for someone to go to the reserva and pose as a buyer of these animals," he said.

"I can't do that," said Fern. "Qualles knows me." Fern's heart jumped when she said Qualles's name.

"Yes, of course" said Renato. "We merely hoped that you might give our agent the information he will need—which bird or animal he might attempt to buy, how best to accomplish the purchase, and so forth."

She hadn't thought about Qualles, on purpose, since she first arrived in Puerto Alegre. She hadn't wanted to dwell on her experience at the reserva. But now that he had come up, she felt her old ferocity rise.

"I don't know how much help I'll be," she said. "But sure, whatever."

Frank broke in. "Hey, I'd be glad to do something," he said. "I don't really know anything about parrots, so I'm not sure what I could do, but I'll help you if I can."

Raquel and Renato looked at each other after Frank spoke, and then Renato thanked Frank for his offer. "Actually, Frank, we already discussed asking you to help with this. But unfortunately, we feel you are too well known in this area." Frank shrugged. "We need someone who can approach Qualles as a foreign buyer of exotic birds," said Renato.

"Okay," Fern said, "So what do you want from me?"

"Just some information on the reserva. Do you have any idea how Qualles located his customers?"

His question discouraged Fern. "None at all. I didn't really know he was selling the animals, not until I came here." They had other questions about the details of the transactions, but Fern knew nothing about these matters, either. Then something occurred to her. "I might be able to find out," she said. They wanted to know how, of course, but she wouldn't tell them. She was thinking of asking Leonin, and she needed to speak to him in private before she said anything. She asked if they could give her a couple of days.

This satisfied them. Renato gave her his card and told her to contact him if she had any other information. The two of them would return to Puerto Alegre the following week. But, before they rose to go, Renato remembered another matter.

"Oh yes," he said. "We had a visitor to our office in Guayaquil yesterday, an American writer inquiring about the same birds that you are studying. A Mr. David Huntington."

Fern nearly groaned. She had, of course, just read this name in the e-mail Pepperbloom had sent her, and the combined effect made her feel very anxious for her work, as if a crew of her countrymen, cameras and microphones and klieg lights at the ready, were arriving any minute to broadcast news of her flock to the world. It *was* her flock, suddenly, and this guy, this Huntington, represented all the forces that had pushed them so far back into the mangroves.

"I've never met him," she said. "I don't know him."

"Of course we didn't want to tell him anything without asking you first," said Renato. This relieved her greatly. "But I believe we will see him again. Is there any information you would like us to pass along—how you might be contacted, or how he might find the birds?"

"No," said Fern immediately. "Thank you." Fern noticed that Frank was listening to all this intently. "I mean, I'd like to meet him," she added, "but I won't have time on this trip."

"Of course," said Renato. It was getting dark by then, and so they took their leave, not having finished their drinks. When they had driven off, Donna came out on the porch.

"What was that about?" she asked.

"Undercover operation," said Frank. "Can't talk about it." But he was only teasing, and they told her.

"I'll do it," said Donna. "Heck, I'll bust their chops."

"Hey, if I'm too well known around here," said Frank, "so are you."

"You just love being well known," said Donna.

Fern didn't say anything. She had relented, a little, in her mood. She'd help the INEVS people, if she could do it without interrupting her work with the birds. But this American guy who was after the flock, she wanted nothing to do with him. And Pepperbloom had told him where she was. She'd have to keep an eye out and avoid him if he showed up. He was trouble.

20

Perhaps some minor X poet, in the days when David's poetry was still turning up in journals, might have thought he was trouble, an invading conqueror. But most of his friends would have laughed at the notion. Peter and Lyle, who had put him on the boat, had feared for him, feared he would be instantly lost and helpless in the world beyond San Francisco. In the world beyond his apartment, for that matter. But here he was, casting a conquistador's shadow in distant Ecuador.

Just that morning he was cowering in the backseat of a cab. His nerve had failed him, by stages, as the journey, so easily considered when it was a matter of moving an inch across the map, went on. The driver could not, for one thing, simply drive southward from Guayaquil, when the only bridge was north of the city. Crossing that span over the wide and muddy Guayas, David felt that he had underestimated the journey and overcommitted himself. He'd been lulled by his success on the phone. The actual world of South America was another matter. The suburbs of Guayaquil fell away and the taxi proceeded into the countryside, into the weird wildness of South America. The ride, slowed by buses and banana trucks, lengthened into hours on narrow roads that turned into the main streets of small settlements.

Farther south the country opened. Wide agricultural fields ran to the distant hills, on which stood enormous, pale, naked trees. And then, abruptly, dense thickets of trees with tangled roots appeared. By then the cabdriver, too, was less than confident of their location. He'd raced southward, when he'd been able to, but on these roads, as the swamp grew thicker, he began to slow down and scowl. The name of the town that was their destination rose from him like an incantation that might magically make the town appear. "Puerto Alegre, Puerto Alegre, Puerto Alegre," he intoned. But no town appeared. The pavement beneath the wheels of the cab ceased, and they crunched along over pale gravel and finally bounced down a rutted dirt road. Then they turned a bend and found a car blocking their path. Two men with crossed arms stood in front of the car.

David's mind was racing. He was imagining that these two men would kidnap and kill both him and the driver and toss their bodies into the swamp. He imagined this in order that it could not possibly happen—nothing happened as one imagined it—but even so, he frightened himself. He could hear Lyle saying, "Dave got killed when he took a wrong turn in Ecuador." The driver got out and began exchanging words with the men, who muttered what sounded like curses and did not uncross their arms.

After they spoke with the cabdriver for a moment, the two men began gesturing toward their car, which, David could now see, was stuck in the mud. The cabdriver walked around it, looking at its rear wheels in a dubious way. David, calming down, got out to look. For a time all four stood with arms crossed, considering it. The car was up to its axles in mud. If these two had not gotten stuck, reflected David, the taxi would have ended up the same way when they drove beyond the point where the road had dissolved.

The cabdriver took from his trunk a length of rope, which David thought too light to be of much use. After many minutes of wordless and muddy work, the men succeeded in tying the two cars together, the rope looped several times around both axles. Then, with the mud flying and both cars roaring and rocking, they succeeding in freeing the stuck car. As the rope was removed, the three engaged in more negotiation and pointing, while David stood mutely by. They got back in the vehicles, backed up until they reached a harder surface, stopped there, and spoke some more. David heard the words "Puerto Alegre." When they turned around, the other car led the way, and David understood that the men they'd rescued were leading them to their destination. So much for murder and kidnap in the wilds of South America.

They had returned to the main road and gone a few miles when the other car pulled over, the driver indicating the next turn. With honking and shouts, the cabdriver bid them farewell and took this new tenuous road into the swamp. Though the surface remained dry, the road became more and more hemmed in by a watery landscape, the strangest David had ever seen in his life: streams and dense forests, marsh and mud. This was the green-dotted condition indicated on the map, no doubt, though perhaps still not the precise part of it they were looking for. And just when he had concluded that they had to be lost again, the road widened, and houses and buildings appeared. *"¿Es Puerto Alegre?"* David asked, and the driver said, *"Creo que sí."* He thought so. But neither was convinced. The road ended in a kind of cul-de-sac, where some boats lay on a gravelly beach.

The driver made sure of the place, calling to a fisherman unloading one of the boats. *"Sí, es Puerto Alegre,"* he said to David. Then moving briskly—seeming eager to get back to his regular urban trade—he opened the door for David, removed David's bag from the backseat, and stood waiting expectantly.

"Oh," said David, when he had unfolded himself in the brightness. *"¿Cuánto cuesta?"* The fare seemed huge, four hundred thousand sucres, though when he pulled out the wad of Ecuadorian currency he had gotten at the bank, he could see that he still had about a million sucres on him, and so gave the guy an even half million, about seventy-five bucks. The cabdriver was delighted with this, so much so that David wondered if he should have bargained with him. The driver thanked him like an old friend, then got back in his taxi and headed out.

It was only as he watched the cab disappearing down the road into the swamp that David, city boy that he was, realized it was not going to be as easy to find a taxi in Puerto Alegre as it had been in Guayaquil. When he did, he called "Hey! Stop!" at the jungle that had already swallowed the car. David listened as the taxi proceeded away, until all was quiet.

Elsewhere, he had dreamed of elsewhere. And now, here he was. He stood in the thick tropical sunshine, his little green duffel bag beside him, in the quiet of a village in the middle of a vast green steaming elsewhere. He stood there awhile as nothing whatever happened. Then he took his bag to the dock and sat down. The fisherman finished doing whatever he had been doing with his boat and went away. After a long time a vendor pushing a flavored-ice cart came incongruously up the road, and David bought an orange ice from the man, who then also went away. David ate the ice from the cone slowly, as it was his only business there, and the long expanse of elsewhere and nothing continued.

Somehow it didn't worry him. He had spent all his panic in the car and now felt oddly complacent, strangely at ease, loose and lazy in the heat, as if the weight of the world had been removed from him. Something would happen, sooner or later, and it didn't seem incumbent upon him to do anything to make it happen.

In another hour, one of the buildings near David disgorged several dozen children, some of whom stopped and looked with alarm when they saw him sitting on the dock. The flavored-ice man reappeared, and the kids clustered around him. A few of the children remained to play, running around the little plaza and ignoring David now as he watched them.

Then he heard the sound of a small engine on the water and, from around a bend in the stream, a blue boat appeared. Sitting in the rear of the boat, steering with the tiller of the little outboard engine, was a woman in sunglasses and a hat with a flap at the back, her shaggy blond hair sticking out under it. She did not appear to notice him. She turned the rudder and scrunched the boat up on the beach. Holding a line, she hopped out and dragged the boat up on the rocks. Her boots and pant legs were coated with dried mud. David thought she looked quite beautiful.

That morning, Fern had again felt the presence of the flock and had the sense that, far off in the mangroves, the birds were looking for her. But it was less strong than the day before, as if the connection were growing dimmer. She was losing it, she thought, as she threw herself out of bed. She couldn't be losing it yet. At the dock, the tide was not favorable again, but she put the boat in the water anyway and moved off down the channel. Soon she came to a place where she knew she would ground the hull if she went any farther. She sighed heavily and turned up a tributary, cutting the engine and paddling through still shallow water into a narrow opening. There she sat, her notebook at the ready as the day's heat intensified, listening for the flock, but hearing nothing.

She felt caught. She couldn't get to them in the daytime, and she couldn't spend another night on the water. Previously she had felt protected, but at this point she felt jinxed about it, as if the spell had been broken, now that the worst thing had been mentioned as a possibility. And it wasn't just her roommates who held her back. It was her mother. Her mother had been furious and weepy the last time they had talked; she just wished, she'd said, that Fern wouldn't be so stubborn. Promise me, she had said, you won't do anything dangerous or go off by yourself. And Fern had promised. So far, Fern had managed to put that promise aside.

But staying out alone in the mangroves, now that the tide was against her, now that Frank and Donna had made an issue of it, this was too much to ignore. Too many things could happen. If she got hurt in the swamp, no one could find her. She fretted about it in the boat, worrying, too, about this other researcher, this guy David Huntington, feeling sure that he would somehow find the flock and get the credit for it. He wouldn't be held back by thoughts of his mother. There was always some guy like this, some macho jerk ready to take over.

But then the mangroves woke her up. In the midst of her worrying, she heard something, a tiny noise. She knew as soon as it reached her ears that it was something new. It was a faint, high-pitched singing from several places at once. She concentrated, then found one of its sources. It was a tiny bee, hovering with others near a low clump of mangroves on the bank. These mangroves were different somehow. Small, pale blooms, each tinier than a pearl, had broken out among the leaves, hundreds of them, and dozens of bees were feeding on them, making that tiny lowing, like minute cows in a meadow.

They had been three feet from her, and she hadn't seen them. She pulled a branch nearer, and wafting strongly from it came that exquisite scent, the perfume of the swamp, her eau de merde. It was the scent of these tiny mangrove flowers. Where had she been? The mangroves flowered in the weeks before the rainy season—she remembered reading that, though she hadn't thought about it for weeks. She reached over the gunwale and into the water, pulling up a handful of the thick muck and bringing it to her nose. But now this scent was too strong, and she couldn't tell if it came from the mud as well. This was not good, she thought. She hadn't been paying attention, and not paying attention was how people got hurt. She was tired. Donna and Frank were right.

She took notes on the flowers and the bees, spurred to her work as the morning wore on. She looked for other species of birds and whimpered when the tide too soon forced her to abandon her place. She pushed the boat back out into open water, poling in the mud with one of the oars, then started the engine and drove back to the dock. At least, she thought, she had got her eyes—and her nose—back for a little while.

When Fern turned the last bend in the channel, she saw amid the group of children on the dock a tallish man with lots of dark curly hair, and though she had never seen him before, she feared she knew who he was. She saw him before he turned around, and then she averted her gaze, pretending not to have noticed him. As she climbed out of the boat and tied it up, she could feel his eyes on her, and when she looked up, at last returning his gaze, she saw that he had an unexpectedly smooth and open face.

But nonetheless there he was, just as she had feared. Only he looked like a geek. From his appearance, she thought, no one would ever guess that he was a rival biologist, ready to steal someone's research. He wore baggy khaki shorts that matched his fancy outfitter's vest, and he had on these odd bright-orange and black running shoes. And no hat. He came down off the dock when he saw her and immediately asked if she were Fern Melartin.

"And if I am?" she said, a little more aggressively than she intended.

He was stopped by her tone for a second. "Well, if you are, then I am David Huntington, or actually I am in any case, and I'm looking for the same parrot that you are."

"The aratinga?" she asked, hoping he wouldn't know the term.

But the guy said, "That's right, the *Aratinga erythrogenys.*" He said it in a precise and scholarly way and confirmed her fears. He had to be a field biologist. Fern said nothing for a moment and the pause fell on them and made them awkward. She wasn't about to tell him anything. She hadn't had much luck seeing them was all she said at last. And this, she felt, was true.

"They're around here, though?" said David, glancing at the dense undergrowth on the far side of the channel.

Fern changed the subject. "You probably know that the

literature suggests that their habitat is higher up than this, up in the foothills. Maybe you ought to try looking up there."

"They're not here, then," he said, seeming disappointed.

Fern looked at him closely, wondering whether he was as naïve as he sounded or was just trying to give that impression, to lead her into revealing something. The latter, she decided, was the safer assumption.

"Who knows?" she said.

He said nothing in answer to this. He just looked a little dismayed, and Fern let a silence settle between them, as she finished unloading the boat.

Then she relented. "Look," she said, "I've been down here all summer, doing this work, and I am really not prepared to share my results with anybody yet. Your best bet is to try the foothills. Do you know how to get there?" He didn't, of course.

She shaded her eyes and looked westward. "Hey," she said. "Where is your car, anyway?"

"I came in a taxi, and it, uh, left. I guess I'll have to call another one."

"You came in a taxi from where?"

"From Guayaquil."

Somehow this information didn't completely convince Fern of David's amateur status. In her frame of mind, this could be simply more evidence that he was a rank opportunist, cutting all corners, not even bothering to check a map or rent a car.

"Well, look," she added. "I don't really know how I can help you." He said, "Thanks, anyway," and she wished him best of luck, and then, as if she were running late, she picked up the gear and, though it was the last thing she hoped to do, said, "See you later," and left him there. She walked down the road feeling a little guilty and upbraiding herself for feeling that. He wasn't her responsibility, she thought, and strode into her house, where she had nothing, in fact, to do but peer out the window to see what he would do next. He didn't do much. He looked around, as if in utter helplessness and wonderment, and then he took his green bag and sat down again on the dock. He was waiting her out, she thought. Well, he could just wait.

When Frank came home from school about twenty minutes later, he said, "Hey, there's a gringo hanging around out there."

"I know," she said. "And I don't want to see him."

"Is it Geoffrey?" said Frank, who knew the story from their dinner-table discussions. "Has he come down here after you?"

"No, it isn't Geoffrey!" said Fern, her voiced raised more than she intended.

"Jeez, bite my head off, why don't you?" said Frank. "Just asking." There was a pause as he went about getting a drink in the kitchen.

"Well, who is it, then?" he said finally.

"It's this guy, David Huntington. He's here looking for the aratinga."

"Oh really, the guy Renato mentioned?" said Frank. "So you didn't manage to dodge him after all." He smirked a little at this, raising her ire. "This place is just getting to be aratinga central." Miserable, Fern just assented.

"I've done so much work," she said. "And he's here to steal it."

"Do you know that for sure?" asked Frank, now peering out the kitchen window himself. "He looks dweebie. The swamp will eat him."

"He called my professor, Pepperbloom," said Fern, "and a day later he shows up here. He seems to know his stuff."

"So what are you going to do?"

"I don't know. Just leave him there, I guess. Maybe he'll go away."

"Whatever," said Frank. He'd gotten his *cerveza* by then and sat down to look at his surf magazine again. Frank read his surf magazines until they fell apart, and even then he held on to the loose pages. After an hour or so, as dusk began to gather outside, Donna drove up. When she came in, she said, "There's some guy on the dock."

"We know," said Frank. "We're waiting for him to leave."

"Who is he? How'd he get here?"

Fern explained who he was. He took a taxi here, she said. From Guayaquil, she added. This news amazed them. Nobody had ever, as far as they knew, taken a taxi from Guayaquil to Puerto Alegre.

"Well, how's he going to get out of here?" Donna asked. Fern didn't know, she said, and she didn't care.

All of them tried to leave it at that, to go on with the nightly routine of making dinner, but it felt forced. Donna, from time to time, looked out the window. "He's still out there," she said, finally. "He's from the States?"

He seemed like it, said Fern.

"Well, we can't just leave him out there. Let's ask him if he wants to have dinner. We don't have to talk about parrots." When Fern said nothing to this, Donna left the house and went to the dock to invite him. After a few minutes, she brought him back into the kitchen, where he stood looking sun dazed. He put his green bag on the floor and blinked in the light, awkward and tired and seeming wary of talking too much. Frank gave him a beer, and Donna drew him out, finding out he was from San Francisco.

"Ah, Frisco," said Frank, who was after all from Southern California.

Dinner was ready by then and they spooned it up. It was the rice and beans and fish thing. They talked politely, about the different kinds of hot weather in Ecuador and California and Arizona and Alabama and Virginia, where they were from—stupid stuff really. The prohibition against talking about parrots hung weightily over the table and made them superficial. Fern said little, but finally she was unable to take it any longer.

"So what do you do, in San Francisco?" she asked David. She could feel the interest of the others pick up.

"Lately," said David, "not too much, to tell you the truth. I was teaching in the spring, but I got this fellowship and I haven't been doing a lot, since then."

Fern wasn't in the best frame of mind to hear this. "Oh really," she said, her suspicions fully engaged again. Fellowships were a sore subject for her ever since she'd been denied hers. Her own money was a worry now. And here he was, funded.

"Actually," said David, seeming to sense her discomfort, "the fellowship isn't for studying parrots."

"It isn't?" said Fern. "What's it for, then?"

"Poetry," said David quietly. "It's for writing poetry."

The remark stopped them all. The fork headed for Frank's mouth paused in its ascent. "For what?" he said, and David had to repeat himself.

"You write poems about parrots?" said Fern. "You're here to write poems about parrots?"

"Actually, no," said David. "I came here to see them, the, uh, conures. The people who gave me the fellowship don't know anything about this," he added. "In fact, I'm supposed to be doing something else. My poems. In San Francisco."

"Well, that's just great," said Donna, looking pointedly at Fern. "So you're not a biologist, then." No, he wasn't. He didn't like to say he was a poet, he said, because it seemed so—he-didn't-know-what—nineteenth century or something, but he guessed that was what he was.

"Well, that's just great," said Donna again, grinning.

Fern still didn't know what to think of this guy, but at least he no longer seemed to be a rival. He was a slacker, sort of. He was avoiding his work back home by looking for birds in Ecuador. This was acceptable. It was the first moment, in any case, in which Fern thought she might not dislike him.

"But why the aratinga?" she said, finally broaching the subject. "Why this particular bird?"

"Oh," he said, seeming shy. "I used to have one once."

"Have? As a pet?"

"Well, not exactly," said David. "As a roommate, I guess." The guy was clearly no scientist.

"Let me get this straight," said Frank. "You had one of these birds, as a pet—or a roommate, as you say—and so you decided to come all the way to Ecuador to see some more. That right?"

"More or less," said David. "I, uh, ejected the one I had." And then he told them his story, of how he got the bad parrot from his father, who wouldn't take him back; of the bird's antisocial habits; of the day that he and Lyle had put the bird out the window.

"I didn't feel good about it afterward," said David. "I

didn't think he could live out there." Then he related the story of his subsequent discovery of the birds in his neighborhood and told them about finding the parrots downtown and finally about meeting Little Wittgenstein again, in his new life as the renegade of the Telegraph Hill flock.

Fern remembered then from her reading that the aratinga had established some feral flocks in the United States. She hadn't thought about it much until then.

"There's a whole flock?" she said. "A breeding flock?"

That's what he had heard, said David. They had escaped from their cages, or had been ejected. Now there were maybe forty birds, of this same species of aratinga, with babies every year.

They hadn't made good pets, he told them. They were too feisty. They were still wild. He figured they'd been captured in Ecuador and sent north. It hadn't been a good idea to import them.

"You called him what?" asked Frank.

"I called him Little Wittgenstein, after the philosopher," said David, getting no reaction from Frank. "But he was called various other things. My father called him Pepito. His full name now, I guess, is Pepito Little Wittgenstein Brando."

This struck Donna and Frank as funny. Frank banged the table and hooted. But Fern listened in astonishment of another kind. She had been making the effort of her life to catch a glimpse of these birds, while this guy had been taking the subway to see them.

Eventually, the table was cleared and the dishes were cleaned. David helped as much as he could, handing things to Frank at the sink. Finally, Donna said to him, "Well, you can't go anywhere tonight, so you might as well use the fourth bunk here." She looked at Fern to see if she had any objections, and Fern shrugged. She'd already thought of this and knew there was no other way. Frank said it was all right with him.

As usual they sat on the porch after dinner, watching the darkness thicken and listening to the insect chorus rise. The birds were not mentioned again. David asked about their reasons for coming to Ecuador. Frank went on about his students and, of course, about the surf. David showed some interest in this. He'd been looking at waves a lot himself lately, he said.

"Where?" Frank asked.

"On a boat. I came down here on a boat," said David.

"What kind of boat?" Frank asked.

"A big boat, a freighter," David said. And by way of explanation he simply added that he didn't like to fly. Across the porch, out of the line of sight of the others, Frank gave Fern a "whoa" look, raising his eyebrows. But this further evidence of David's eccentricity served finally to convince Fern that he was all right, that he wasn't out to steal her research.

So as they prepared for bed, Frank having to unload a bunch of surf paraphernalia from the unused bunk in his room, Fern came to say good-night to the two of them, with one final question for David.

"You know how to swim?" she said.

"Yes," he said hesitantly. "But I hope I don't have to."

"Me too," said Fern.

21

That night, as always, the planet rolled in the rays of the sun, turning into the dark and then back into the light. And in the cool pale moments before dawn, when that sense of the flock visited Fern again, she felt subject to this movement. The earth itself had woken her and the flock with the same continual gesture.

She lay considering these matters, as Donna breathed evenly and deeply in the bunk below. The sound of snoring came from the other end of the house. The place was full now, all the beds filled, and the intensity of that presence was quite strong as well. She slipped out of bed quietly and went out onto the porch. The village was stirring. Cooking smoke hung in a thin line above the rooftops.

Across the road, the door opened at Leonin's house, and he came out, dressed for work. When he saw her, he smiled broadly and stood in the road, holding his bicycle. She was pleased to see him. Since she had begun her work in the mangroves, she'd seen Leonin in passing. Sometimes he came over, but usually they had greeted each other as they came and went. She felt a strong bond with him. She knew that she would never stop feeling grateful to him for delivering her to Puerto Alegre, for keeping her project alive. There were moments they had shared, particularly their early morning hike up the ridge on the day she'd been fired, which she'd always remember.

That morning she didn't ask anything of him; she simply told him that the INEVS officers had some information on illegal animal sales at the reserva and that they were looking for a way to get more evidence. They wanted to arrange a sale of their own, and they needed to know how to do this. Leonin listened to all this seriously, without giving away what he was thinking. He nodded, not agreeing to anything, only letting her know that he understood, and they parted. He mounted the bicycle and rode out of the village.

Back in the house, the others were up. Frank was under the shower out back, and Donna and David were in the kitchen. When Fern came in, Donna told her that she was taking David to her office, where he could use the phone to find a way to get back to Guayaquil. Or he could take the bus, Donna said, which stopped on the main road. Fern said nothing to this. She was still considering matters. By the time she'd had her tea, she'd made up her mind. He really doesn't have a clue, Fern thought. He'll never see these birds, if I don't help him. Besides, she knew that she could use some help.

"Would you be interested in going into the mangroves today?" she asked him. There was a possibility he could get a look at the flock. But they would have to spend the night out there. Donna gave her an arch look.

He said yes in a solemn way that was reassuring. He wasn't taking it lightly. She couldn't know, of course, that until that year, David hadn't taken a walk around the block lightly.

"I need somebody to help me with this stuff, anyway," she said.

"Sure," he said, seeming to contain his enthusiasm. "What do I have to do?"

"Mainly, you sit in the boat." She asked him a few questions, discovering that despite his experience with the freighter, he didn't know anything about handling boats. "Definitely you'll sit in the boat," she said. When Frank came in, his hair still wet, Fern asked him if he could lend them a few things for David. "He needs a hat and water gear," said Fern. Frank said, "Absolutely," in his cheeriest manner, letting Fern know that he was delighted that she wouldn't be going out into the mangroves alone again.

By the time Frank and Donna had left for work, they had made a project of getting David ready for the swamp. Frank lent him his Surfriders Foundation hat—"Please don't lose this," Frank implored him—and found him sunblock and shades. From Frank's boat they retrieved extra flotation cushions. And then, with the gear piled up and the others gone, the two of them sat down on the porch to wait for the tide to fill the channels.

Fern still had her doubts. "You came to the tropics without sunglasses?" she asked him. He didn't like sunglasses, he said. They changed the way things look.

"They're supposed to do that," she said.

She wondered, too, if the birds would cooperate. She couldn't resist the feeling that the birds had allowed her to see them. Maybe his presence would keep them away.

He asked about the flock—where it was, how they could see it. She told him that the place was deep in the mangroves. That was why the tides had to be just right. It had taken her weeks to find them at first. There was a chance they wouldn't be there.

"We may not see them, you know. The last time I saw

them was the best, though," she said. "They found me, really. Right at sunrise. They just came pouring through. Something like a hundred birds."

"Orange under their wings, right?" said David.

"Yes," she said.

"That's how they looked when I saw them," said David. And it surprised Fern again that he had witnessed an actual flock.

"It's weird that they're there," she said finally.

"Where?"

"In San Francisco." She didn't know whether to be disappointed or not, or what difference it made.

"It's weird that we're here," said David. "It's like the whole world is trading places."

"I know why I'm here," she said, after a pause. "And I guess I know how you got here—you talked to Pepperbloom in Boston, right?" David acknowledged this. "But *why* are you here?"

He was as surprised about that as anybody, he said. This was not anything he thought he might be doing. But his life had been at a standstill before, and everything that had happened since his father had given him the parrot was fated, in a way. Supposed to happen.

"There's a guy who takes care of the flock on Telegraph Hill," said David, "and he thinks that the flock, the whole flock, wherever it is in the world and as far back in time as it has lived, is sending us some kind of message. And it's picked out anybody it can—me, even—to help them. To ask that we think with their mind for a bit, before it's too late."

"Do you believe this?" said Fern, knowing she believed it herself.

"More and more," said David.

That convinced her. "Here's the thing," she said. "We sleep in the boat. It's not comfortable. But we'll be there in the morning for the birds. That's how I saw them before. Otherwise the tides won't work, anyway. Is that going to be a problem?"

"No problem," said David, though not quite firmly. He didn't seem to understand the question of the tides, so she tried to explain it to him, which didn't help much. He just said, "I've come this far, and I might as well go through with it."

"Okay, then," she said, impressed again by his gravity. They'd rest through the heat of the day and then they'd go.

They took an extra can of gasoline and some food that she had packed even before she had asked him that morning, as well as a couple of flashlights, the cooler, and the other gear. David looked alarmed and unsteady getting into the boat, and for a moment Fern put her fingertips to her forehead, saying to herself a one-word prayer: Please. Then she pushed the boat off and got in.

The water flowed against them, rising in the channels as they went out. David sat in the bow, looking at the mangroves as Fern steered. His amazement at all of it made her realize how comfortable she'd become there. She drove the boat confidently, gliding down the watercourses, sure of her way, pushing on, noticing the tide reaching its peak, then feeling it begin to draw them on as the channels began to drain. She opened the throttle all the way whenever the depth allowed it: she was hurrying to reach the cove. Behind them the sun dropped toward the ridgeline, casting its glow into the trees ahead. She had to slow the boat to a walk in the last minutes, taking care in the shallower water, until at last the stream opened and she recognized the broad place, the cove. She let the boat drift, then dropped the anchor, testing the rope length at several points to see where the water was deepest, where they might float clear of the mud-flat at low tide.

The water and the nearby trees had begun to gather the dusk already, though the top of the canopy and the sky remained bright. She watched David as he took in the surroundings, noticing the spoonbills roosting on the roots at the far end of the cove, where the channel angled off into the trees again. It was a peaceful, beautiful sight, but he didn't seem relaxed. He gripped the seat. Then as they ate the cold dinner—the same fish and rice and beans from the night before—Fern noticed that his plate shook a little. He couldn't be cold in the steamy air.

"Are you all right?" she asked him.

"I guess so," said David. "This has to be the farthest out that I have ever gotten in my life, though."

"Oh," said Fern. Great, she thought, just great.

"What happens when it gets dark?"

"Jaguars and pythons and alligators, that kind of thing," she said.

"No, really," he said, with a quiet plea in his voice.

"Really," she said. Then she recalled the fear she'd felt when she'd first gone into the mangroves and relented. "But mosquitoes are a bigger problem."

They had already been biting him, David confessed. So, after they ate, Fern put up the mosquito netting, draping most of the little hull. She gave him the bug stuff for his face, so he wouldn't have to get under it entirely.

"Is it always this loud?" David asked. He was talking

about the insect noise, and she heard it as if for the first time again. The whirrs and chirps and whistles rang on all sides of them, a million parts making one pulsating texture. Fern remembered when she'd first heard it. It was a sound like nothing you could imagine back home, like the calls of crickets on a summer night in Minnesota multiplied by a thousand. It could sound like dozens of sleigh bells.

"Listen," she said, "there's a low note in it, a kind of weird spaceship sound." She imitated the deep oscillation. "If you listen to that hard enough, it kind of gets to you." They listened a minute, as the sound she pointed out grew more intense.

"It is getting to me," David said, and the earnest way he said it made her laugh.

"What do we do if there's a problem?" asked David. Fern felt inclined to dismiss his fears, but she'd brought him along to be safe, after all. So she showed him how to use the oars to keep them in midchannel if there were any difficulty. If she fell out of the boat in the dark, she would yell and keep yelling until he found her, she said, adding that he, too, should do that.

"No problem," he said. "None at all."

She lay down in the rear of the boat and he tried to do so in the front, folding his long legs and trying to get the cushion somewhere it might help. It was not going to be a comfortable night.

"This is so strange," he said, after a while. "You know, I used to think I knew exactly what my life would be like. I thought I could see it all in front of me. It was what I was doing, what I knew, and it would just go on and on."

"Did you like feeling that way?" she asked.

"Yes," he said. "That's what I wanted. That's what I wished for."

"So what happened?"

"I don't really know. Life took over."

"That's what happens to a dominant species."

"What?"

"Life takes over. Variation continues until it fills all the available niches," she said. "Eventually even a dominant species becomes a host. Somebody finds a niche."

"That's funny," he said. "That actually happened to me. I mean with Little Wittgenstein. He exploited my niche."

They laughed about this. "Science in action," she said.

The moon rose and they watched it in silence. It was waxing toward full and cast a yellow light over the dark tops of the trees and the surface of the water, which was still and clear.

Fern thought that she should probably feel strange, less than comfortable there in the middle of the wilderness with this man she had only just met, but she didn't. He was smart. She could talk to him. Plus, he was the nervous one, which put her at ease. Beneath his nervousness, he was as awed by the place as she was. Being there was important to him.

And it was she who broke their silence again, asking him about his poems. "Do they rhyme?" she asked.

"Once they did," he said. "But I guess you could call the poems I've been writing since college experimental."

"What was the experiment?" asked Fern, like a scientist.

"Nobody ever asks that," said David. "Maybe the experiment was an attempt to see just how little you could say and still write a poem."

"Was it successful?" she asked.

"Yes, you could say it was. I wrote poems about almost nothing."

"Why?"

"I guess I felt that everything had already been said, and so I worked on saying nothing."

"It seems like saying something might be important in a poem," said Fern.

"It was felt," he said—trying to defend himself a little, she thought—"that any meaning would have reflected an outmoded way of thinking."

"So you wrote nonsense," she said.

"Well, not nonsense, exactly," he said. "Nonsense is consistently nonsensical and is still rational that way."

"So nonsense would have been too sensible for you," said Fern.

"In a way, yes."

"Oh my god," said Fern. "No wonder your niche got exploited."

He laughed at this, as if it were patently true. "Wittgenstein, the guy I named the parrot after, he said that language was a cage. No matter how much you wanted to be in contact with the world, you couldn't get past this cage."

"How horrible," she said.

"Now it seems like that idea could come only from someone who'd spent too much time in some little room somewhere," he said. "I couldn't keep doing it, anyway. And once I'd seen the flock, I didn't even want to."

"Now you can write about everything, instead of nothing," she said. She said it lightly, but he didn't dismiss it, though he didn't respond in words. He said nothing, and his silence opened into a broader one, as they watched the moon climb above the trees.

What was she going to do next? he asked.

She'd go back and try to get a dissertation out of the notes and pictures she'd taken. "It doesn't seem like enough," she said. She'd spent half the summer in the wrong place, working in a kind of zoo.

"Thank god I got fired," she said, "or I would never have done anything." She told him the story of Qualles then, even the part about him coming over with his wine bottle and suggesting that she might move into his house.

"Now that's horrible," he said.

Fern said she would probably have to pack it up in a couple of weeks, when the rains began. She had been hoping to observe more of the flock's behavior, though she would probably only get a few more sightings, at most. She didn't know. She wished she could stay another year.

"You aren't looking forward to going home?" he said. No, she confessed. Graduate school was hard, and her situation at home had changed since she'd left. She'd broken up with her boyfriend, she added, trying to preempt his questions. Then as flatly as she could, she said she didn't know where she would go when she got back.

"You were living with him?" he asked.

"Uh-huh," she said, seriously.

There was another silence then, before David said he didn't know where he'd be going, either. He told her the story of Bozuki and of getting evicted and how his friend Peter had found him a place where he could store everything in a ship container at the docks. He told the story in a funny way that made her say "You're kidding!" several times.

"So neither of us have a home to go back to," she said when he'd finished.

"Yep," he said. "We're both homeless."

"That sounds terrible," she said, though she felt goofily delighted by it. For her, it was a truth she'd been resisting. "Well, for the moment there's the boat," she said, tapping on its wooden hull for good luck. David tapped, too.

As the darkness increased, he told her about the ship, speaking easily now about his voyage to South America on the freighter. He told her about the Indian officers and the huge ocean and the seabirds and the flying fish off the bow.

"You'd think such a huge ship would seem artificial, you know, outside of nature," he said. "But on the ship it occurred to me for the first time that there is no outside of nature. It doesn't stop. It isn't elsewhere. It comes through us. It *is* us. I guess that's obvious, especially out here, but it had never occurred to me before. These birds had learned to hunt fish in the wake of a giant freighter, as if even huge steel ships were natural. And maybe they are. Now I wonder how I thought it was otherwise."

The moon had risen high above them and rode over the space of water between the trees. "Look, it's got a ring," he said, and they stopped talking and looked up at the halo around the moon. It was a broad ring, like a huge open eye, with its shining pupil in the center. And then he recalled the moonbow he had seen ahead of the ship and told her about that.

But she had grown quiet. To her the ring around the moon meant rain coming, and it reminded her of the end of the season and the end of her time in Ecuador. She thought about the story he'd told her of the aratinga in San Francisco, and it sounded odd and ironic to her.

"Brando?" she said after a while.

"Yeah, Brando, Little Wittgenstein, Pepito, whatever," he said. "Those were our names, not his." Then he said nothing for a long time in the dark. She heard him breathing deeply at his end of the boat and knew he'd fallen asleep. The sound of his breathing comforted her, made her feel safe. She wasn't in bed with him, but it reminded her of what it felt like to lie awake with a man asleep beside her. She felt then that she could close her eyes and sleep, too.

And then it was another morning, or not quite another morning. David startled at something in a dream and opened his eyes. In the pale light beyond the mosquito netting, the thicket pressed in. It hurt to move, so he stayed where he was, his back numb where he had lain. Fern was somewhere nearby, lying in the bottom of the boat between the rear seat and the motor, still asleep. He pieced it together as he awoke, already feeling a thrill of amazement at all that had happened, and especially at her presence.

He recalled the day before in delicious detail, remembering Fern's practiced and workaday way of getting the boat into the water, getting him into it, starting the motor, and pushing them off. Everything that had happened to him in the past year had brought him to that moment, moving across the water in this far and strange place. What was most unexpected, most wonderful, was this woman herself, and yet somehow her being there did not feel accidental either. From the first time he'd seen her, rounding the bend in the stream in her blue boat, steering with the tiller, she'd looked so beautiful and so familiar.

Even the mangroves, those odd trees going on and on, miles of twisted roots and slender trunks rising so close to one another, even these he seemed to recognize, for all their strangeness. Mollusks clung to every sunken tree trunk. In the shallows, wading birds stalked; in the tops of the trees, birds sang. A kingfisher flew by, outpacing the boat, the legs of a crab dangling from its bill. On one branch a huge green lizard stood alert, watching them, so near that David noticed that the ends of its toes broadened into pods.

He'd never been anywhere like this, and yet he knew it. This was the ancient stronghold, the heart of the world, an impenetrable haven, a place where, no matter what had happened elsewhere, wild energy moved and stirred and folded and continued. Somehow, sometime, in some form, he'd been here before.

And Fern, wonderful Fern, had driven them steadily on, down one watercourse and another, steering expertly and exactly, keeping them in the center of the current. For him, the shores rushed by in a bewildering swell of detail. He had no idea where they were going or how he might get back. He had to trust her and he had trusted her, though he was glad, when at last she had slowed the motor. They'd glided silently along in water so still that the hull parted the dark trees over an inverted sky. As if she were parking a car, she had maneuvered the boat, lowering and raising the anchor several times until she found the spot she wanted.

And then they had simply talked, David giving in to her assumption that the extraordinary reality hemming them in was nothing to be alarmed about. In the midst of it all, they'd talked about poetry and evolution and relationships and getting evicted and the trip on the freighter, conversation they might have made anywhere, until he had suddenly relaxed and fallen asleep. David, who had slept badly in his earplugs in his apartment for years, had zonked out on the hard hull, the moonlight on his face, as the rich dark and the alien insect drone poured over them.

David watched the sky lose the pearly shade it had before dawn and take on its blue color. He couldn't remember if he had ever seen this before. Then he heard it, the same cry that had so startled him when he had taken the bird his father had given him up to his apartment, a shocking shriek from such a small creature. This was a full-voiced version, a trumpeting that moved and echoed through the thicket. Before it had even fallen away, it was answered by others, by five, ten, twenty others. It rose like a fire in the trees.

"Fern!" he called. "They're here!" But she was already awake, sitting up in the boat and pulling the mosquito netting away.

The sound of the cries built and broadened, then broke into one sustained bird shout, which moved and drew nearer. Fern raised her camera and planted her elbows on the rear seat of the boat, as David stared at the barricade of trees.

Then there they were, flapping vigorously and silhouetted against the pale sky. As they came into view, they veered toward the boat, at first just a few birds and then a bunch and then a living current of them. They flew directly overhead, drumming the air with vibrations of their wings. The bright blurred bodies rushed past. Beneath the torrent of avian energy, David felt taken out of himself, as if some part of him had risen into the pale air with the birds and could look back at the two of them in the boat, at his own eyes staring up, his mouth open. This flock had many more birds in it than the group on Telegraph Hill, and the cry, the sense of electric knowing was bigger, deeper, but the familiarity was the same. David knew again that ancient singularity that was the one flock, always.

The main body flew through the space over the water, then diminished, as the birds seemed separate again, now a few dozen flying overhead, then fewer, until at last the stragglers crossed the open water and disappeared behind the screen of trees on the far bank. Fern kept snapping pictures, even of the empty sky. Then she exclaimed, "They're gathering! They're putting the whole flock together. The fledglings are out. This is maybe twice the number of birds I saw before."

The two of them whooped and yipped, celebrating what they had seen, and he crawled back over the seats of the boat and took her hand and she clasped his. They had not touched before. Charged with exultation, David had a potent impulse to take her in his arms then, to touch and kiss her, to make love to her right there in the blue boat. But he held back. The moment of seeing the flock was important, and he didn't want to make it seem like a means to anything else. Still, she didn't let go of his hand, but held for a moment longer than their exhilaration required, until he knew that she'd acknowledged him, that she'd known his thought.

In another moment they had returned to their separate selves. She wrote up her notes, and he sat taking it in, feeling as if he had finally arrived, as if he had awoken that morning after a sleep of years. They ate and drank a little as the sun rose and the steaming heat of the place began to press upon them. She kept exclaiming at the size of the flock—there were maybe two hundred birds, she said, as she folded the net and then raised the anchor. But that was it for the day, she explained. The birds would be inland.

She started the engine and took them up the channels. He was amazed by her again, as she found her sure way back through the swamp, moving them along as stream after stream opened in the banks they passed, many of these wider, more promising, it seemed, than the one she chose. He had no idea how she could know the way, or where they were, and laughed out loud when then the dock came unexpectedly into view.

"Pretty good, huh?" she said.

22

Returning to the house, they found it vacant. There was a note. "Went to the market and the waves. D and F." This was their Saturday routine, Fern told him. Frank went surfing for the day, dropping Donna at San Lorenzo and the market. The house was full of sunlight, and Fern felt awake to the presence of this man and the possibilities of their being alone as she had not before. When they'd seen the flock together, something had changed for her. Now she wanted him. It excited her to think of it. She said and did nothing, though. It was too soon.

She made him tea, her ritual even in the heat, filling the kettle from the jug. He sat at the table as she moved around the kitchen. She felt nimble, happy, a little giddy. After they had their tea, they showered. She insisted that he go first and listened to him gasp out in the yard, as the cold water from the cistern fell on him.

And a little later when she got out of her own shower, he was waiting for her in the kitchen, and she stood before him, feeling naked beneath her robe. And it was all she could do then not to go to him. He was hesitant, too. There was an awkwardness between them, a reluctance both to proceed and to part. He took refuge in formality and thanked her again for taking him to see the flock. He said he guessed he'd get some sleep, and she said she would, too. Still, she had to bite her lip as she turned into her room and dropped her robe and climbed into her bunk alone. Her body rang with the possibility, and it was a while before she could let herself drift off. When she closed her eyes, she could still see the dense, raging passage of the flock they'd witnessed at dawn.

A knocking pulled her from a sweaty sleep in the heat of the afternoon. At the door she found the INEVS officers, Raquel and Renato. She stepped out on the porch to speak with them, noticing that the air outside smelled different. Clouds had come in, not the towering thunderheads of summer, but a lower enclosure, a frontal mass from the sea, marking, or at least presaging, the change of season.

She knew what the two officers wanted. They were returning to Guayaquil and had stopped by to see if Fern had any further information on the matter they had raised two days before. They appeared very anxious to proceed with the operation at the reserva and were visibly disappointed when Fern told them that she had no more for them. She still needed to hear from Leonin.

Then David came to the door and peered out, his hair standing up from his sleep. To Fern the sight of him suggested that they had been sleeping together in the house, and she blushed, even though it wasn't true.

Renato said, "*Buenas tardes,* Mr. Huntington," in a matter-of-fact way, a practiced courtesy that allowed no inferences about the situation. "I see you've found your way to Puerto Alegre."

"Oh," said David. "Hello. Yes, I made it. Thanks for the information."

"And have you also managed to find the bird you were looking for?"

David had come out onto the porch, and he looked at Fern, as if wondering what to say. She rescued him from having to give anything away.

"Actually, we saw them this morning," she said. Then she paused, letting him answer. Fern had known how to find them, he said. He grew enthusiastic, describing their journey into the mangroves and the passage of the flock, from their first cries to how they looked in the air, trying to describe that sense of the flock as a living current or stream. The two INEVS officers listened intently, Raquel drawing out her notebook and nodding to Fern to see if she minded.

She asked some specific questions about the size of the flock and the time and place they had seen it, and Fern found that she really didn't mind sharing the information. Having seen the birds with David had shifted her attitude, as if the flock were no longer her own private experience. It was good if other people, the right people, anyway, knew about the birds.

"And what will you do now?" Renato asked, when David had finished. "Do you have other plans?" David had to admit he really didn't have any. Would he be returning to Guayaquil? David said he didn't know.

"He came here by taxi," said Fern, teasing David a little. "And he'll have to find another one to go back."

She regretted saying this immediately, as Renato—of course—offered David a ride back to Guayaquil with them. They were just going there, he said, having finished their weekly business in San Lorenzo. David hesitated. But he had no other way to leave and Fern had not asked him to stay, so he accepted the offer.

And then, too suddenly, it was time for David to go. The two officers exchanged numbers with Fern—she gave them Donna's—and Renato said pointedly that they hoped to take some action on that other matter soon. They wouldn't be returning to San Lorenzo until the following week.

"Uh," said David, "I guess I need to get my things."

"Certainly," said Renato, adding that they would wait for him in the car.

Fern followed him inside and watched as he stuffed the duffel bag. "I guess it's best that I go," he said. "I just dropped myself on you, in the middle of your work, and you had no choice about it."

"You know, you don't have to leave," Fern said. "Frank and Donna don't mind, I know. And I don't mind. We could see the flock again."

"No," he said. "I mean, I want to see the flock again. And you, too. But as it is now, you have to put me up because I stranded myself here."

"It's not like that."

"It feels like that to me, anyway. I just want it to be right."

She didn't want him to go, but she could see what he meant. "Well, okay," she said. "But if I invite you back, you'll come?"

He would, he said.

"When?" she said, a little more eagerly than she intended.

"When do you want me to?"

"Why don't you see if they will bring you back when they come back next week? And bring some stuff so you can stay awhile. I mean, I need help with the boat."

"Oh, I'm a big help in the boat," he said. Then he was

done putting his things in the bag, and some paralysis gripped them both for a moment.

"It was perfect," he said. "I know it was the reason I came to Ecuador. I feel so lucky."

"I do, too," she said. He hadn't expected her to say that.

She found a pencil and wrote down the number and the e-mail address at Donna's office. "I left Frank's hat and stuff in the kitchen," he said, asking also if she would thank Frank and Donna for him.

Then she said, "Consider this my invitation." And kissed him. He kissed her back, letting it linger for a sweet moment. "As soon as you can," she said. They went back out on the porch together. He took her hand and let go of it. Then, in a stunned way, he stumbled toward the car and got in. Renato started it up.

David had the chance to wave just once before Fern disappeared into the great green elsewhere of Ecuador. He felt stupid for leaving and already wanted to be back. If she had asked him to stay after she had kissed him, he would have put down his green duffel and stayed. For a time he sat in the backseat of the car and could say nothing. He was overwhelmed by the events of the day, seeing the flock and having her kiss him like that.

"If you don't mind my asking," said Renato, breaking the silence after they had driven for a while, "have you been studying parrots for some time?"

"No," said David. "Just for the past year. And, really, only reading things."

What things? Renato wanted to know.

David didn't know quite where to start. He still didn't feel like telling them about Little Wittgenstein, so he told them about the log of Columbus, of how Columbus had actually mistaken huge flocks of birds for the new continent. The two were interested, so he continued to talk as they drove. He told them about discovering the parrot flocks of the Caribbean, and about the Carolina parakeet, the only North American parrot, observed by Lewis and Clark, and now extinct. They had been conures, David told them, the same kind of birds as the ones he had seen that morning with Fern. When he stopped talking, Renato and Raquel exchanged a brief acknowledging look.

"Mr. Huntington," said Renato. "David. We've been wondering if you might be interested in undertaking a little job for us."

Fern sat on the porch for a long time after David left. Frank and Donna came home from their errands and found her there. She explained to them that David had gone back with Renato and Raquel, back to Guayaquil. "So it didn't go so well, last night in the mangroves?" said Frank.

"Oh no," she said. "It went great."

"Then why'd he leave?" asked Donna

"They offered him a ride, and he seemed to feel he should take it."

"So he had enough of the mangle?" said Frank.

"No, he was a little freaked out on the water, but I think he loved it. He just wanted it to be right, being here. You know, not to be imposing or whatever."

"You think he'll be back?" said Frank.

"Hope so."

Donna had bought a chicken and was going to make all four of them dinner. Frank said he'd help her make it anyway and they left Fern on the porch. She watched the setting sun flare and glower in the clouds, then heard the rain begin to fall, spattering on the palm leaves. She had expected rain and had not planned to go back to the cove that day. Being there with David that morning, seeing the flock at its full strength, all the fledglings gathered up, seemed to have capped her observations that summer. She was at peace with this fieldwork, even with the rain. She would see the flock again, she hoped, but she was no longer so frantic. She knew she had observed them in their full array. She had proof of their existence in the mangroves. She'd have something to write about. Maybe it wasn't so much, but it was something, and she remembered another thing Pepperbloom had told her. Better to prove a small point than to push a grand theory, she'd said. The grand theory would wait.

"Hey, rain," said Donna, as she came out onto the porch.

"Yeah, rain," said Fern quietly.

Donna was quick. "Somebody's blissed out," she said "What is it? You like him?"

"Uh-huh," said Fern.

"You like him!"

"I like him."

At dinner she heard about the day's waves. They were so overhead, Frank said, ignoring Donna, who said that they were always so overhead. Nice big long rights, said Frank. Free speech? Donna teased. Freedom of the press? Still, the women listened to him when he talked about the local kids at the beach, who, just bodysurfing, fearlessly took on the biggest waves. For her part Fern told them that Renato and Raquel still wanted to get the goods on the reserva. But she hadn't done anything about it.

"Well, we need to do something about it," said Donna. "Qualles is giving all of us *norteños* a bad name."

The other two left her to bring up the subject of David and

her night in the swamp. After a couple of glasses of wine she told them everything, about funny David and his terror, about how oddly comfortable she had been alone with him in the boat, and about the magnificent passage of the whole flock.

"Jeez, he lucked out," said Frank. "Some grem always shows up on the perfect day."

"It wasn't like that," said Fern. "Actually, it was better with him there."

"Hmm," said Donna.

"How'd you pee?" Frank wanted to know.

"Frank!" said Donna. But she wanted to know, too.

A voice calling *"¡Hola!"* from the door interrupted this high-minded discussion. Leonin looked in through the screen. They greeted him loudly, Frank yelling, *"¿Qué más?"* his usual greeting to Leonin, which meant something like "What next?" The young man came in rather shyly and sat down. He politely refused a glass of wine, then announced in his formal Spanish that he had something to tell them. He wanted to work with the INEVS people, he said. He wanted to help with the investigation.

Leonin had found out the name of a man who dealt in tropical birds in Guayaquil, who often referred customers to Qualles. If the INEVS people wanted someone to play the part of a foreign buyer, Leonin said, they should have him contact this man, who called himself Ramón.

Leonin spoke with determination, and the three others, understanding the risk he was taking, grew serious. He was supporting a family on his pay from the reserva, and if things went wrong, he could end up losing his job. Donna, finally, was the one who congratulated him.

"This is good," she said. "This is the right thing to do." All three of them told him the same thing. Whatever they could do to help him, he could count on it.

David returned to Madame Cherchenko's, astonished by what Renato had asked him to do. They'd asked him to go undercover. They'd wanted him to try to buy an illegal parrot from this man Qualles, the same man who had dismissed Fern from her job. In the car David had told Renato that he wanted to do it, but that he doubted he could. He could speak only a few words in Spanish. He couldn't even get around.

None of that would matter, Renato had told him. In fact, it would be helpful. It would convince Qualles that David was really an American traveler looking for an exotic bird. This was the reason they had thought of him for the assignment.

"You're not supposed to know anything," Raquel said. "You're supposed to be new here."

"Well, I don't know anything and I am new," said David.

"Precisely," said Renato.

He'd decided to do it. He wanted to, for Fern. And he had his own reason, too. He'd be righting the balance, compensating for throwing the parrot out the window. That act had brought him, eventually, to this one, and now it was not only right but also necessary to follow through. So when he'd gotten out of the car he'd said yes, and Renato had told him that they would contact him on the following Monday.

Arriving at Madame Cherchenko's, David went to his books. He would have to know about parrots if he were to appear to be a knowledgeable collector. That night, in spite of his long day, he stayed up late and studied parrots as if they were the subject of his graduate qualifying exam.

The next day was a rainy Sunday, and he felt held in suspension, thinking of nothing but Fern and this thing that he'd been asked to do. He tried the number at Donna's office, but he couldn't reach anybody there. He looked again at his parrot books, but saw nothing he didn't already know. He didn't know when it would happen, but he wanted to move, to go already. The restlessness was strong in him now. He couldn't stand being indoors. He walked out into the rain and came back. And all day he felt her close to him, as if her scent filled his room. Late in the day he went out again. The rain had stopped for the moment and the city streets glistened and steamed. He walked to the river and looked south across the water to the mangroves, where she was, where the flock was. The low green horizon pulsed with that presence.

The next morning Madame Cherchenko came up to tell him he had a phone call, and it was Fern, her voice full of excitement. She had just spoken to Renato, who had told her what they had proposed. He was going to do it, he told her.

"I was so hoping you would," she said. Renato had some new information, she told him. "You should call him," she said. "I think he wants to do this right away. But whenever it happens, bring your things and come here afterward. Will you do that?" He told her he would.

23

That very afternoon, David took up his assignment. After David called the INEVS office, Raquel picked him up. She wore jeans and sunglasses, and she coached him as she drove through the city streets. He was to say that he was visiting Ecuador from the United States and that he wanted to buy a Buffon's macaw—a local but endangered bird. It would be no problem if he spoke only in English, or if he were nervous. Then, as she stopped at the curb, she warned him. "Remember, these people are not so polite and friendly. They might act that way. But if something bad happens, just get out of there." She'd wait down the block, she said.

David found himself in a new part of the sprawling city, on an avenue of shops. Peering through the gleaming windows of the nearest, he saw, sitting on three wide swinging perches, three large pale parrots. The birds were familiar to him, though he had never seen them in the flesh, so to speak. Two were African grays, beautiful dove-colored birds with red tail feathers. The other was a white cockatoo with an extravagant yellow crest. Cockatoos came from the South Pacific, David thought, but for a moment he wasn't sure, and this gave him a jolt of anxiety about going into the shop. He stood there on the sidewalk, looking in at these birds, which shone in the display windows like rich merchandise. Cockatoos, he thought, racking his brain. Where were white cockatoos native? Indonesia, he recalled at last. Only then did he put his hand on the chrome door handle and go in.

Inside, the chirps and calls of birds rang off the high ceiling, and various bright parrots preened on their perches. Dozens of golden finches hopped around in a case that took up most of one wall. When a clerk approached him, David said, in English, that he was looking for a particular kind of macaw. The clerk, looking confused, said *"Un momento, por favor,"* and disappeared through a door behind the rear counter. Then a mustached man in a tan business suit emerged from the back offices, asking if he might be of help.

When David said he hoped to purchase a Buffon's macaw, the man fell silent and looked David over, then simply said that they did not sell that kind of parrot. Money was no problem, David said. The man shrugged, rubbed one eyebrow, and said, "Come, let me explain this to you," and led David through the rear door, down a short hallway, and into his office, a large room with a thick beige carpet and drapes and a bar. The place was silent and shaded, thick wooden shutters shielding the windows. A large desk, of shining metal tubes and green glass, braced one corner of the room. The man ushered David to a kind of living-room suite opposite, where he introduced himself as Ramón, the accent strong on the second syllable of his name.

David sat down on the couch, feeling less nervous than he had imagined. It was easier, oddly, to pretend to be someone else than to be there for real, as himself. When Ramón asked if David would like a Coca-Cola, he accepted the drink. He thought it might help him appear American, though he never drank the stuff at home. Ramón produced the Coke and a glass with ice from the bar. David, wide awake in his tension, noticed everything, even that the Coke came in an old-fashioned bottle, an object he remembered from his childhood, though this bottle was worn and battered as if it had been many times reused.

"The parrot you are looking for," said Ramón, as he sat down across from David, "cannot be sold in Ecuador."

"But they come from here," David said. "And I've come all the way from the States to find one."

There was a pause then, as the man considered. David sat forward on the couch in his hiking clothes, hoping he looked like a bird-watching tourist seeking an expensive pet. The man evidently decided that he did.

"This will have to be a strictly confidential matter," he said. David nodded. Satisfied, Ramón said that he would have to make some calls. Where might he reach David? Surprised by the question, David had to fumble in his wallet for the slip of paper bearing the phone number at Madame Cherchenko's. As he did, he realized that his fumbling looked good.

"When can I expect to hear from you?" David said. He was hoping, for one thing, that he wouldn't have to be away from Fern for too long. Ramón said he would call him in the morning.

At nine the next morning, David and Renato and Raquel and Madame Cherchenko sat in her parlor sipping tea and not saying much. Renato looked at his watch every few minutes. An hour passed as they waited for the call. At last the phone rang. When David took the receiver from Madame Cherchenko, he heard Ramón's smooth urbane voice on the line. The item David was seeking might be available after all, he said. But the price was eight thousand dollars, U.S. That seems fine, David said, surprising himself with the ease of it. But he would have to see the bird first, of course.

Certainly, said Ramón. This bird was not in the city, though. If David would come by the shop, he would take him out to see the bird.

"Could we go today?" asked David.

"Of course," said the man. Even that morning would be fine.

And where would they be going? David asked.

"To a special collection, out in the country," said Ramón. David wouldn't have to drive; he would drive. They arranged to meet at the shop. Ramón told David to bring a cashier's check for the amount. The business would take much of the day.

Ramón's windowless van smelled like the inside of a birdcage. Outside, the rain had stopped. The day was clear, and though puddles stood on the shoulders, the road was dry. The road was familiar to David, as it was the same one that the taxi had taken. It was the road to Fern. Ramón drove fast on the narrow highway and passed recklessly on curves. Still, they continued without incident for an hour or so. Then they turned left, up a road David didn't recognize, and passed a sign bearing a big red macaw and the words BOSQUE PRIVADO. The driveway wound into some low hills. Presently they reached a small guardhouse, where the attendant simply nodded and sent them through.

Inside the compound at the top of the curved drive stood a red-haired man, who waved to them. As David got out of the car, the man thrust out his hand and greeted him heartily. The man was slight and looked wasted, his cheeks sunken, the flesh beneath his eyes slack and tinged with yellow. "Welcome to Ecuador, Mr. Huntington," he said with an American accent. He introduced himself as Dr. Leonard Qualles. David shook Qualles's hand, reminding himself of what Renato had told him, to deceive Qualles on only a few key details and otherwise to make nothing up. Mostly he was not acting, but being himself, being natural, as it were. Qualles took them into a building to his own dim and book-lined office, where he offered them ice tea and, again, Coca-Cola. This was how one made Americans feel at home, evidently. David took another one, just to be consistent.

"How was your flight?" Qualles asked him, and David explained that he had not arrived by plane, but by boat.

"How nice," exclaimed Qualles, casting a glance at Ramón. "Did you sail here yourself?"

"No," said David. "There was a crew for that."

"How very nice," said Qualles. He assumed that David had sailed to South America in his own yacht, and David did nothing to discourage that idea.

He understood that David was looking for a very special bird, said Qualles. Yes, said David, a Buffon's macaw. Why that particular bird? asked Qualles.

David didn't have to pause. He said that he had several macaws already, from various parts of South America, but that he wanted one from the region of western Ecuador, to complete his collection. Qualles nodded, seeming to believe this, but asked, as if casually, what other birds David owned.

He had a blue-and-yellow from Panama, said David, and a military from Mexico, and a scarlet that he'd gotten in Venezuela.

"All birds I picked up on trips," he added. "Oh, and a little red-shouldered from Guyana. *Ara nobilis.*" He also said that he had a number of other birds he'd purchased in the United States, an African gray and several Amazons. But the macaws were his favorites. David elaborated easily, drawing on the information he'd taken from his reading. All those days in the library in San Francisco, during which he thought he'd been avoiding anything serious—it was all proving useful. In fact, he could have cited some of the page numbers from *Parrots of the World*.

"You've taken these other birds back on the boat with you?" asked Qualles.

"Yes," said David. "It avoids complications."

Qualles bought it completely. He stroked his chin and nodded like a fellow connoisseur, ready to deal. "Would you like a look at my collection?" he asked.

Behind the office building lay the shaded zoolike grounds of the place, where they found the cages. Two of them were aviaries as big as houses themselves. Qualles escorted David quickly past several cages to show him the prize of the collection first. The tiger appeared asleep when they came to the bars, though he lifted one eyelid as Qualles spoke and gave the three of them a look of deadly contemplation, a look that intensified David's sense that he, too, was hunting prey.

Qualles took them back past the other cages, moving more slowly and explained what was in each. Next to an enclosure that contained dozens of monkeys stood an attendant, a young man with a head of thick dark hair. Qualles called to him, and he walked over, saying nothing and following when Qualles told him he needed some help with the macaws.

In a cage near the office were four large birds, at the sight of which David felt Fern's presence. She'd been there. Two of the birds he recognized as scarlet macaws. They perched in the lower branches of a tree, looking huge to David, as big as collies. Two other macaws sat higher up on the perch. These were smaller birds, green with muffs of scarlet at the tops of their black bills. The undersides of their tails were a subtle burnished golden color, with a trace of sky blue in the upper feathers. They were beautiful birds, and they looked at the group of men with calm suspicion, as if they were the only ones there who knew everything that was happening. To David, they looked ancient and wise.

"And here are the Buffon's," said Qualles with a flourish, gesturing to the top of the perch.

The nearest of the big scarlets screeched, fluffed his feathers, and said distinctly, "Don't give me any crap." Qualles smiled weakly at the bird's insult. "I don't know where he got that," he said.

"Will you bring one of the Buffon's down for Mr. Huntington?" said Qualles to the young man. Inside the cage, the guy set up a ladder and, carrying a net, climbed until he was close to one of the Buffon's. He spoke to the bird softly in Spanish, and held out only the handle of the net. To David's delight, the macaw stepped onto the handle, and the young man was able to bring the bird gently down the ladder and over to the visitors.

Up close the Buffon's macaw was stunning, its white face dramatically striped, its wings a bold turquoise. It looked at them nervously, with one eye and then the other—a gesture David remembered from Little Wittgenstein. It squawked and raised its wings, but did not leave the handle of the net.

"There, you see how tame," said Qualles. And David very much wanted to buy this bird then, not to possess it or to keep it captive, but to get away from Qualles, whom he viewed with real distaste.

"How much?" said David, cutting to the chase.

"Oh," said Qualles, "I couldn't let this bird go for less than fifteen thousand." The man called Ramón grew alarmed at this, and broke in, asking for a moment with Dr. Qualles. They moved across the pathway to the monkey cages and spoke in Spanish. David heard the words *"ocho mil"* and *"avión."* He could guess from Ramón's tone that he was explaining that he had mentioned a lower price to David. David also assumed that it made a difference that he was supposedly taking the bird out of Ecuador by boat, something he had not mentioned to Ramón. As the two men conferred, the young man stood inside the cage with the macaw and looked at David through the bars of the cage. He gave David a small and subtle wink.

When Qualles and Ramón returned, Qualles said, "I understand that Señor Ramón here quoted you a different price for this bird. But he was mistaken. The price remains fifteen thousand."

"That's disappointing," David told him. David had decided to bargain with him, as it might look too pat otherwise. Qualles was on the hook, though, there was no doubt. He had a gleam of greed in his watery eyes. David first warned that he would have to give him a personal check for any amount over eight thousand dollars, as he'd brought a cashier's check, the check that he and Raquel had drawn that morning. Qualles had no problem with this. Then David offered him ten thousand dollars. Qualles considered this a moment and said, "Twelve five." David agreed, and they shook hands. Qualles's small dry hand felt repulsive, embalmed.

Back in Qualles's office, David gave him the cashier's check and wrote out his own for $4,500. It would have been good, had Qualles tried to cash it. David had a momentary feeling of fondness for the Wadsworth Foundation, which knew not what it had done. Qualles looked at the check closely and asked if David might show him an ID. Just a formality, of course. David produced his passport, glad then that he had not tried to use a pseudonym. Then they arranged for Ramón to take the bird and hold it at his shop until David's ship sailed, supposedly on the following Tuesday.

They left the office together, Qualles effusive as he escorted the other two out of the building. When they reached the van, they opened the back doors. Looking forlorn in the dimness, the Buffon's macaw sat quietly in Ramón's rectangular cage. David thanked Qualles and had to shake his lizardlike hand again as he said good-bye. They drove past the smiling guard and out the gate. David glanced at his watch. The whole business had taken just an hour.

When they reached the main road, they found it blocked by wooden barricades, behind which stood soldiers with automatic weapons. Military vehicles were pulled over on the shoulder, and around them stood several officers. David saw Renato standing among them. At the sight of the van, the soldiers sprang to life, raising their rifles as one of them waved the van to a halt.

David had one bad moment, wondering how Ramón would react. But he simply muttered and applied the brakes, as if he had seen such roadblocks a thousand times. The soldier in charge ordered both of them out, as two soldiers walked behind the van and opened the doors. At the side of the road, Renato conferred with the officers, who gestured that David should join them. Quickly enough, he did and watched from the shoulder as the soldiers put handcuffs on Ramón and placed him in one of the army trucks.

Renato, who was very tense, asked David if he could identify the bird in the back of the van. Inside, the bird shifted from foot to foot, seeming uneasy but unharmed, and David told him that this was indeed the Buffon's macaw he had purchased. Then Renato told David to wait there, and he and the commander took two of the army vehicles back up the road to the reserva.

The insects buzzed in the heat, and the soldiers relaxed and leaned on their vehicles, having stacked their guns on the tailgate of one of the trucks, like so many umbrellas at the library, David thought. After a while the cars came back, this time with a lone passenger in the backseat of the second vehicle. It was Qualles, who looked out his window at David with rage and astonishment. David gave him a little wave, just for Fern.

The group then broke up. Renato bid David a quick goodbye, saying they'd see him later. One of the soldiers, a thin, red-haired kid in glasses, gestured to David, and led him to a truck, in the back of which were all five of David's bags, everything that Peter and Lyle had helped him put on the freighter back in Oakland. David got in, and the soldier jockeyed the truck around a U-turn, passed other soldiers who were now loading the barricades, and headed south. The kid drove fast, and through the open windows of the truck the warm air buffeted them. David had that fabulous feeling of being out of school for the summer. Soon they came to the mangroves, the bright water flashing in the trees. Then citrus orchards appeared on the left of the road, and they made the turn David recalled—he could have driven it himself by then—into the mangroves.

Fern must have heard them coming, for she was off the porch and in the yard when they pulled up at the house. He shouted, "It worked!" as they stopped. She yelled and hugged him when he climbed out of the truck.

"They got him?" she said. "They got Qualles?"

"Took him away," said David, and she gave another yip.

The young soldier insisted on unloading David's luggage for him and carrying it to the porch. He did the work seriously, as if under orders. They thanked him and he left.

"Nobody's home," she said, pulling him through the door. He put his hands on her shoulders. She turned and held him eagerly as they kissed, a long kiss during which the sweet smell of her skin, which had scented the air ever since he'd left her, rose in his head. Then in a rush they pulled off each others' clothes, the shirts damp from the heat, shorts and jeans and socks and underwear—beneath her work clothes, he discovered, she had on little panties and a delicate bra, both royal blue. They left them on the kitchen floor and went to her bed, climbing to her top bunk and plunging against each other powerfully, passionately, with a need that sprang from long months of loneliness for both of them.

She was quick and ready and they made love for a long time without pulling back once, locked into each other, with no sense of reserve or observation, as if they were a single creature swimming or flying, eager and sure. For him, her sweet animal warmth and presence was home, a place he'd finally reached. They said nothing and came together, crying out wordlessly. Then folded around each other, melted into each other.

David realized again and again his delight at finding her strong, small body still there, and he kissed her and stroked her, each moment new. He remembered his dream—if it had been a dream—of floating over Ecuador in darkness, feeling the land as it rose and fell, knowing for a certainty its palpable existence, its actual life. They made love again, and then she suddenly remembered that Frank would be coming home and leaped up to retrieve their clothes from the kitchen. He lay there alone a moment, so happy and grateful to have left San Francisco, to have gone into the world. He'd had one ounce of courage, and it had repaid him with a whole new life.

Frank did come in from school soon after that, though he left again, understanding what was going on. Then the two got up and took turns screaming under the frigid outdoor shower, made tea, and began dinner for the others. They sat on the porch with their tea as the tropical sunset shed its glowing light over the village. They welcomed Frank and Donna when they got home, and David told them the whole story of his assignment.

"That was Eisenhower!" Fern said, when he told them about the bird.

"And that was Leonin!" said Frank.

"He winked at me," said David. "In the middle of everything."

David basked in the company of the three housemates, feeling more comfortable with people than he had in years. Donna looked at him with a sly smile.

Leonin himself rode up and shouted and shook hands with David. Leonin laughed as he told them how completely David had fooled Qualles. Eisenhower was safely back home, he said. Then Renato and Raquel drove in, and it became a party. Donna brought out what food they had, and Frank went to work in the kitchen to make more. The rest of Leonin's family arrived, with his uncle Enrique.

In the midst of it all, David thought of Mike and his idea that the flock was communicating with them. And maybe it had been, thought David. He couldn't deny that, had it not been for Little Wittgenstein and the events that had followed upon his arrival, none of this would have happened. Maybe David had been meant to go to Ecuador, to do this assignment for the INEVS people, to help the flock.

Frank made a batch of the sweet rum drink called *canelazo* and all of them drank. They played disco music on Donna's boom box and, as the evening drew on and became more festive, danced on the porch. Others from the village joined them, as the kids looked on. David was reluctant to dance, but Fern pulled him out of his chair. She knew the music—these were the same songs she'd heard all year, the dance music of the South. And when the party wound down and the guests had gone home, Fern and David kissed goodnight for a long time on the porch, swaying in their embrace, their heads swimming with rum, before they went to their separate bunks.

24

The next afternoon the two of them were back on the water. Again they spent the night in the cove, this time making love in the blue boat, holding each other with such passion that neither felt the mosquito bites or the cramp of lying in the bottom of the hull until afterward, when it made them laugh. The next morning they saw the flock again, and got a better count—214 birds, Fern thought—and more pictures. They returned to the house, slept together in the bunk during the day, and set off in the boat again in the afternoon.

By then the parrots were showing off for them. On the third morning, the lead birds turned as they entered the clearing above the open water, and the whole flock wheeled in the air above the boat, shooting upward in a charged display, flaring and intertwining, releasing and regathering. Their sustained call radiated through the flock and rang in David's ears, pure here, celebratory, free of all rage and complaint.

The rains, which had paused, allowing them these added days with the flock, were to be denied no longer. Even as Fern and David headed home that morning, winding through the serpentine maze of the mangroves, the downpour began. The drops pocked and mottled the water's surface. It was wonderful, the rain, David thought, letting it soak him. The low clouds swept in from the western ocean. These were winter rains, not summer squalls. They set in with determination, storms that might last for weeks.

By the time they reached the *malecón,* the water was running in streams through the street. They dropped their gear in the house, shed their wet clothes, and went to bed again. When they awoke in the afternoon, the rain was drumming on the roof. They couldn't go back to the cove that night, and Fern had a premonition that the sight of the flock that morning, when it had saluted them, would be her last glimpse of the birds, at least for that year.

Donna came home that evening bringing news. Renato had called. Both Ramón and Qualles had pleaded guilty to charges of trafficking in wildlife. Ramón had to pay a big fine. Qualles was being deported to the United States. It was all they could do, Renato had told Donna. He had hoped for stiffer penalties. The court had placed the reserva under the auspices of INEVS, to be run as a research facility, dedicated to reestablishing native species in their original habitats. They had even begun inquiries about returning the tiger to India.

"And guess who's going to run the place?" said Donna.

"Leonin?" said Fern.

"Yep, Señor Leonin."

The next morning the downpour continued. Water ran in spouts off the big leaves of the palms. Frank and Donna put on ponchos and went off to work, and the other two stayed indoors. They missed the birds, but it was so sweet to be together in the house in the wet. They made love again, slept again, got up to eat, went back to bed. The rain came down.

Fern was sure now that the end of her stay in Ecuador had arrived. She thought of the cove and the flock, and it made her quiet. The entries in her notebook, the rolls of exposed film in her suitcase, this would be all the documentation she'd get. She hoped it would be enough. It helped to recall Pepperbloom's words, that this project was the first step of her work, not the last.

She wondered, too, about her future. What would happen with David? Though she hadn't known him long, she already felt connected to him. Apart from everything else, he'd seen the birds with her. They shared a feeling for the flock that few others would ever understand. Now leaving Ecuador would mean leaving David as well.

"I think it's over," she said, as they lay listening to the rain.

"What's over?" He said this with a slight tone of worry, which was the way she hoped he would respond.

"My time here. It's done. I can't work in the rain, and I've got to go back, anyway."

"I thought you said you were homeless," he said.

"Well, not quite," she said. But what was there for her in Tucson? she thought. She had finished all her classwork and had only her dissertation to write. Until it was done, she'd have no official business at the university. God knew Ron wouldn't miss her. And she had been dreading having to see Geoffrey again and having to clear her things out of the old apartment. At least there was her job at the tree nursery, though in truth that did not seem enough to go back for. She fell silent in his arms, thinking about this.

For his part, David was feeling his old fear rise again. Something frightening had occurred to him. There in Ecuador, with Fern this close, he knew he had reached the edge of his daring, and yet there was no stopping here. This was his life now. Everything he had done was bringing him to yet another next step. Still, he'd had some nerve, he thought, and he might as well have some more. He took one deep breath and then he said it.

"You could come back to San Francisco with me."

She sat up to get a better look at him. She had a funny surprised smile on her face. "Are you joking?" she said.

"No," he said, "I mean it."

After a moment, she answered, "I don't know if I can do that."

Then it was his turn to fall silent. At last he said, "Why not? Do you have some reason to go back to Arizona?"

She had to admit that she didn't. "But my work," she said.

"You could study the birds in San Francisco," he said.

"I'm writing about the aratinga in the mangroves," she said. "Watching escaped pets in a city park seems—I don't know what—not exactly serious."

Though she was still hesitant, hearing this he suddenly felt that it was going to be possible. If she had said, "We don't really know each other," or "I can't be with someone like you," he would have had nothing to say. That would have been her choice, an understandable one, he thought. But she hadn't said that, and on the subject of the birds on Telegraph Hill, he had plenty to say.

"Look," he said. "A: They're nobody's pets, never were, never will be. B: They're the same birds. We can keep watching the flock, every day."

"You're getting carried away," she said, laughing at him. "These birds are just exotics in San Francisco."

"How can you say *just exotics?"* he asked. "The whole world is exotic at this point. The flock in San Francisco finds plums on exotic trees that people have imported from China. They're eating exotic apples from New England."

"But they shouldn't be there," she said.

"Should, shouldn't," he continued, delighted at the turn the conversation had taken. "They are. And aren't *we* responsible for moving species around and making them exotic in the first place? Besides, what could be more exotic than human beings themselves, African apes on every mountaintop and every beach in the world?"

"Riding every wave," she said pointedly.

"Exactly," he said. "*We're* exotics. Me especially."

"I can't argue with that," she said. "But you're not talking like a biologist."

"I don't care," David said. "Nature has *us*—we don't have nature. It doesn't just stop at the city limits."

She laughed at his vehemence. "You're defending the flock, you know."

He laughed, too, knowing it was true. The flock *had* recruited him, as Mike had said. She looked so beautiful, sitting over him, intent on the argument. He coaxed her to lie down again, and together they listened to the rain some more.

"Anyway," he said, not willing to let it go, "it just seems like there are going to be only two kinds of wild animals now. Those in the most remote places, like that swamp out there, where people can't go—regular people, I mean—and those who can find a way to live among human beings, to exist through human culture."

"And which kind are you?" she said, mocking him a little.

"I'm trying to find a way to live among human beings," he said, going with the joke.

"Exploiting their niche," she said.

"That's right," he said. "Look, this is the real new world. The flock is pioneering it. And you can witness this, as a scientist."

"You've been thinking about it a lot," she said.

"Yes, I have," he said. "I mean, about the parrots. I've been thinking about almost nothing else for months. And if that's your only problem with going to San Francisco, I think I can talk you into it."

"You do, do you?"

He nodded, still vehement. She kissed him, then said, "And what if I can't do my work there? Would you come to Tucson?"

"You'd want me to?" he said.

"Mm-hm."

"Then I would," he said, feeling the gravity of that.

"Okay, then," she said. "Maybe I'll go to San Francisco. But just to see the birds. Then I'll decide."

He was ecstatic, so excited he couldn't lie there any longer. "Hey," he said. "Let's go walk in the rain."

"Sure," she said. "We can check the boat."

So they dressed and put on ponchos and went out. They walked to the *malecón,* holding hands, the rain spattering on their plastic hoods. The water in the channel had a beautiful, pale, even appearance, smoothed by the rain. Together they tipped the hull of the blue boat, pouring water out over the stones of the beach. Then they turned the boat over to keep the rain out of it and embraced, laughing as they slid together in their wet ponchos.

"So you'll go with me?" he said.

"I'm still considering. My plans didn't include this."

"We could take the boat," he suggested.

She looked at the blue hull, which lay like a turtle on the rocks. "I'd really like to," she said wistfully, "but it won't fit in the luggage rack."

"No," he said, "I mean the big boat. I mean *it* can take *us*. You can save your plane ticket and come back here on it sometime."

"Now that," she said, "sounds like an idea."

The freighter, in fact, was on its way north, returning from Chile and due to arrive in Guayaquil in a few days. During that time, as the rains continued with barely a halt, Fern let her provisional decision stand while they packed their things and said good-bye to their friends. Fern made Enrique a gift of her little blue boat, entirely redeeming herself in the eyes of his wife. For his part, Enrique promised that Fern would be able to use it whenever she returned to Puerto Alegre.

Then, too soon, the day arrived, and Fern said farewell with tears and hugs to Leonin and Donna. Frank drove them to the dock in Guayaquil, where Renato and Raquel had come to see them off. At the ship's railing stood the Indian officers, Roy and Surojit. They had received David's messages—relayed by e-mail through Donna to the line's offices in Santiago and then by radio to the ship itself—and were glad to see him again.

Frank and Renato and Raquel went aboard with them, helping them get their luggage up to the same cabin that David had occupied before, and then they, too, said farewell. They'd all see each other again, they promised. Fern cried hard as the three went back down the gangplank and waved before they got into their cars.

That night they slept on the ship as it lay at anchor. In the pale dawn, the same dawn they had seen so recently in the mangroves, they awoke in the small bunk to the throbbing of the engine belowdecks. David held her, feeling both the astonishment his former self brought to that moment and the new happiness he'd found.

From the upper deck they watched the mangroves recede, vividly green under the low clouds. They tried to guess when they had come downstream to the point nearest Puerto Alegre—there was no telling from the mangroves themselves—and listened for the sound of the flock rising. Then the ship chugged on as the Gulf of Guayaquil widened. Later that morning, they turned north into the open ocean, and the verdant coast fell away.

That night David suddenly remembered Little Wittgenstein's feather. He searched in his bags until he found the right book, then shook the pages until it dropped out, twirling onto the floor, the green-and-yellow tail feather that he'd found when he had swept out his apartment. He gave it to Fern, and from a clear plastic pouch clipped into the rings in the back of her notebook, she produced another feather, the remex that had fallen to her from the branches at Las Manos. The feathers could have come from the same bird.

It proved to be a wet voyage, the sea and the sky often indistinguishable, the horizon melted in grays of water and cloud. When they arrived in San Francisco, it was raining there, too. The city was freezing after the south, and they took the blanket from their bunk and wrapped themselves in it to stand on the deck and watch the ship come to port. The skyline opened, building by building. David pointed out Coit Tower and Telegraph Hill, and they listened again for the sound of the flock.

For the time being, they found a hotel on the waterfront and took a room with a king-sized bed and a view of the bay. The next morning they made their first pilgrimage to the flock, and the birds were there to greet them. Fern was astonished to see her aratinga again, crying out with the same flight calls that she had heard in the mangroves and flying in configurations exactly like those she had seen in the wild. David introduced Fern to Mike, who wanted to hear everything they had learned about the flock in Ecuador. He and Fern talked for an hour, excitedly comparing observations.

They stayed at the hotel for two weeks, as the year wound down. For her part, Fern was still reluctant to relinquish her plans, though she loved San Francisco and found life with David sweeter all the time. She took an hour each morning to write up her notes from Ecuador. She wrote to Pepperbloom to get some advice about finishing her dissertation.

But she watched the flock every day, as David watched her, wondering if this new life would take. Then one day, as they watched the birds circle and land in the big cypress on the point, he noticed on her face a rapt expression that he'd seen in the mangroves. The next day, when she brought her camera and notebook up the hill, he said nothing, just continued to hope.

Then he had to take another chance. On Christmas Eve, David took Fern to dinner at an Italian place. They walked there, up the hilly streets of North Beach. He was nervous all through the meal, and finally, after the zabaglione, he brought out a ring and asked her to marry him. She said not even yes, but of course. "Of course," as if there'd never been a doubt.

That spring they were wed on the waterfront, his San Francisco friends, even Lyle, in attendance, and Fern already secretly, blissfully, pregnant with their baby. They were the couple the parrots had brought together, Mike told everyone. Some people were meant to meet, said Peter. David's father took all the credit, for giving him the parrot in the first place.

After they were married, they rented a place they found with Peter's help, on Telegraph Hill, a two-bedroom apartment with a terrace that overlooked the Greenwich Stairs. It was expensive, of course, but David took an offer to teach, and he still had his Wadsworth. And Fern did finish her dissertation that spring, sending it first to Pepperbloom, who loved it, and then to Ron, back in Tucson, who told her he'd let the graduate secretary know that she had fulfilled her requirement.

Inside, on the wall of their living room, hung a picture, which they'd had enlarged and framed, that Fern had taken of the flock in the mangroves in Ecuador, wheeling as one in the sky on the last morning they'd seen it. Outside, every morning and several times a day, they heard and saw the same flock, the northern branch, and among them the bird that David had called Little Wittgenstein. He, too, was now living in a larger world, part of a family, a regular member of society. David could always pick him out among the others, even far off, and after a time could even distinguish his call amid the cacophony of the flock, that raucous and familiar cry he now knew to be a shout of joy.